ORB

DAVID E. ARP

THORNDIKE PRESS

A part of Gale, a Cengage Company

GALE
A Cengage Company

Farmington Hills, Mich • San Francisco • New York • Waterville, Maine
Meriden, Conn • Mason, Ohio • Chicago

Copyright © 2018 by David E. Arp.
Thorndike Press, a part of Gale, a Cengage Company.

Thorndike Press® Large Print Christian Mystery.
The text of this Large Print edition is unabridged.
Other aspects of the book may vary from the original edition.
Set in 16 pt. Plantin.

LIBRARY OF CONGRESS CIP DATA ON FILE.
CATALOGUING IN PUBLICATION FOR THIS BOOK
IS AVAILABLE FROM THE LIBRARY OF CONGRESS

ISBN-13: 978-1-4328-6305-0 (hardcover alk. paper)

Published in 2019 by arrangement with Pelican Ventures, LLC

Printed in Mexico
1 2 3 4 5 6 7 23 22 21 20 19

175

ρ

ORB

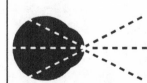

To my Savior for not giving up on me.

1

Thursday night, April 4

Meshach suffered from a bellyful of Lubbock, Texas. The city sprouted on a flat plain with a view of nothing but sunup and sundown, unless the wind blew. Then, gusts stirred enough dirt in the air to make the noon sun disappear and cause the streetlights to come on. Today looked like pictures of the Oklahoma dustbowl. It was impossible to escape the smell of dirt. Grit covered his face and arms, every inch of him. People lived here and liked it.

Nighttime didn't bring relief. The quartermoon protested, refused to peek through the dust, and added to the darkness.

Not much for playground equipment in the little park. A metal slide and two plastic creatures mounted on coiled springs. When the gusts hit them, they looked like horses galloping. A small merry-go-round sat next to that. Kid powered. Push until dizzy then hop on and ride it out.

He walked to the swing set just beyond the creatures and opted for the lowest of three rubber seats swaying on the end of their chains. He sat and stretched out his legs as a chill eased up his back. His black shirt would have been warm enough on a sixty-degree night, but not in the buffeting wind.

His dog tugged the leash to its end and then sat in the dirt and whined. The mutt cost him ninety-five dollars and a round-trip drive to Amarillo. The longest four hours of his life. Like driving across the moon. The broad who ran the shelter for wayward canines cited a long list of maladies the vet had treated when the dog arrived, as if to justify the sale price. Would have been more but Mr. Maxwell, she'd called him with all due reverence and respect — the dog, not the vet — had already been neutered. Poor thing. Dropped off on a country road, what was he to do? She'd welled up with tears when Meshach left with him. She should have bought the cur and took him home herself.

Maxwell had short brown hair, big ears and weighed twenty pounds. He looked like a Chihuahua on steroids and acted twice as spastic. His boney tail stayed tucked away and rarely made an appearance.

Meshach glanced at his watch: 11:18. If what he'd witnessed the last three nights held true, he had five minutes. He'd timed the walk from where he sat to the driveway. As soon as the car turned the corner, he and Maxwell would take a little stroll. Should put him there just right.

In the distance, two headlights probed the dusty night. The vehicle he was waiting for only had one lamp on the driver's side. He knew because he broke out the other one with a rock two hours ago. Meshach stood and pulled the dog toward the slide just in case.

A streetlight five houses down revealed the two beams belonged to a black-and-white. Meshach gave the cruiser a cursory glance then focused on his prized mutt. To one of Lubbock's finest peacekeepers, he was just a man outside to let his dog tend to its business before bedtime. The cop slowed then continued around the park and disappeared down another avenue.

Ninety-five dollars well spent.

A second car appeared . . . His.

Fifty seconds.

He crossed from the slide to the curb and stepped onto the street. Maxwell kept the leash taut, running around in a circle, pulling every direction except the right one.

Meshach strode across the pavement and stepped onto the sidewalk in front of a plumber's house. The man had crawled out of his work truck a little after six on the past three evenings, hugging what looked like the love of his life — a twelve-pack of beer. The place on the other side of his target sat vacant.

Maxwell took Meshach's pause in the darker area under a tree as a cue to piddle. The car turned the corner behind him, illuminating the playground. Max flipped around, bowed up and bug-eyed, as if he didn't know whether to bark or run for his life. "Easy, pooch, easy," Meshach whispered.

The headlight lit him, and his shadow jumped out and stretched down the sidewalk. He hunched his shoulders, looked straight ahead and walked. The dog shied then followed.

The garage door on the next house rumbled to life. The opener dragged the white wooden panels on squeaky rollers. The car slowed and turned onto the driveway fifty feet ahead. The single light lit the dark recess. A blue mountain bike sat on one side of the walk-in door and a small plastic trash-can on the other side, both outlined against slick white walls. The wind carried a white paper cup, bits of trash, and dried grass on a tour of the garage then stirred the lot in a small eddy on the concrete floor.

The red Honda eased into the garage. The door slid down the rails. The moment it reached the halfway point, Meshach dropped the leash and sprinted across the driveway. At the door, he laid out flat and slid through the last sliver of opening into the space behind the car. The door immediately reversed direction.

What the . . . He'd missed one little detail. He'd blocked the beam on the safety device meant to protect pets and kids from being crushed.

His mother's prissy, ever-preaching voice screamed at him like it was yesterday. *Best laid plans, honey!*

Now what? Exposed to the street and nowhere to hide if someone drove by, he pushed onto his knees, then his toes, in a crouch below the car windows, and made sure he was out of the eye's beam.

The dog stood in the middle of the street looking at him. That was an appropriate place for Maxwell. The dog didn't like him, and he didn't like the dog. The relationship worked in Meshach's favor because if the mutt ran to him . . .

11

The white backup lights came on. The broad had put the car in reverse. If she gassed the engine, he'd have no choice but to run. That would ruin their date.

The Accord rocked slightly as the woman's weight shifted inside. She had to be thinking about the door, looking back, pondering the workings of a mechanical device she didn't have the first clue about. Her car door opened. A radio voice . . . *bringing you another fifteen minutes of uninterrupted . . .* The backup lights went out and the engine died. The metal of hot exhaust pipes creaked. The garage door lurched and screeched its way down the tracks again, finally closing with a groan. Silence. Shoes scuffed on the concrete. The headlight went out. A thump as the car door closed. *The dome light stays on for how long? Too long.* A strong gust shook the paneled door and sucked air from the confined space with a weak whistle. He used the noise to cover his movement and duck-walked along the passenger side of the car. Her shadow grew larger on the wall and edged toward the door leading into the house. Darkness consumed the garage. He stood. A dainty cough and a strong breath followed the tap of shoes and the jingle of keys. The knob clicked, and he moved into the doorway.

Light lit a laundry room. She faced away.

He knew she was pretty, smelled pretty, a hint of lemon, slim but shapely, brown hair pulled back into a ponytail, wearing tan slacks and a green pullover. She'd just waited on him at the restaurant two hours earlier. Her nametag read *Bethany.* She'd been nice.

His hand covered her mouth.

Meshach held tissue paper over the lens of a small pen-light. He clicked it on and pointed the muted beam at his trussed-up victim and then eased silently across the light-colored carpet through the house. A floor lamp next to a dark couch and chair flanked by two end tables, all arranged to face a medium-sized television, made up a small living room. Blue light glowed from the satellite receiver on the shelf below the television. Cardboard boxes littered the guest bedroom. The master bedroom, her bedroom, smelled lemony, like her. *Your mom would be disappointed you didn't make your bed, Bethany.*

A picture in a chrome frame stood next to a clock/radio glowing with the time: 1:11, in green, atop a small bedside-table. Bethany and two other women posed with their arms wrapped around each other against a blue sky. *Her BFFs.*

Like the couch, stuffed animals covered the bed. The pink bear, the blue-and-white dog, the brown cat, like a boy's baseball pennants and football posters tacked to the wall, were all attempts to prolong childhood. Stupid.

He picked up her pillow, buried his face into the cool cloth and breathed deeply. She'd recognize the strange scent later. He could imagine her reaction and utter disgust. He smiled.

Back in the kitchen, he opened the fridge — bottled water, leftovers from Chili's, a plastic carton of 2% milk, sandwich meat, cheese, condiments, and four wine coolers. He smelled the milk, opted for a berry cooler and carried the bottle to the kitchen table and sat down.

A billionaire's kid renting a forty-year-old house in the older part of town was what, a lesson in life?

Her cell rang. He opened the side pocket of her handbag and checked the caller. "So, his name is Matthew, eh?" he whispered. "Not Matt, but Matthew. Is he on his way to see you right now? Nod yes or shake your head no. His life depends on it."

She shook her head.

He placed the phone on the counter next

to what was left of the roll of duct tape he'd used on her. The phone stopped ringing and vibrating after a few seconds. Now, Matthew would wonder why she hadn't answered. Must be serious about each other for him to call so late. Or he was the assuming, jealous type and wanted to make sure she was home right after work.

Meshach glanced at her lying on the floor and twisted off the cap on the drink. Careful not to touch the rim to his lips, he tilted his head and poured a cool shot into his open mouth. He set the bottle on the table and knelt next to her. Her chest heaved slowly at first, then faster and faster. The bellows fanning her fears of the unknown. He slid his gloved-hand over her arm, down her waist, and let it rest on her hip. She tensed, and a whimper escaped her throat as he leaned close, breathed in deeply through his nose, and whispered with his lips, brushing the duct tape covering her ear, "The boogie man visited you this night. You heard his voice. Be grateful. Most don't."

2

Sunday afternoon, April 7

Wes Hansen arrived fifteen minutes before the scheduled three o'clock appointment. He'd never met Cole Blackwell, but from the scant bit of information he found on the Internet, the oil man didn't appear to be a person who abided amateurs.

Cole had picked the Ship Tavern, one of four restaurants in the famed Brown Palace Hotel, in downtown Denver, as the venue for their meeting. Wes usually searched for information about a place he'd never visited to get a feel about what and where, but he'd driven by the Brown a hundred times. He'd heard the place was ritzy, but what he saw when he entered the lobby surprised him. Dainty clinks of porcelain cups. Painted nails and extended pinkie fingers.

Rattling saucers and teapots arranged on small square tables littered with scones and finger cakes. Looked like he'd stepped back into the 1920s in time for High Tea.

He didn't particularly care for tea, hot or cold, so the draw eluded him. The ladies appeared to be in high form.

Wes navigated the lobby and entered the wedge-shaped restaurant, leaving the light piano music and muted female whisperings behind. He scanned the booths along the wall, the four-place tables around the floor, and the long oak bar. Of the forty or so patrons, he picked out three lone men, all bellied up to the bar with empty stools between them. None matched Cole's description.

A college-aged kid dressed in a black suit, white shirt, and black tie approached. "Good afternoon, sir. A table for one?"

"Two, please." Wes said. "A business associate will be here soon. I'd like to have the table at the end of the bar, if that's OK. Looks like the most secluded."

"It is. I'm Brent."

"Brent, I'm Wes."

Brent took his job seriously. The proper butler, direct and formal, but then Wes didn't run with the likes of the Brown Palace crowd, so maybe he played his part well.

His host led him past the replica of a ship's mast standing floor-to-ceiling in the middle of the room and then waited for Wes to choose a chair at the table. "Kevin will be your server. Can I start you off with a beverage? Something from the bar?"

"Black coffee will be fine for now. Thanks."

"Very well." He gathered up two of the four place settings and returned to his post at the entrance.

A description of Wes's state of mind rarely included the adjective *apprehensive,* but he'd never met a billionaire, much less sat down with one for a job interview. He told himself Cole was just a man. As his high school football coach used to say about the opposing teams, "They put their pants on one leg at a time just like we do."

A man who fit Cole's description entered the restaurant and looked around. As Brent zeroed in on him, the guy removed his camouflaged ball cap, used it to indicate Wes, and walked to the table. "Wes Hansen, I'm Cole Blackwell."

Wes stood. "Mr. Blackwell, my pleasure." Cole's firm handshake and direct green eyes gave the same message: pure confidence. He obviously knew Wes by sight. The mention of his name wasn't a question. Cole had either done his homework or made an assumption. Wes didn't believe Cole made many of the latter.

He smiled. "Call me Cole." He slid out the opposite chair and sat.

The traits Wes had subconsciously attributed to the man since their first phone conversation two days earlier flew out the window. His six-foot, one-eighty frame sporting Wranglers, khaki shirt and scuffed cowboy boots walked straight out of the backwoods. This was no pinstripe-suited millionaire with a cloud of attentive male aides and doting blond secretaries floating around him everywhere he went.

The waiter approached and placed Wes's coffee on the table in front of him. "Good afternoon, Mr. Blackwell. Nice to see you again. Could I start you out with something to drink?"

"Good to see you, Kevin. Water, with a twist of lemon, please."

"Something from the grill?" Kevin looked between them.

"Nothing for me. Wes?" Cole said.

Wes held up his cup. "Thanks, but I'll be fine with coffee, if you don't mind topping this off when the time comes."

"Yes, sir." The waiter left.

Cole watched the young man as he made his way along the bar. He placed the Bass-Pro Shops cap on the seat of the chair to his right. A tinge of gray singed the edges of his light brown hair. Wes knew the man was fifty-five, but he looked ten years younger.

Cole focused on Wes. "As you heard, I'm here often enough to be on a first name basis with the hotel's staff. I'm in Denver a couple times a month on business. I love this place. You know, several presidents have stayed here, Teddy Roosevelt for one, and the Beatles, the 'Unsinkable' Molly Brown, no relation to the builder, a Mr. Henry Brown. Quite a history going back into the 1890s."

Kevin brought Cole's water and a carafe of coffee.

The information surprised Wes, the part about the hotel's name in particular. He thought the title derived from the color of the stone exterior. "I used to live not far from here, but this is my first time in the hotel. I was shocked when I walked in. I never dreamed the place was like this. Impressive. Gives you a rare glimpse back, but I suppose the reality of back then was less nostalgic than it is now."

Cole took a long drink and set the glass on the table. "Wes, I appreciate you making time for me today."

The man didn't dally getting to the point of their meeting. "Mr. Blackwell, Cole, you had my attention when you mentioned Bubba. He and I go way back." Not like anyone needed to know, but he'd be off his rocker not to make time for a billionaire.

"You served together in Iraq."

Again, it wasn't a question. "We did."

"He said you're an excellent investigator. I'm counting on it. In the oil business, we drill what we call tight-holes. Are you familiar with the term?"

"No, sir, I'm not."

"We keep 'em secret. The information and what's discovered, if anything. Bidding against the competition for adjacent properties or leases can cost millions, so we guard the information we obtain. We call such projects a 'tight-hole.' I'll wager you didn't find much about my personal life in your Internet search." He raised an eyebrow.

Wes nodded, which confirmed he'd found nothing and had done a search.

"I like it that way. Tight-hole anyone asking questions." Cole slid two business cards from his shirt pocket and placed one of them on the table. "I received that in the mail two weeks ago."

Wes picked up the white card. Printed in bold, large caps was the name or acronym MESHACH, evenly spaced over a bare eyeball. The eye was black with no lashes, lids or brows. On the back, printed in pencil, was *You'll pay.* "One of the three guys in the fiery furnace."

Cole shook his head. "One of the four. The Lord joined the first three if you'll remember."

"Yeah, you're right, and it's not a name I've ever heard in reference to anyone otherwise."

Cole tapped the second card on the table. "Look, since the Deepwater Horizon burned and sank in the Gulf of Mexico, I get a threat a week on average. Or I should say my company does. That card is the first threat I've received at my home."

"You've been to the police?"

"So many times I'm like the boy who cried wolf. Most of the threats are rambling manifestos and don't name me directly. No individuals or organizations take the credit, so there's nowhere to look. The envelope the card came in bore a fictitious address and a few prints, but none matched previously booked individuals. Then there's this one." Cole slid the second card across the table.

Wes examined a card identical to the first one, but with *I'm watching you* written on the back, again in pencil, in the same block letters. "By mail too?"

Cole's jaw set. His green eyes suddenly held a look Wes had seen many times in some very dangerous men. Call it determination, resolve, the will to inflict grievous bodily harm to another human being. "My daughter, Bethany," — he paused then finished through clenched teeth — "found it in her purse."

Now that was personal.

"She's twenty-two, going to college at Texas Tech, in Lubbock. Her boyfriend, Matt, got worried about her when she didn't answer his calls. He found her Friday morning bound and gagged on the kitchen floor of her house." Cole sat back and took another long drink of water then continued, "The man got into her rental house somehow. No forced entry. No prints. No witnesses."

"Your daughter?"

"Fine, physically. Uninjured in every respect, including what goes through everyone's mind when a reprobate assaults a woman. He used duct tape on her hands, feet, even her mouth and eyes. She's missing a number of lashes and won't need to pluck her brows for a while. She said he whispered. Never said a word out loud. He told her the boogieman had visited and she was lucky she heard him. He stole her car, but only drove it two blocks." He took a deep breath and let it out in one strong puff. "Yesterday, Beth found that card in her purse. Now, she's a wreck."

Wes had his ideas about the man whispering. Beth would recognize her assailant's voice if she met him on the street, or in a lineup, and a voice in the night would humanize him. Obviously, the man wasn't human, at the least, not humane. Who did stuff like that to other people?

Leaving the card in her purse had an eerie twist. "The card is an aftershock. He knew she'd find it sooner or later, and his intrusion would become real again. If she'd found it next week, or the week after, she wouldn't know how long it had been there, since the first assault or ten minutes. And every man she sees walking the street could be him."

"He opened and drank a wine cooler too." Cole sat up in the chair and glanced around. The wish-I-could-get-my-hands-on-him look returned. "Lubbock P.D. is investigating. They're checking for DNA on the bottle, but I don't think he's that dumb. I believe he's long gone. It's obvious he took her car to get back to his car. A man walking the streets after midnight would attract a cop."

"Yes, he would. That gets me to wondering how he entered the house. Anyway, I believe he's after you," Wes said.

"You think?"

Wes nodded. "There's no easier way to upset a family man than by going after his family, his wife or his kids. He had your daughter but didn't hurt her, at least not physically. He likes control. He feels he's in control. He relishes the thought of your reaction and distress."

"Well, he knew where to kick me, and he holds all the cards because I haven't got the first clue as to whom or why or where to even begin looking. Disgruntled ex-employee," Cole scanned the ceiling, "or I don't know. I'm lost."

"Or someone who doesn't like what you do for a living."

Cole nodded and fingered his empty glass. Wes waved at Kevin who refilled the glass and took his leave.

"There's something else." Cole tapped the tabletop with his index finger. "He's been stalking Bethany for a while. He tried to engage her, friend her, on a social media site a month ago. It's not like you can forget the name Meshach. Not if you're a Christian and have heard his story."

"Did she accept, remember a profile, see

a picture, or notice anything we can use?"

"Nope. Not that I'm aware of. I've warned her about the social media stuff. I have to say she's been good about what she shares with her friends. I still don't like it."

"That's a place to start. I have a guy who'll be all over it." Wes pulled out his cellphone, took pictures of the front and back of both cards and returned them to Cole. "I'll get you a proposal together today."

Cole shook his head and thumbed a third card from his shirt pocket. "I don't need a proposal. Get on him. Get him. Do what you need to do. I don't care what it costs. Take this." He handed over his business card — Cole Blackwell Jr., Deepwater Energy. "I have two aircraft. My personal pilot and plane are at your disposal. His cell number is on the back. Brooks, Jordan Brooks. He's in Salt Lake City, and he's expecting your call. He'll take care of you."

"Cole, I don't think —"

"Wes, a man always wonders if he would be able to pull the trigger on another human being to protect his family. I'm in a situation I've never been in. Now, I know I could hunt this guy down and shoot him on sight."

"Yes, sir, and they call that murder, not

26

self-defense."

Cole took the saltshaker and shook out a portion onto the table. Then, he slowly, methodically, used the bottom of the shaker to grind the salt into a fine powder, one white crystal at a time.

Wes knew the feeling, the helplessness and frustration of not being able to put a face or name to an enemy. Every grain of salt had *Meshach* written all over it.

Cole's nostrils flared as he thumped down the shaker and swept away the salt with his balled fist. "Exactly! Right now, I'd take the Lord's vengeance and make it mine. Find him." Cole grabbed his cap and slapped it on his head. "OK, I have to fly to Texas and pick up a dog."

He finished what he had to say as abruptly as he'd started. "A dog?" Wes said.

"Yeah. Matt said the thing was sitting on the porch when he arrived to check on Bethany. He had on a collar with a leash attached, but no ID. He's the ugliest creature walking on four legs I've ever seen. So homely he's cute. His tail wags him, not the other way around. I told my daughter she has to advertise. Someone lost him. She knows I'm right, but she's latched on to him anyway."

So a witness to Meshach's entry into

Bethany's house existed. Too bad dogs couldn't talk. He didn't want to say it, but he'd just acquired his first lead. He had a good feeling she'd be able to keep the dog. No use in telling Cole his thoughts. Might ruin his daughter's relationship with her new pet if she discovered who the previous owner had been.

3

Sunday evening

Wes didn't want to appear anxious, but by the time he shook Cole's hand and left the hotel lobby, he'd caught his client's fever. Whoever this character was, by whatever name he used, he had to be found and locked up.

Just the type of job Wes could sink his teeth into.

As he walked to his pickup, he slid the unlock bar across his iPhone, went to favorites, and tapped Tony's name. His only employee, a consultant he used when the technology got too deep, was never out of pocket. Junkies didn't stray far from the source of their addiction, and Tony's was a Mac. He answered before the ring-back tone sounded in Wes's ear. "Hey, Wes. How's your pulse?"

"Pitter-patter, pitter-patter. How's the

weather in Flagstaff? Any snow in your fore-cast?"

"I hope not. Winter is supposed to be over. We've had enough hard water for one year."

"Hard water?"

"Ice, dude. Hard water spelled with three letters. What's on your mind?"

"I've got a project I need to get on, pronto. Can I enlist your fulltime attention and persuade you to meet me in Denver tomorrow morning, at the Embassy Suites by the airport?"

An I'm-thinking-on-it-hum traveled the connection. "At my full rate?"

Sometimes, doing what was right didn't pay well. Soldiers, police officers, and firefighters had a sense of servitude, and their pay didn't fit the risks or the effort they gave their jobs. Tony had helped Wes when the task was more important than the pay. Like last year when they spent two weeks looking for a runaway teen for a single mom who lived paycheck-to-paycheck. This time, Wes would make sure Tony received his due. "Plus twenty per-cent."

"Must be important."

"It is. I'll explain more when I see you. For now, I'm going to send you pictures of the front and back of two business cards.

See what you can find out about the name on them."

"What name?"

"Meshach."

Paper rustled on the other end of the connection. "Like Meshach Taylor?"

"Who? No, like Shadrach, Meshach. Who's Meshach Taylor?"

"He's an actor."

Wes opened the door and climbed into his white Silverado pickup. "Huh, never heard of him. Anyway. This spelling might be an acronym because the name is printed in large caps, but no periods were used, so who knows."

"It's a long acronym if that's what it is."

"I think it's a man's name or his alias. You might start with social media sites."

"I'm on it. I'll get a flight."

Wes tapped *End* and sent the pictures of the cards in a text message.

He didn't like to use *hacker,* a term normally associated with illegal activities, but for lack of a better word, Tony was a hacker. The best Wes could find outside of prison walls. If information existed about Meshach, Tony would chase it down.

Before he could start his pickup, the techie called back. "I only found him on a new site called Chirp. The eyeball is his avatar.

He Chirps some weird stuff. Got a couple of followers."

"Avatar? Chirp? You're kidding me. What's Chirp?"

A quick sigh traveled the connection. "Avatar is a photo or image a person uses or identifies with. His profile. It's the same eye as pictured on the card. A dead, creepy-looking thing that gives you the elusion it's following you when you move. Chirp is like texting, but with the potential for a global audience, and users aren't limited by character count."

Wes started the diesel pickup and pulled out of the parking space. "You're quick."

"You could've discovered the same info on your cell phone."

"There's a reason I call you when a computer is involved. Anything else?"

"Not for now. Just thought I'd let you know before I booked a flight."

"Wait on the flight. I'll call you back." He signed off and pulled Cole's business card from his shirt pocket. He'd had fighter planes and helicopters at his disposal before. They'd dropped ordnance on enemy targets he and his spotter identified in the Iraqi desert. He steered the Chevy into the next available parking spot and tapped the numbers for Jordan Brooks on his phone.

Maybe he'd actually get to meet a pilot this time.

Tomorrow, during regular business hours, he'd have Tony scour the Lubbock-area animal shelters to see if he could get a line on a man who liked ugly dogs.

Monday, April 8

Midnight tolled before Wes got Cole's pilot and Tony together and checked into the hotel. He was spent and wanted to sleep, but tossing in the king-size bed, two o'clock strolled to three then crawled to four. Meshach had the same effect on him as a hit of caffeine. What kind of mind thought like that?

He'd asked for a spacious suite when he checked in. The hotel didn't disappoint. A large oak desk in one corner flanked a television cabinet centered at the foot of the bed. Toward the door, between the bed and the kitchenette, two orange-cushioned chairs and a matching couch surrounded a marble-topped coffee table. He and Tony wouldn't step on each other's toes trying to work.

By five o'clock, he had coffee brewed, a cup poured, and his computer booted. He was never one for the social media stuff. He'd thought about it, hoping to keep better tabs on his daughter. He'd searched for her, but without success.

A broad search for Meshach turned up a music band and dozens of individuals.

His cell phone vibrated, a text from Tony — *should b there by 8.*

Jordan was in Salt Lake City, so from north central Utah to Flagstaff for Tony, then to Denver by eight. Some serious flying on short notice. They'd been at it all night.

He opened Chirp. Great. He had to join to enter the domain. Lack of an account stymied him. In order to search the site, he'd bite the bullet. After typing in his name, he erased it and sat back. Did he want to be himself? Maybe a female name would work better, someone off the wall, looking for love, or selling a product. Monica, Monica Carson. Monique Crayon. Mysterious. He typed the name in the space, picked an easy password and hit *submit*. He noted both the fictitious name and the password on his legal pad. Once inside, he set up his new account and then sat back again. What to post? Sex? Sales? Sex sold, but for now, inconspicuous might be the better approach. Posting could wait.

The same double name took him to Meshach's account. The eye greeted him.

34

Meshach had followers — a Mr. R. Lamech and J. Sullivan. His only post, *in joan,* was time-stamped about the time he and Cole wrapped up their meeting. Wes clicked on Lamech. Again, only one post — *anjali to see joan for oleos jordan with hemmingway.*

Wes reread the post four times. He didn't get it. Tony had mentioned some weird stuff. More like off-the-wall.

Lamech and Meshach had ties in their posts. Sullivan followed Lamech, but not the other way around. Sullivan followed Meshach, but again, Meshach did not return the favor.

Wes opted for Monique to follow Meshach and clicked on the button. He went back to Monique's profile page and picked Omaha, Nebraska, for her hometown.

What next? Profession? Agenda?

He typed *Help save the planet from ourselves. Global warming is real. Join me at the Whitehouse. If we speak as one, they will listen. One voice! Before the ice is gone and polar bears are extinct!*

He reread the rambling and posted it. Tony would be proud of him.

The Avalanche Journal came up in a search for Lubbock newspapers. He opened the site and checked the archives for Bethany Blackwell. *Tech student accosted in her*

35

home. Crime Stoppers offering reward for information leading to the arrest . . . No useful info.

Criminals left signs of their passing, just like animals left tracks in the dirt or in the snow. Meshach had already made one mistake by leaving the dog. Bet he never dreamed his cover would end up with the victim — if the dog had served the purpose Wes believed.

A knock at the door shook his attention from the computer. He gave his watch a quick glance: 8:35. He'd lost track of the time.

When he opened the door, Tony was standing in the hall with a red backpack on his shoulder. Wes had forgotten about the man's taste in clothes. Pants and shoes he would alternate. One day red shoes and yellow pants, one day yellow shoes and lime green pants, or like today, green-and-white checkered shoes and orange pants, but he never wore anything other than a black hoodie. Never. Tony had the physique of a desk-jockey. He wasn't overly heavy, but he was pudgy and soft. The hoodie fit his round, five-nine build like a plastic trash bag.

Wes grabbed Tony's hand and shook hard. "Come in. Long time no see. How was your flight?"

"First class. Nice aircraft."

Wes walked back into the room. "I'll bet. Did you check in?"

Tony plopped the backpack computer bag onto the bed. "I did, and I stood at the counter long enough to smell bacon cooking. Though I know I don't look like it, I'm starved. Let's eat. You're buying."

"Yes, I am. I'm hungry too. I've been waiting for you. Then, we'll get to work."

Tony followed him into the hallway and stepped up beside him as the door click closed. "I don't know what we're going to accomplish."

Wes had to think about the comment a second. Tony's job didn't include physical labor, unless packing a laptop around fit the description, but he was far from lazy.

"Wes, there's nothing out there. I mean nothing. We're going to need something else. You might as well start ghost busting. Looking for this guy is the same thing."

"I agree, but we can't sit and do nothing. We have to look. That's what we do. It's what I do. For your first task after breakfast, I'd like you to call the animal shelters and pet stores in and around Lubbock and obtain a list of all the dogs sold the past week."

"You're kidding."

"Nope."

"That's it? All the dogs, pups, and old dogs, males and females alike? No description of the canine suspect? Is the dog's name Meshach too? Why are we looking for this Meshach person anyway? And for *whom,* if I may ask, are we working? Obviously, a wealthy someone."

"Cole Blackwell. As for the dog, he's brown, four paws, male, and he has a long tail."

"You're funny." Tony stopped mid step. "I know that name. Blackwell, Blackwell. . . ."

"Deepwater Energy." Wes tossed him a hint.

"That's him. What do an oil man, a dog, and a fiery-furnace dude have in common?"

"Meshach accosted Cole's twenty-two-year-old daughter in her home. Cole received in the mail one of the cards I sent you pictures of. His daughter, Bethany, found the other one in her purse two days after her attacker wrapped her in duct tape and abandoned her on the kitchen floor. They found the dog on the front porch of her house, wearing a collar and leash, the same morning Bethany's boyfriend rescued her."

"I can guess which card she received. The one with *I'm watching you.*" Tony's head bobbed. "We're looking for a bad dude. The police have any leads we can chase?"

"Nothing Cole's aware of. That's something we need to do this morning. Check with the Lubbock Police Department."

"She at Tech?"

"Correct, but I don't think she's the intended target. He had her, but he walked away."

"One of the many uses for duct tape. To think big-gov is trying to ban guns."

"That's an off-the-wall comparison."

Tony shrugged. "Yeah, well, think about it. Is the tape in the hands of a crazy less at fault than the gun in the hands of a crazy? You think he's after Cole?"

Wes pushed the *down* button at the elevators. "That's my guess."

Tony leaned against the jamb. "I think social media is the key. Have you been online and seen Meshach's response to Lamech's post?"

Wes nodded. "I have."

"They're up to something. Those two cats are using the site to communicate. I can feel it in my bones. We just have to figure out what language they're speaking. Another thought. Why would two people go after a woman in Lubbock, Texas? What's she into? This is bigger than some college kid. A somebody-Sullivan is following the other two and some broad named Monique who posted baloney about global warming forty-five minutes ago is following Meshach."

Wes smiled at him and patted his own chest. "T'was I."

"You're kidding?"

"Nope."

"Good idea. Though, I don't know what good it will do us. They're not going to communicate with her. Excuse me, with you."

Tony was right, but that wasn't Monique's intent, not his intent. "Right now, Lamech or Lamesh, however it's pronounced, and Meshach are linked by their posts. Sullivan is following both, but they're not following him. 'The guilty flees when no man pursues.' If the three of them follow Monique, say, to keep tabs on her, maybe that will tie in Sullivan. I don't know. We have to try something."

The elevator bell dinged and the doors opened.

Tony entered and propped himself in the corner of the car. "I think we're going to need some help. I have someone in mind, a wordsmith who does crosswords in minutes. Smart as a whip. Might help us break their code, if that's what it is."

"Hire him. Get him here."

"I took liberties and already did. Hope you don't mind? She, Jessica Wahl, lives in Boulder. She's meeting us for breakfast."

4

Wes sipped his coffee and scanned the newspaper. Denver had the usual big city aches and pains. Murder, breaking and entering, assaults, robberies and domestic violence took up a full page. One item caused him to wonder about the sanity of at least half of Colorado's electorate. Marijuana had been legalized, opening myriad problems. Not the least of which: possession was still a federal offense.

He put aside the paper. Tony had his cell phone cradled in his laced fingers, tapping and swiping with both thumbs. Twiddling carried to the nth degree.

"Tony, what's got your attention?"

"Monique."

"Monique? My Monique?"

"Yep. I'm following you, sweetie. Just set up my phone to get alerts. I've never been one for reading the mundane ramblings of some narcissists, so I didn't do it before.

Now, I'll get their comments. Meshach's, Lamech's, all of them, as they post." He let go of the phone with one hand and took a sip of orange juice. "You want me to fix yours?"

"No, thanks. I'll let you handle the social media monitoring duties from here on. My phone does enough pinging and vibrating as it is. Anything else of interest?"

"Nope." Tony glanced around the room then went back to his phone. "Jessica should have been here by now. Traffic might have held her up."

"There's time."

A waitress stopped with the coffeepot and refilled Wes's cup. "Are we eating today?"

"We are. We'll be a few minutes. Still waiting on one more," Wes said.

"More juice?" she addressed Tony.

"I'm good." His attention remained focused on the phone.

Wes wondered about introverted people like Tony. The man didn't mean to be rude or appear rude. He just didn't know any better. If he thought to be polite and say *no, thank you* and didn't, then yes, he was at fault. The thought never registered. He missed a measure of empathy somewhere in his makeup. Only technology kept his attention longer than thirty seconds.

Tony glanced over Wes's head. "Ah, you're here."

Wes pushed back and stood before turning to greet the woman. He had a pink hoodie and thick, black, framed glasses in mind.

One glance into her striking blue eyes roiled feelings in the pit of his stomach. A sense of guilt that a married man with any values or conscience felt when his wandering eyes mixed with amorous thoughts. A sense of betrayal, loss and heartbreak all rolled into one, and all because of one woman — his late wife, Teri.

He thought time healed all.

"I'm Wes Hansen." He held out his hand.

She grasped his hand. "I'm Jessica Wahl. Nice to meet you, Wes."

Shoulder-length dark hair framed sharp features, a slightly crooked nose, high cheekbones, creamy-clear complexion and a permanent tan. She stood five-eight, maybe five-nine, with a one-hundred-thirty-pound runner's build. He guessed her age at forty, maybe thirty-nine, two years his junior.

Her eyes were . . . alluring.

He pulled out a chair for her.

"Hi, Tony." She unzipped her red jacket, revealing a yellow top, let it slide off her shoulders, and draped it over the back of the chair.

Tony scooted back his chair and stood. "Good to see you again, Jessica. Hope you haven't eaten. We're starved." He patted her on the shoulder and headed for the buffet line.

"I have not. So you've been waiting on me. Sorry I'm late. The traffic is terrible. I should have left the house earlier. I know better."

"No worries. Please, after you, unless you'd like to order something from the menu. I'll get the waitress."

"The buffet is fine. Thanks."

Wes held out his hand, open-armed, for her to lead the way.

They dished their plates and returned to the table. Wes had his usual eggs, sausage, and toast. Tony chose the entire buffet, one of everything, a plateful. Jessica used a small plate for a modest helping of cantaloupe, pineapple, and one boiled egg. The melon was out of season, but looked inviting.

She bowed her head for a three-count before picking up her fork.

"Jessica," Wes said. "Tony told you about our project?"

"He mentioned you're a private investigator and had a code to break, but he didn't elaborate."

"Thought I'd leave the specifics up to you," Tony said.

Wes cut and forked a bite of egg. "If you can call it a code. We think the man we're looking for is communicating with others, his cohorts or his boss, via social media posts. We're not sure. For now, our only leads are two cryptic messages, a dog, and two business cards."

"He's a ghost," Tony said. "We're real ghost busters."

Jessica looked between them and smiled. "That's different. Sounds intriguing."

"You active on social media, Jess?" Tony talked around a bite, staring at his phone.

"No. My life isn't that interesting. I like my privacy."

"Speaking of privacy. Our employer asked that we keep his in mind at all times." Wes's phone vibrated. A text. He unlocked it. *starbucks 270 & quebec near bass pro 10am if u can.* The phone displayed 9:15 above the message. What timing.

The text was either the answer to a long-recited prayer, or . . . he'd have to make the appointment to find out. He replied with *c u soon.*

"I have to leave you two for a bit."

Tony laid his fork and phone next to his plate. "Something wrong? You look like someone stole your dog."

"No, I'm fine. I won't be long. Don't wait on me for lunch when the time comes. Jessica, I'm sorry for the interruption, but I have to take care of this."

She stood when Wes did. "I'd like to help with your investigation. Can I leave you a number, references, a resume? Though I don't know what good my CV would do in this line of work."

He pocketed his phone. "We need another set of eyes on this one. Tony thinks you're the one for the job, and I agree. Are you free to travel?"

"I'm single. No ties. I'm willing to go anywhere you need me to. I don't have a passport."

"I don't think we'll need passports." He slipped Tony the keycard to the room. "Set up shop in my suite. Give Jessica anything she needs, including information, all of it. Our employer and the reason we've been hired. Don't hold back. She's on the team. Then start looking. Our guy is in his twenties, early thirties maybe. Look for off-the-wall stuff, like tree sit-ins or occupy protests, that kind of thing. Check with the Lubbock PD. I think you'll get a cold shoulder, but see if they've uncovered any clues they might be willing to share. Run down the canine link. Keep me posted if anything turns up."

He headed for his pickup. All of a sudden Jessica and his late wife weren't the only females distracting him.

5

Wes ordered a tall vanilla latte from the skinny barista kid behind the counter and took a seat in a chair at the first small table, closest to the entrance. The last person in line at the counter didn't have to worry about being last for long, as a revolving door of customers entered to purchase their morning hit of overpriced caffeine. Every time the door opened, the cool Colorado air rushed in and carried his way a hint of cinnamon and nutmeg from the condiment bar.

Glass walls gave patrons a view of the street and the entrance to an extensive strip mall. Jessica Wahl had struck him in a way he'd not been hit since his wife walked into his life. All his feelings were the result of one glance into her blue eyes. He didn't know her from Eve. What was he thinking?

He'd dated a couple of times in the years after Teri's passing. Nice ladies, but his heart wasn't in it. His lack of feelings for them wasn't anymore their fault than the emotions he felt in Jess's presence were hers.

He'd gone on a blind date one time, which was something he'd never done. A well-intentioned friend had arranged the evening. The moment he shook her hand, he knew her designs far exceeded his expectations for the outing. A week later, again, he had to do something he'd never done before: tell her to get lost. She wouldn't take *no* for an answer.

So what was Jessica's story? Widowed? Divorced? So crazy no one would have her? The latter was not readily apparent. What were the odds she'd never been married and if not, why?

She'd bowed her head before she ate. Seemed as though he was seeing more and more of that these days.

He sipped his coffee and scanned the lot for his daughter. Every passing car drew his attention. Lisa's text read ten o'clock. He had twenty minutes to wait, but he didn't know what for. The last time he'd seen her she'd been eighteen. The parting wasn't good. Time could heal wounds or allow them to fester. His pain had done neither. The ache in his heart was more like a deep cavity in a tooth that wouldn't hurt until he had sweet thoughts about her.

A display case next to him held some pricey items. Coffee beans at $40 a bag and cups at $15. Plastic cups and small bags too. One stainless espresso machine priced to sell at $1,200. They'd lost their minds. He wondered how many of those moved off the shelf.

Like the green square in an automatic camera picked out and focused on different faces and objects in the same frame, his daughter's face emerged from between the bottom shelf and green bags of coffee. She smiled, held up her hand in front of her face, and waved.

He wondered how he'd missed her as he crossed the shop to her table. He would recognize his own child.

"Hi," she said.

He was numb. Dumbstruck. Pregnant?

"Sorry to startle you, Dad."

"Do I look startled? I'm, I don't know, elated." Five years ago, she looked like she'd fallen face first into a fishing tackle box. The studs and piercings in her ears, eyebrows, and nose were gone, and her natural brown hair had replaced the gothic black. Not startled but thankful. "I'm sorry, Lisa, but, but, I don't . . ."

"It's OK. I didn't mean to be sneaky. I

51

went to the restroom. When I came out, you were already seated. Looks like you've got a lot on your mind. I watched you through the shelves. Gave me time to think about how to introduce myself. I've been doing that for weeks, since our first correspondence, thinking about seeing you and what I'd say. I was as lost for words as you look to be now."

"You were on my mind, but I watched for you outside. You're so, so —"

"Different?"

She was different. Unexpectedly. Giving her a hug and a kiss crossed his mind, but given their past and the years gone, he thought he'd wait. "You look great, honey. I-I'm sorry, but I don't know where to begin."

"Neither do I." She indicated the chair across the table from her with a nod. "Maybe sitting would be a good start."

He felt self-conscious and didn't know why. No one was watching the exchange, and whose business was it anyway? He pulled out the chair and sat. Her eyes were bright, like those of the little girl he remembered before their lives fell apart. She'd gained weight, as expected, but not too much. She looked happy, radiant. There was something special about the aura of a woman with child.

"Dad, you're staring."

"I can't help myself." He held his gaze and smiled.

She closed the laptop, clasped her hands on top of the computer, twirled the simple silver wedding band with her thumb and forefinger and searched his face. "I'm sorry, Dad."

"Lisa, we don't have to go back there."

"I do. For a minute, yes I do. I —"

"Lisa —"

"Stop. Please stop." It wasn't a plea.

Her green eyes didn't waver. She was her own person, a woman with the same strong will she'd always possessed. If she had something to say, then he would listen.

She must have sensed something in his resignation. She leaned forward. "I know you weren't responsible for Mom's death. She was. Though, looking back now, looking at my own problems controlling my hormones and depression, honestly, I'm not sure she was in control of herself. And it's not your fault I dove off the deep end. I said some terrible things. I missed Mom. It's taken me a long time to learn to live without her . . . and to find myself again."

He'd braced for the worst and hardened his emotions, but now he wasn't sure if he could talk. He reached for her hand, took it, and squeezed. She squeezed back. Tears crept down her cheeks.

"You're pregnant."

"I am, Grandpa." She smiled and wiped her cheeks with her fingers.

"That, my dear, and seeing you again so happy, makes my day. Your mom would have been proud of you. I'll bet Josh is proud." He immediately knew he'd made a mistake.

Her smile turned into pursed lips and a set jaw. She squinted at him, and her gaze left his face for the ceiling. "We haven't talked about my husband. Or if I'm even married."

"You're wearing a ring, and you're pregnant. A good assumption on my part."

"I am, and I am, but how did you know his name?" A long breath escaped her lips. "You've been snooping."

"Snooping is what I do for a living."

"On me?"

"God forbid, but eighteen years from now, when the child you're carrying is in high school and should turn his or her back on you and walk away for five years, you will do anything within your power to make sure that child is safe. It's called love, not control, like I mentioned to you five years ago."

She shook her head and put her hands on her stomach. "I don't know how to feel about you checking up on me. I suppose I should feel good, but I don't."

He usually kept a better handle on his tongue. He'd looked for general information about her, and nothing he'd done was illegal, even though, through Tony, he had the means to pry as deeply as he wanted. Some things a father neither wanted nor needed to know about his daughter. She'd walked away and he'd let her go — physically, not mentally or emotionally. Some of her wounds had healed, but not all. "Have you decided on a name?"

She sat up and glanced at her watch. "Not yet. We have a list, but haven't picked one."

Changing the subject wasn't working too well. "Boy or girl?"

"Josh thinks the surprise is part of the fun. One of those since-the-beginning-of-time mysteries a man and a woman shouldn't cheat themselves out of. I don't care either way, but I went with him on it. We'll wait and see." Her voice remained flat, matter-of-fact.

"Run some names by me."

She let out another long breath he recognized as frustration. Something she, as a teenager, would readily express when he didn't understand. "For a boy, Levi, Chance, Chase, Yancey, Colt, or Colton. For a girl: Addison, Chance again, Rilee, with two Es and Kylee with two."

"Yancey is a cool name. I've never heard of it before."

"You can't be serious. Men think alike. Josh likes it too. I'm going to insist upon Levi. Different websites have a mix of meanings, but from what I've found, Yancey is Native American for Yankee. He also likes Kylee if it's a girl, but that's Aboriginal for boomerang, so she won't be called that name either."

She surprised him. She'd done her homework. "Why Levi?"

"Josh and I have had our problems, my problems mostly. Levi has united us. That's what the name means — 'united' or 'connected'."

"So, you think it's a boy?"

She placed her hands on her stomach again. "I know this moving, living person inside of me is a boy."

"Well, I'm not going to argue. Your mom knew you and named you before you were born."

She searched his face, glanced at her watch again and opened the laptop. "Dad, I

56

have to go. I have a class in forty-five minutes."

"You're going to college?"

"To Denver University. You already know that if your nose sniffed into my life as deep as I suspect. College is hard. For me it's hard. I'm starting to wonder why I'm there."

That was one tidbit he didn't know. "Can I help? With tuition, with —"

"Josh takes care of me."

"That's not what I meant." He stood when she did.

She grabbed her backpack, a small one that looked all but empty. When the screen went black, she closed the computer and shoved it into the pack. "I really have to go."

"Can I walk you out?"

She nodded.

He opened the door and then stepped out behind her into a cool gust. The wind had shifted to a northerly direction, driving clouds into the area. The forecast had called for snow the past couple of days. So far, they'd been spared. Might get a dose after all.

His daughter didn't waddle. The baby still rode high. He'd guessed seven months. Close. He realized he'd missed an obvious detail. She wore green bibs, like the Oshkosh

57

brand young kids wore. She'd had a pair as a child. They were cute on her. Today, she wore a yellow long sleeve shirt, something she would have never done five years earlier. Even in freezing weather she would have worn short sleeves to display the tattoos on her forearms.

At the curb she stopped and faced him. "Dad, e-mail me, text me. I'll write back. I'll let you know how Levi is doing. He won't be here until the first week of July. Can we go slow?" Her eyes searched his face again. This time, pleading for the right answer.

He held out his hand and she took it. "As slow as you need to, Mrs. Bell."

Her lips hinted at a smile to show pleasure at the mention of her title. She kissed his cheek and walked away. Her lips left a small spot of moisture just below his cheekbone on the right side. It felt cold in the breeze.

6

Monday, April 8

Meshach stayed right on the I-10 loop when the highway forked toward downtown New Orleans. High-rise banks, hotels, and assorted office buildings loomed ahead. Beyond the city proper, the Greater New Orleans Bridge spanned the Mississippi River. Cranes, ship-loading facilities, factories, and warehouses lined both sides of the lazy, muddy river.

Traffic moved at every speed but the posted sixty miles an hour. He set the cruise control at sixty-two and planted the black sedan in the center lane. The car had 4,000 miles on it. For all practical purposes, a brand new vehicle, but he'd checked the taillights and turning signals before he left the drop. He wanted to stay under the radar in every respect. A cop with nothing better to do than critique signal lights would be a problem.

The same with obeying the speed limit — never exactly on the number and never under it. A guy his age drove under the limit when he had car problems or something to hide. He'd heard stories about southern, good-ole-boy towns where issuing tickets funded Christmas for the sheriff's passel of kids. One mile an hour over the limit: speeding. One mile an hour under: drunk.

Once across the river, he took Highway 23 southeast through Belle Chase. The highway was the only route along the Mississippi River to Venice. He paid particular attention to the massive ships on the river. Towering vessels, some seven hundred feet or more in length, sat in their moorings or traveled the river road.

Sixty miles later, he saw the sign *Fish Camps 4 Rent.* He turned right onto a graveled track, ascended the levee toward the ocean and stopped when he topped out. The levee he parked on protected the population who lived along the highway from the ocean to the south. Its twin to the north held the river at bay. The middle cabin of the five in front of him would be his home for the next few days.

He followed the gravel road as it looped across the back of the houses. He stopped in a turnout behind cabin C and got out with his computer bag and backpack. A pleasant seventy-five degrees greeted him. The wind couldn't make up its mind what direction to blow. A puff from the right smelled like the grass left in a mower bag for a week, a puff from the left like rotten fish mixed with shrimp. He wondered which odor was normal.

He preferred desert. Arid rock and dirt didn't smell like anything unless it rained or the spring flowers and cacti bloomed.

Like most of the structures along the coast, all five of these places were built on poles twelve feet or so above the marsh to keep a hurricane from washing them away.

Water lapped at the arc of wooden walkways, docks and boat slips in front of the cabins. The only boat rocked gently in the middle slot across from his house. If he had to guess, the craft came with the place and was his to use for the week.

He trotted up the steps. After a minute of searching, he located the key in the hidden groove along the edge of the jamb and let himself in. Now, he'd see just how far Lamech's sphere of influence reached.

The kitchen and living room combo with sweeping French doors led to a large deck and made the place airy. Two big fans hung from the ceiling. The white sink, black microwave, matching dishwasher and stove made for a simple kitchen. The sink sat in an island with four padded barstools on the opposite side. Three bedrooms and one bath made up the rest of the house. Like the outside, all the woodwork was cypress.

He placed his cell phone and computer on the island and walked into the back bedroom to drop his backpack on the king-size bed.

His phone chirped. He trotted back into the kitchen, glanced at the number, and snatched the phone off the counter. "Have you lost your mind?"

"Excuse me?"

"I didn't stutter. No phone calls. If you have something you want to say to me, use the net." Meshach walked to the couch and dug behind the cushions until he felt cold steel.

"I'm paying the bills."

What arrogance. Meshach pulled the .45 Kimber semiautomatic pistol from behind a cushion. It was clean and smelled like gun oil. The butt held a full clip of jacketed hollow points. He eased the slide back to reveal the round in the chamber. "I don't care. I'm doing the job, risking my life. We've never met in person, but if you call me again, we will."

"That's funny. You're threatening me, and you don't even know who I am."

"You keep that line of thought. Make yourself feel safe. Who you are means nothing to me, but don't ever make the mistake of assuming I can't find you. I've got an area code to start searching. Listen to me. Are you listening?"

A hard breath sounded in his ear. He held the phone out and pushed *end.*

You'd better get the message.

Heat rose in his face. That moron might be paying the bills, but Meshach was no one's employee, period. If Lamech didn't have enough sense to know not to use the phone, he'd better find some, quick.

Meshach didn't know the man's true identity, just as Lamech didn't know Meshach's, but the seed had been planted. Lamech would have trouble sleeping now. He'd be looking over his shoulder at every turn wondering if the boogieman was about to pounce.

A new box of .45, ACP ammo lay under the right cushion. He tossed it on the island, stuffed the pistol in his belt and pulled down his shirt to cover it.

He eyed the kitchen drawers. Monty Hall came to mind. *Let's Make a Deal. Mom's favorite. Which door do I want?* He jerked open the middle drawer next to the sink and ran his hand along its bottom. Wrong door. He pulled open two more before he found the bundle of cash. He sniffed the banded pack of fresh bills, peeled fifty Ben Franklins off the top, and stuffed them into his pants pocket. The five grand remaining, he tossed into the freezer. Another forty grand was stashed in the house. He'd locate the rest later.

He locked the door on the way out.

7

Wes walked into his room, and Jessica looked up and smiled. She sat at the little desk in the corner, eating yogurt from a small container with a plastic spoon.

He turned one of the chairs next to the couch toward her and plopped down. "Where did Tony run off to?"

She finished a bite and pointed over her shoulder with the spoon. "In search of a burger and fries. He's been gone ten minutes. How was your outing?"

"All well. I guess you're up to speed on our employer, who we're looking for and why?"

"I am. Strange case, or at least it seems so to me. I don't feel productive. I mean I'm working, looking, I just can't identify a specific item I would call completed."

"You're correct about the strange part. Don't worry about your progress. This type

65

of thing takes time. Anything new on our man or the points I mentioned this morning?"

"We inquired about the dog at SPCA, the Humane Society, and various animal shelters. Even looked through the pet classified on various lists. You wouldn't think describing a dog to someone would be so difficult. One lady wanted to know what kind of personality the 'dog in question' had. I think the root word in personality was lost on her. We may need a mug shot of him. No pun intended. On the police side, Tony talked to a detective who seemed willing enough to share information, but he didn't have much to share. He said no DNA or prints were found anywhere at the scene, including on the glass bottle." She closed a laptop that had to be hers because Tony wouldn't own a PC, and sat back in the chair.

Wes grabbed his pad and a pencil. "What are your first thoughts about the posts?"

"Off the wall. The name Anjali is foreign and foreign to me. The post is random, like Lamech just grabbed names out of the air and plugged them into the sentence."

"Tony thinks they're communicating. A code of some kind with no good end in mind."

She nodded. "I would agree. The names

66

are too random for it not to be a code, and based on that assessment, I think we should include Sullivan and Lamech in our searches. This is a conspiracy of some kind, and we might identify and locate Meshach through those contacts."

Spot on. Wes was impressed. "Did you mention that to Tony?"

She shook her head. "He'd already left, but I was in the process of looking up J. Sullivan. Even with the J for the first letter of the first name, if that's legit, the individuals are endless. Plus, other than the Meshach angle, what do I look for? I'm afraid I'm Internet challenged compared to Tony. It takes me longer to go through the lists."

Jessica moved her handbag from next to her computer to the floor by her chair. A small tag with her name printed on it hung from a side pocket. Seemed like every convenience store had a rack of them on the counter next to the cash register. Jessica's resembled a Colorado farm vehicle license plate: white letters on a forest green background.

Could Meshach's code be that easy?

"Jessica, do me a favor and help me chase an idea. Are you online?"

She opened her computer. "I am. Shoot."

"Search for popular baby's names and

definitions."

She held the yogurt in her left hand and typed with the other. "Got it. An A to Z compilation."

"Check for the name Levi. Give me a definition."

She typed. "United or connected. It's Hebrew. Oh, I know the origin of Levi. That was Leah's third child. I don't think she was Jacob's favorite because her dad deceived him and sneaked her, the ugly older sister, into his tent on his wedding night, instead of Jacob's real love, Rachael. Some real strange marriage rituals in those days. But anyway, after Levi . . . Oh, sorry, I'm off track."

She seemed to know the Bible well. "Try Meshach," he said.

She typed, paused, typed again and looked up. " 'Draws with force'."

Before he could suggest another one she said, "Lamech is Hebrew. It means 'strong or powerful'. Hang on, Joan, Joan means 'gracious'. Sullivan means . . . one second . . . 'dark-eyed one.' Jordan means 'flows from a river.' "

He wrote down the definitions. "What about Oleos?"

"Is it a name? I think of butter."

"I don't know. You tell me."

She set aside the yogurt and engaged the other hand. Wes sensed they were onto something, but what?

"Oleos isn't listed on this site. Let me check somewhere else. One second . . . ah, it's Spanish for holy oil. My niece looked up names for her kids. Is this code as simple as the meaning of names?"

"Maybe, but where's the key? What about the other two names, Anjali and Hemmingway?"

After a minute she looked up from the screen. "Anjali means 'proposing' and Hemmingway is 'someone who lives by or near Hemming's Way.' Not really a definition, but . . ." She shrugged. "Hang on. Let me search each name by itself."

As she concentrated on her computer, Wes wrote out Lamech's post, inserting the literal meaning in place of each name and underlined each meaning. *Proposing to see gracious for holy oil with man who lives near hemming's way.* Unbelievable. He rearranged them in his head. *Proposing man who lives near Hemming's Way to see gracious for holy oil.*

Nuts.

"Are you ready?" Jessica asked.

Wes nodded.

"Lamech is a company in Houston in the

metal building business. Cedric Lamech is a Frenchman who produced some videos about . . . who cares. I can't read it. Janet Lamech wants you to follow her blog."

"Next. Pick another one."

"OK, Meshach. An actor. Meshach Taylor. A hunter, Meshach Browning, lived in the 1800s and wrote a book about hunting. And, of course, the Meshach of Bible fame."

"Look at Joan."

"Joan, Joan is Joan, wait . . . Joan Jett, Joan Crawford, Joan Collins, Joan of Arc, and Joan Baez. Movie stars, singers and another French national. All women. There are millions of references to search."

Maybe he was off track. With no second name, something had to give. He unlocked his phone. He needed to call his old friend, Bubba, thank him for the reference, and pick his brain. A federal prosecutor would have access to other databases too.

He'd never been to Lubbock, Texas. Might be time to fly down for a visit and snoop around.

"You know." Jessica held up a finger. "Lamech posted to *see Joan,* like a person, but Meshach posted he was *in Joan.* I'd say I'm at the supermarket, but in Denver or in Houston. Meshach is either in or at somewhere, a place, not with a person. Joan of

Arc laid siege to Orleans, in France, in the 1400s. Ernest Hemmingway wrote *The Old Man and the Sea.* I'm just guessing, but do you think he's talking about New Orleans, Louisiana?"

Wes set his phone onto the coffee table. "Girl, you're brilliant. You know what else? The name *Oleos* doesn't have a thing to do with holiness. I hope you brought a suitcase. We're leaving."

Monday evening

Meshach counted his chips once more — eleven hundred dollars — and then let them slide through the fingers of his right hand into the palm of his left hand over and over. The dull, rhythmic clunk played to him like a soothing melody.

Bet inside or outside, even or odd, red or black, or straight up on one number?

Six gamblers and a dozen onlookers stood around the roulette table. One broad eyed his chips and leaned toward him to say something in a raspy voice. Smoke emanated from her red lips as she spoke. She used the hand with the red lipstick-stained cigarette between the fingers to wave and accent her point. Whatever that was. She'd been looking him over since he'd started playing. He thought of her as the painted lady. More like war paint. Lashes, brows, lids, and lips, not a spot of bare skin visible. The thick layer radiated cracks like a dried riverbed. Twenty years and a thousand packs of smokes earlier, she might have landed a high roller. Now, she looked like she'd settle for anything breathing.

The dealer spun the wheel and thumbed the white ball along the groove in the opposite direction. Nothing in, nothing out. Meshach placed the chips on thirteen just as the man called, "No more bets" and waved his hand over the roulette table.

Thirty-seven to one. Meshach liked long odds.

Gamblers and spectators watched the wheel. Their heads wallowed consciously or unconsciously as they followed the wheel one direction or the ball as it traveled in the opposite direction. The marble fell from the slot and bounced over the numbers, finally resting on black twenty-six.

Four grand lasted long enough for him to drink two cocktails and weak ones at that. His luck at the tables had been running thin lately.

A skinny man sporting a wife-beater T-shirt and bibs held a lighter to another menthol cigarette for the painted lady. Looked like a good match.

Meshach exited the casino, strolled down Canal, and hung a right onto Bourbon Street. The place didn't know Mardi Gras had ended two months earlier. Vaudeville, burlesque, a traveling circus with a tin man, a clown, a midget, and a fat lady performed on every corner. Some had talent and some did not.

The blare of a trumpet drew him into a small, open-air establishment. He found a spot to lean against the bar where he could see the street and then ordered a Hurricane to drink. The trumpeter gave it a good effort. His cheeks puffed up with air like a chipmunk's full of acorns.

"Hi, darling, what's your name?"

He glanced right. A scantily dressed waitress had slipped up beside him and posed with her back against the bar, arms up, elbows propped on the bar top behind her. "Hey. My name's Paula." She held out her hand.

The little tuft of white feathers she wore in her hair reminded him of Gamble Quail. Meshach took the slim fingers then stared at her, eye-to-eye. "I'm Meshach."

Her gaze wandered over his face, but like tinted windows of a car, he knew his dark glasses wouldn't allow her to see who was looking back. He stared her down for a long six-count before she pulled her hand back and turned her head away.

He left her there, leaning against the bar, stepped onto the sidewalk, and gazed down the street. Paula, she said her name was. Didn't take long to ditch her.

Meshach saw his old school mate first, turned too quickly, and bumped into a lady who made it an issue when her drink spilled. The commotion drew Lane's attention. "Elgin, is that you?"

Meshach ignored him and walked away.

"Elgin, it's me. Lane, Lane Woodard."

The crowd provided perfect cover. Meshach weaved in and out at a ground-eating pace, trying not to be too obvious in his escape. Lane had approached from the Canal Street side, forcing Meshach to walk farther down Bourbon. He entered another establishment at the first intersection and cut across a large, open area in the corner of the building. Once out of view, he shed his red jacket, draped it over an empty chair on the way out the other side, and turned his hat around backwards. He circled, walked to the opposite side of Bourbon, and moved in behind three thirty-something women. He spotted Lane fifty yards ahead. One of the two guys with him stood well over six feet tall, wore a yellow ball cap, and made them easy to follow. They crossed the littered street, changed course, and proceeded down the sidewalk toward Canal. Lane looked back twice. Not a casual glance, but an obvious search of his back trail.

The absence of the red jacket changed the game. The human eye always picked up the last visual cue. Whether shape or color. He'd be harder to single out. Now, he was a dutiful husband in a white shirt tagging along behind his better half.

Barriers blocked traffic at the corner of Canal Street and Bourbon Street and every intersection northward, making the street the sidewalk. Music blared. No pattern to the flow of human traffic. A group of sweaty black kids beat out a tune on plastic buckets while two kids in wife-beater T-shirts and low riding jeans break-danced on the sidewalk. A handful of admirers gathered and clapped. Small change littered a plastic trashcan lid on the pavement in front of them.

A woman in tall heels and fishnet hose strutted along in front of the Hustler Club. A burley bouncer in a black suit watched the oglers with a wary eye in case someone decided to quit gawking and handle the merchandise.

Leaving the rental house was stupid. He'd been safe, out of sight, and unknown, but he couldn't have guessed that fifteen hundred miles from home, he'd bump into a guy he went to junior high with. Dumb luck.

He thought of himself as a professional, but professionals didn't make mistakes. Not if they wanted to stay employed or under the radar and out of prison.

Twelve years had passed, but he'd recognized Lane. Worse yet, Lane had recognized him. They'd been buds once. Meshach liked him. He'd wished his old friend would have walked away and he did, but then Lane looked back. He shouldn't have looked back.

When Lane and his two buddies reached Canal Street, where Bourbon ended, the taller man turned left, east, and was quickly absorbed by the noisy crowd. Lane and the third man waited for the light to change, crossed, and continued west on Canal.

The sun had set. Crowds thickened. People emerged from the dark outlying areas like bugs drawn to the lights of the big city.

Meshach walked close to the curb, using light poles, signs, and people for cover.

Lane's companion talked a lot. He was the animated type who'd have trouble communicating with his hands tied behind his back. At Baronne, a one-way street south, they turned left down the east sidewalk.

Meshach crossed to the west side of the street and increased his pace to pull even with them.

At Union Street, Lane clapped the other man on the shoulder, shook his hand, and they parted ways. The deep rumble and pop of a motorcycle passing through the intersection drowned out their dialogue. The second man crossed the street in front of Meshach and entered the Wyndham Hotel.

Lane strolled like he had nothing to do, but in the middle of the next block, a neon sign glowed *Comfort Inn and Suites.* If the hotel happened to be his destination, the time had come. His old friend was alone and approachable. Another sixty feet and Lane would pass a recess in a building. Meshach checked both directions. Not a soul. The stars were lining up.

He removed the glasses, put them in his pocket, and crossed the street, walking straight at Lane. Timing meant everything. If Lane saw him short of the dark alcove, he'd have to regroup. Thirty feet, twenty feet, ten, a shoe scuffed on the sidewalk, and Lane glanced back and stopped.

Just right.

White teeth in the darkness. A smile. Expression didn't matter. Whether recognition or question, he didn't want to know. The wide, four-inch-long blade went in with ease at the base of the throat. No way for the man to scream. Meshach grabbed him in a headlock with the crook of his arm across Lane's eyes, turned him, and shoved hard, forcing him into the recess, against the rough brick wall, in the dark corner. Lane's grip felt like iron. He struggled, valiant, but much too late.

Meshach held on and squeezed him like he had the birds and rabbits he'd caught as a kid, so the chest had to work to expand, until the heart beat its last. Death wouldn't be long. If the tip of the blade reached a gap in the spine and severed the cord, only seconds. If not, then maybe a minute.

Patience, but not too much, someone would walk by soon. Removing the blade or slicing the throat would be stupid, too much blood. Hard to explain bloody clothes.

The stench of a fleeting life drifted up as the bowels and bladder turned loose, and he knew the soul had left. Tension eased and the hands gripping his forearm fell away. He let the body slide into a sitting position and removed the knife.

Now, the wallet and cell phone. No phone.

He tried to think back. Had he seen Lane with a phone? Everyone had a Smart Phone. He remembered Lane as geeky. He'd have one, but where? He did another quick search. Too dark. Nothing. Voices. He jerked the wallet from Lane's hip pocket and then stepped out so he could see down the sidewalk. To the right, a couple, arm-in-arm, ambled toward him forty feet away. He turned to face them, staggered and made a show of zipping his fly. Their conversation ceased. They were wary. He'd created doubt. They didn't want to be near him, not now. They crossed the street, creating distance between themselves and the unapproachable.

He grinned then bit his lip. He'd just made a big mistake.

8

Monday evening, April 8

Wes called Jordan to arrange a ride. No answer.

As he packed, his mind raced from confidence to doubt. Jess's interpretation of the post made sense. Or did it? Tony's earlier comment about Bethany's involvement in a conspiracy with two unknown cyber identities against her father held little weight, but nagged him. Like the Hearst heiress, Patty. Daughter hates daddy, so she conspires with her kidnappers and robs banks. No. Cole was due an update. That thought would be absent.

Moving shop to Louisiana risked what? Time and money. The move made sense. He tried to call Jordan again. Went to voicemail. He disconnected and it rang. "This is Wes."

"This is Jordan." The pilot didn't sound like his chipper self.

"I'd like to bum a ride to New Orleans if you're available."

"Hate to say it, but I'm ill. I normally fly with an attendant. She's been off sick. Now I know what she's got."

"I'm sorry to hear that. I'll leave you be. I'm going to arrange a commercial flight on the first thing smoking."

"Sorry. I'll call you when I'm on the mend. I'll call Cole too. You might warn Tony. This bug is not amusing."

"Yes, sir, I will. Thanks." Wes hung up.

He plopped down in the chair at the desk and opened his computer case. *Never bounce until you hit a bump.* He just had.

Tuesday morning, April 9
Meshach woke, kicked off the sheet, and rolled out from under the covers. The clock on the nightstand displayed 5:32. He stood and stretched then dropped and started a set of pushups. *One, two, three . . .* Seconds lapsed, a minute, two minutes . . . *ninety-five, ninety-six, ninety-seven.* At one hundred, in a swift, fluid motion he moved into a crouch and stood.

Gray dawn provided the light for him to make his way down the hallway without turning on a bulb. As he passed the bathroom, he caught a glimpse of his movement

81

in the wall mirror and stopped. He didn't need a light to appreciate the reflection.

The fans in the kitchen cooled the sweat on his bare chest and back. He started the coffeemaker, grabbed his laptop from the counter, pushed open the French doors, and stepped onto the large deck overlooking the docks. During the previous evening, three boats had joined his twenty-five-footer in the slips. Two of similar make and a fancy, sleek beast that looked like it would take a cool million just for the down payment.

Contentious gulls squawked and fought with each other over a scrap of trash. Their noisy bickering grated on his nerves. A snowy egret winged south into the humid breeze like it couldn't stand them either.

He decided the normal smell for the area leaned toward a mower bag full of wet grass. When the wind blew out of the southeast he got a whiff of the abnormal, a raucous stench from a fish processing plant a mile away. He wondered what useable product man had discovered from the source of such a foul odor.

White, lightly constructed steel and aluminum patio furniture was arranged around the deck. He placed his computer on the glass tabletop, pushed the power button, and left for the kitchen and a cup of black coffee. After returning, he logged onto the net. Nothing new from his admirers, but they'd want to know his status. He posted *patience??* then searched for New Orleans news sites, opened WWL-TV, clicked on the heading *Crime,* and scrolled down. *Man killed baby daughter who wouldn't stop crying. Man charged with raping four-year-old. Reward offered for information leading to . . . Arrests made in a string of burglaries.* The list went on, forty items total, ending with *Nevada man found dead on Baronne. Seeking information . . .* He opened the story and read. *Lane Woodard, 25, of Las Vegas, Nevada . . . homeless man in custody . . . lacking motive.* The article didn't mention a cause of death or missing wallet. The police chose to omit those tidbits. They always left something out of the public disclosure, so some moron could hang himself with his loose tongue.

Lane's driver's license and credit cards lay on the table inside, next to the couch. The missing formal ID didn't stop the NOPD from identifying the body. They either canvassed area hotels for absent patrons and put two and two together, or Lane's fingerprints were on file. No matter, he would be another cold case gathering dust with a

thousand others in a dingy basement somewhere if the old drunk Meshach planted the
knife on wasn't convicted of the crime first.

A door slammed. The neighbors to the
west, three men in light shirts, shorts and
boat shoes walked down the cypress steps
to the dock carrying coolers and bags. Two
of the men liked to eat. Their shirts hung
over their bellies creating an eave to shade
their feet. The third guy looked buff, at the
very least physically capable. The key was
his will to succeed, to win at all costs. At-
titude made small men formidable adversar-
ies.

They turned down the first slip and approached the fancy boat. Someone yelled a
greeting and stepped out of the cabin.
Owner, guide, or both? The men boarded.
After a minute, its engines started with a
low rumble.

Meshach didn't want or need a guide. His
boat had all of the electronic GPS guidance
equipment he needed. Navigating the gulf
would not be a problem.

Looking at the weather forecast, he had
two days, maybe until noon on Saturday.
Then, the gulf would be rough with twenty-
knot winds, seas five to eight feet, and a
forty-percent chance of thunderstorms.

The big boat's engine tone changed pitch.

Water boiled around the stern. She backed out of the slip and made her way through the watery streets dredged through the marsh, toward the open water of the Gulf of Mexico. *Goin' South* adorned the stern.

He sipped the coffee and pecked at his computer. He opened a blank Word document and typed *Mars, Nakika, Ursa, Devils Tower,* and *Thunder Horse.* Of the many deep-water oil production facilities, these had made his short-list. After a second, he typed Ace of Spades in bold and underlined it. Then, he closed the file without saving it and opened Chirp again. Lamech had posted *ur isle of choice.*

Perfect.

Avoiding contact with his neighbors would make life easier. That meant leaving before sunup or after they left to fish. Darkness suited Meshach, but he'd be nuts to navigate the watery streets through the marsh when he couldn't see, at least on his first trip out. Once the GPS logged his initial excursion, he'd be able to follow the stored track and use the instruments to come and go as he pleased at any hour.

He stepped away from the window, opened the freezer, and removed the cash he'd tossed in the night before. Three large bills would pad the seven in his pocket. He stuffed them away, then tucked the remaining Franklins behind a package of fish in the back of the freezer.

He grabbed his small backpack, an ice chest he'd prepared with water and snacks, and made his way out the door, down the steps onto the dock. He'd yet to pilot the twenty-five-foot ShearWater Bay boat and looked forward to the experience. The 300 horsepower Yamaha, V6 outboard mounted on the transom of the V-hulled craft promised to be nothing less than exhilarating.

Before reaching the boat, he scanned the two houses east of his place. The nearest one sat empty. The second one had four male tenants, a night-going, noisy lot who didn't leave the slip in their boat until after eight o'clock. Seemed like a late departure for fishermen. Their labored trudge down the dock to load and board the boat hinted at a long night in a bottle of something stronger than soda pop. No surprises at either house. Nothing moved. The fourth place, the westward one closest to his, housed the men who'd boarded the baby yacht at dawn. A red car, parked in the small graveled area behind the fifth and last abode, hinted at an occupant, but Meshach hadn't seen anyone stir.

He stepped aboard the ShearWater, set down the cooler, and took a seat at the center console. The four-stroke engine hummed the second he turned the key. The navigation gear booted. He opened the backpack, removed a handheld GPS device, and turned it on. The coordinates displayed by each matched. He marked both with his waypoint, and titled them *camp*.

"Good morning."

So much for avoiding the neighbors. The brunette approached from his left, his blind side. She stood on the dock, at the bow of the boat, one hand on her hip. She was barefoot and bare from head to toe except for a camouflage bikini her shapely curves wore well. She seemed more than comfortable, half-dressed and approaching a man she didn't know.

"Good morning back," he said. He gave her just a hint of a smile to acknowledge her teasing pose.

"So, nice boat. Are you going out this morning?" She shifted her weight, moving her hips from one side to the other like a willow swaying in a gentle breeze. Actresses earned hard cash for worse performances. She was good . . . real good. She purred in a low, barely discernible whisper, forcing a man to lean close to hear only her. He knew the type. The kind who should have a tat on their forehead that read *woe-man.*

"I am. It's a cool, beautiful day. Seas are calm."

"Where's your fishing gear? I've never seen a guy come here who didn't want to, uh, catch something nice."

The hint didn't slip by him and why not? He'd just be another man boating with his girl. With what she displayed, no one would notice his presence. "I'm not much of a fisherman. Just trying to get away from the rat race and relax a bit."

"Would you like some company? I'm Shanteel."

She strutted the length of the slip then leaned over to offer him the back of her slender hand. He took it, but not as the prince she might have expected; he squeezed gently and glanced at the naked ring finger on the left hand she'd planted on her knee as she reached for him across the small gap.

He smiled. "Call me Meshach. Come aboard."

Her tongue swept over full lips, leaving them moist and redder. "Meshach? Cool name. Baby, give me two minutes. I've got a lunch and drinks packed." She spun and trotted toward the end house. A red and yellow butterfly tattoo rode the tanned, smooth skin on her right shoulder.

He placed the GPS inside the backpack. Still in the pack, out of sight, he eased the action back just enough to expose the chambered round in the .45, then holstered it and zipped the pack.

9

Meshach entered open water and pushed the throttle to the stops. The 300hp engine romped. The Kevlar-reinforced hull planed out on the glassy ocean surface immediately, like cruising a sheltered lake. The boat handled well, responding to the slightest movement of the wheel.

The craft wasn't a Rolls Royce, but it had a hood ornament. Shanteel was perched upon the bow, her lithe, tanned body gleaming in the sun she seemed not to get enough of. So far, he liked her. She was a display, eye-candy for any man who wished to gander, and not a talker. Give her a smile and she'd preen and pose as though pageant judges were critiquing her movements.

He steered east toward the mouth of the Mississippi. The muddy highway held freighters, fishing boats, oilfield workboats, crew boats, tugs, barges, and the occasional cruise ship whose home berth lay adjacent to downtown New Orleans.

The Laurel Lee, a small freighter, as freighters go, had her bow pointed out to sea. He pulled in behind her and slowed to match her speed, keeping five hundred feet between them. The ship travelled steady at twelve knots — a little over thirteen miles an hour.

He turned the horses loose again, pushing fifty-eight miles an hour, what looked like max for the boat, and sped toward her stern. The six-foot wake from the steel beast rose slowly on each side as he neared. He eased in close, into the edge of the turbulence produced by the twin screws churning just below the surface on each side of the massive rudder. The bay boat wallowed in the roiled water.

Shanteel faced aft, away from the freighter. She seemed oblivious to the change in wave motion until the shadow of the freighter engulfed them. Then she twisted in the seat and raised her eyebrows at Meshach.

He shrugged and turned right, scaling the moving wave with ease. As the ship's bridge loomed above them, he slowed again to match her speed. The hull was slick, no ladders, nothing to get a toehold on between the sea and the handrails skirting the outer edge of the ship. The deck stepped down in height from a good thirty feet tall at the bow to the lowest point aft, behind the bridge, no more than eighteen feet. Closer to fifteen. Loaded, those heights would be significantly less.

The deep, vibrating bellow of the ship's horn shook the air. Shanteel gave her best wave to three men standing on the uppermost landing. Goofy broad thought they'd honked at her, and maybe they had, but Meshach knew his boat was close, too close. The bay boat would splat against the hull of the Laurel Lee with no more notice than a bug hitting the windshield of a speeding car. No one would feel the impact or notice a scratch on the paint.

The men outside the bridge looked official. Blue coveralls, blue ball caps with white patches on the crowns, and all three stood at ease, military style. The ship's crew compliment ranged from eighteen to thirty persons of various responsibilities. Chief engineer, able-bodied seamen, electricians, motormen, mechanics, and the most important in Meshach's mind, at least one certified radio operator worked twelve-hour shifts.

He edged the boat ahead and veered right, angling south away from the vessel. A siren penetrated the wind and engine noise. From the left side of the freighter, a Coastguard boat moved to cut him off. Where had they come from? He could kick himself. He'd missed them.

Running would be dumb. Shows guilt and there was nowhere to go. He might outrun the much larger boat in the narrow lanes in the marsh, but out here, no way. They had a chopper at their disposal, only a radio call away too.

They'd seen him approach the freighter, or someone had reported him. In either case, they had him. He pulled the throttle back to neutral. The bay boat settled. A second later the siren stopped.

He made a mental note of the location of the lifejackets in the compartment under his seat and the two fire extinguishers mounted on each side of the center console. They would ask. Safety was always first and missing lifesaving equipment would warrant additional snooping. He had nothing to hide physically. The gun was legal. Everyone carried firearms. They could give him a ticket if something was missing. An Internet search would reveal the citation, and he'd be a blip on the radar screen.

Shanteel took her seat in the front and eyed the large white boat speeding toward them.

The boat slowed then turned and stopped two hundred yards away. A small crane lowered a rubber-craft with four puddle pirates dressed in blue coveralls over the side. It sped Meshach's direction. A woman's voice blared over a bullhorn, "Sir, please turn off the engine. We're coming alongside."

Two coasties moved to grapple the bay boat.

Meshach gave his best smile to their commander, a short attractive woman with her hair in a perfect bun topped with a blue USCG cap. "Something wrong, officer?"

Shanteel leaned back against the side of the boat, spread her arms wide across the top railing, and stretched her long legs out in front of her. She didn't hide her head-to-toe assessment of the other woman.

All four wore side arms. A stocky kid who looked like he'd played his last high school football game a week earlier put one leg over the gunnel, resting his foot on the rail of the bay boat. "Sir, you took a chance approaching the Laurel Lee the way you did. Do you have mechanical problems that need to be addressed? Or a steering or throttle malfunction?"

"Nope." Meshach gave Shanteel — who had yet to give the female coastie a break from her evaluation — a sideways glance. "I was distracted, if you know what I mean, and I let the moment interfere with my judgment."

The kid's gaze followed Meshach's to Shanteel and lingered a long moment before coming back. He gave the knowing smile of a worldly eighteen-year-old.

Meshach grinned. "Yeah, I'm testing this boat. Thinking about buying it. Thought I'd take my girl for a short cruise this morning."

As the three men glanced at Shanteel again, he assessed them. Pistols secured, but handy. One man had his thumbs hooked in the pockets of his coveralls. All three distracted. Easy to get the jump on. Not the woman. She watched him. She'd been around.

To her credit, Shanteel grinned and, most importantly, kept her mouth shut.

Meshach nodded at the tallest man. "How's your golf game?"

The guy blinked and patted his chest. "You talking to me? It's OK. Have we played together?"

"No, but I see you're a lefty and you play quite a bit." Meshach pointed to the man's hands. "The back of your right hand is white, with a brown V from the gap in your

95

glove. The other is tanned."

The coasties exchanged looks as the guy scanned the back of his hands.

The female nodded toward the center console of the bay boat. "Could I see your preservers, please? Show me that your fire extinguishers are charged?"

Meshach raised the seat cushion revealing half a dozen orange lifejackets and waited for her nod of approval before dropping the seat back in place. Then he opened the clips holding the ten-pound extinguishers and held them out so she could see the needles hovering in the green, charged area.

She tilted back her head far enough to look at him under her sunglasses. The stitching on her coveralls read *Moore.* "Very well. Thanks for your cooperation. Please try to observe the *Rules of the Road.* It's a good practice anytime, but especially between the sea buoys. Big vessels can't leave the lane, might run aground, and well, as you can imagine, it can take them several miles to stop. I'd hate for one to ruin your outing."

"Yes, ma'am, as would I." Meshach gave them a mock salute as they pushed away. He started the bay boat and engaged the motor.

Shanteel rose and moved in beside him as

he opened the throttle again. She slipped her hand under his shirt and let her long nails scratch their way up his spine to the middle of his back. She said something, but the wind snatched it out of her mouth.

He leaned into her. "Darling, that little purr isn't going to work at this speed. You'll have to speak up."

She looked back at the coastguard boat. The smaller boat had already been retrieved. "I said that was interesting, and you're a big fat liar."

He pulled his glasses down and peered into her deep green eyes. "Do you care?"

She seemed to wander his face then focused on his bad eye and flinched. "Where are we going, sweetie?" Her fingers slid down to the small of his back.

He looked ahead and replaced the glasses. *Smart girl. Get closer and change the subject.* "Not far. Maybe go out fifteen, twenty miles, goof off, see the sights, have lunch and enjoy the day."

"Cool." She glanced to their left. The Laurel Lee's hulk had turned eastward. "I've never been so close to one of those big ships. What's it carrying?"

"Nothing, she's empty. Look at her, riding high, the top of the screws nearly out of the water. See the change in color about halfway up the hull, from dull to bright red, that's the waterline when she's loaded."

"What does it carry?"

"Who knows? The ships leaving here are usually loaded with grain, soybeans, sulfur, coke, any number of things."

"Coke? Like cokes you drink?"

He knew she was going to ask. Clueless. "No, an oil refining residue. It's those huge black mounds you see stacked along the river here and there, near the refineries."

She nudged her shoulder in front of his arm, one of those let's-get-cozy moves. "You know a lot about ships. Are you a captain?"

"No, but I'm going to pilot one soon."

"You are?" She sounded surprised, like they'd known each other for years and she'd never heard such an absurd idea.

"Yes, I am. Only bigger." He looked toward the northwest where the Marathon refinery loomed. "Much bigger. Hopefully, one that's full of crude oil."

She leaned into him this time. "I didn't hear you, baby."

He smiled, eased his arm around her bare shoulders, and squeezed. She melted against him.

No, and for your sake, it's a good thing you didn't.

10

Tuesday afternoon, April 9

Wes stepped out of Louis Armstrong International Airport into a sauna. In two hours they'd flown from the threat of snow to a humid, musty-smelling eighty-five degrees. He preferred the former. Donning a coat smothered the chill, but nothing short of an air-conditioner relieved heat.

Jessica dragged her bag up beside him. Wes had noticed the lack of a wedding ring. She'd stated she was single. He'd missed that she didn't wear any jewelry, period, and no makeup. Not a puff of powder to be seen. With her complexion, she didn't need it, but the thought crossed his mind she might abstain for religious reasons.

"Woo, I bet Tony sheds his hoodie in this," she said.

He smiled. As long as he'd known Tony, the man had worn a black hoodie like a ritual robe, winter and summer. Wes had

Jessica at a disadvantage but for fun. "How much?"

"Really? A bet? I was kidding."

He held out his hand to shake. "I wasn't."

She looked back as Tony plodded through the automatic doors. "OK, a dollar."

"A, as in one?" he said. Her eyes really were mesmerizing, but he got their message and made a fist. She tapped his knuckles with hers.

Tony approached with two hard-sided cases in tow. "Our guy is chirping again. Posted one word, patience, followed by a couple of question marks. And whether it's an answer to Meshach or not, Lamech posted 'your isle of choice.' It's nuts. They're nuts." He heaved a big sigh and looked around. "Where's the taxi stand?"

Wes pointed down the street to their right. "The hotel is two hundred yards that way, across the street. It's an easy stroll. I've been there before."

Tony looked left through the covered drive. "It's hot. Too hot. If you're walking, I'll meet you there. I'm not dragging these anchors any farther than I have to." Before he shuffled away, he zipped the jacket and flipped the hood over his head.

Patience. A question accented with two marks. Isle of choice. None of it made any sense. Nuts? Yes. But no more than chirping. Who would have thought? Wes glanced at Tony again, then at Jess, and held out his hand, palm up.

She looked at his open hand then to his face. Azure eyes, or a mix of turquoise and teal, he didn't know how to describe them. "What?"

"The bet. See the hoodie." He pointed at Tony.

"You are kidding me. One dollar?"

"A bet is a bet. Every penny. I can take it out of your first check if you'd like."

"I'll have to owe you." She smiled and swiped at a dark strand of hair blowing across her face. "You're hard."

"Business is business. Come on. This way." He winked and then led her down the sidewalk to the traffic light, across Airline Drive, and left toward the hotel.

Tony strolled through the front door in time to meet them at the elevators, the hoodie still in place.

Wes handed his employees their keycards as they waited for the lift. "We're in a row, three-thirteen, fifteen, and seventeen. I'm in seventeen. Relax tonight. We'll get started in the morning."

They entered the elevator — Jessica with one suitcase and a computer bag first, then

Tony and his anchors, as he referred to them. Wes held his arm across the door and stepped in last.

"I meant to ask you about something before I fell asleep on the plane," Tony said. "That epiphany you had about the names; that just occurred to you out of the blue?"

"No . . ." In a way, Wes and Cole Blackwell were a lot alike when it came to their personal lives. Wes had never mentioned his daughter to Tony. What was there to tell? *Oh yeah, she hates me. Doesn't want to see me again, ever.* With his computer skills, Tony would have gathered his own dossier on his occasional employer long ago. He'd know about Teri and Lisa, but to his credit, he'd never uttered a word.

Wes swallowed the urge to keep his mouth shut. "My daughter, Lisa. She's expecting. When I asked her about names, she told me what they'd come up with. She'd researched the origins and meanings of a dozen or so, for boys and girls. That got me to thinking about our guy and his code."

The ding of a bell and the slide of elevator doors opening interrupted Tony's look of contemplation, air-filled cheeks and half-closed eyes.

"So," Tony continued as they strolled down the corridor, "you're going to be a papaw, eh, Papaw?"

Wes had been thinking about Levi's arrival all day, and not once had he felt the excitement that coursed through him when Tony mentioned *Papaw*. He smiled and gave Jessica a quick glance. "Yes, I guess I am, but I think I'll ask him to call me pops."

They arrived at room three thirteen. Tony fished out his card from the hoodie pocket. "I'm glad you're talking. Must have been good to see her again after so many years."

Jessica pushed by without a word, inserted the keycard, opened her door, and disappeared inside her room. The door clicked shut leaving heavy silence.

Tony's comment and Jessica's actions shocked Wes. Tony knew a lot more than he'd suspected, and Jessica just acted like a spoiled teenager. Not so much as an *excuse me*. What in the world had set her off?

Tony's cheeks filled with air again; then he let it escape out of the corner of his mouth. He shrugged and opened his room door. "I'll see you in the morning."

Wes found himself standing in the corridor alone. Was it something he'd said?

After opening his door, he pushed into the room and shoved the travel bag against the wall. He plopped down on the bed with the computer case on his lap and looked around — television in the center of an oak armoire, matching desk and swivel chair next to it, suitcase caddie against the wall, pint-sized closet with an ironing board and iron next to wooden hangers and plastic laundry bags, two green cushioned chairs, and a small coffee table. Hotels were all the same, and yet again, he occupied one alone. What scared him the most: he was becoming comfortable with the solitude.

He shuffled to the desk and removed his brown leather day planner from his computer case. Tony chided him for not having all the info entered into his smartphone or computer, and maybe he should, but he could lose the phone. Or one day it would spontaneously combust and all the info would go up in smoke. He could misplace the book too, but barring that, his notations would not disappear into cyberspace or wind up on some hacker's computer.

Over the next hour, he chronicled his team's activities and drafted an e-mail to Cole, citing what he hoped was a big step in finding their man. He included the supposed code names and their meanings and why they'd moved office to New Orleans. He stopped short of conjecture. He still didn't know if they were on the right track.

Invoicing the billionaire would be next,

but he'd have to think about the sum for a day or two. His rate for finding a runaway teen for a single mom and finding — maybe confronting — someone willing to do what Meshach had done, were two different things.

He drew out a simple flowchart on a white legal pad. Below the box titled *Meshach and associates,* he branched out to three additional blank boxes, then three more lines to empty boxes below the first three. Twelve boxes total. In the upper three, he entered their names. In the first box below his own name, he wrote *law enforcement.* In Tony's he added *backgrounds* and in Jessica's, *definitions.* The rest of the boxes remained empty. He looked at the scribbling a second then tore the sheet off the pad, wadded it up, and missed the trashcan in the corner with his toss.

He went over their next steps in his head, but those thoughts tumbled like clothes in a dryer. Where should they look now that they were in New Orleans? He needed to call Bubba, pick his brain, and catch up. Too many years had passed. He needed to pay a visit to the NOPD and establish a rapport. Let them know why he was in town. They needed another break, another revealing social media post or a mistake, something to point them in the right direction.

His cellphone chirped. "What do you have, Tony?"

"Nothing about the case, but I've been thinking about what Jessica did. Something I said about your daughter hit a nerve. You and I have never talked about Lisa or your late wife, but I know what happened. I know you've been estranged from Lisa a long time. I know, too, Jessica's ex-husband is some kind of high-powered lawyer and, as it turns out, a wife beater. She's said some things in the past, the whole story isn't clear, and I've never searched it out, but she still carries some old feelings around."

Seconds ticked. So she had an ex. What about children?

"Boss, don't hold it against her."

"Thanks, Tony. See you in the morning." He clicked off, stood, and looked out the window. Below, a surge of traffic sped down Airline Drive when the traffic light turned green. Another jet took flight. The intensity of the power it took to hurtle the aircraft into the air shook the hotel.

He tried to remember Tony's exact words. Something about seeing Lisa again, or how good it was to see her. Did Jessica think he'd abused his daughter?

He unlocked his phone, tapped *Messages*,

and reread Lisa's text of instructions for their meeting. He looked at his watch — 9:15 in New Orleans and 8:15 in Denver. She and Josh would be . . . what? Watching sitcoms? Painting the baby's room?

He ached to know.

11

Tuesday evening

Meshach ascended the metal stairs. The platform looked well maintained in the easily accessible areas. A fresh coat of paint covered the deck, handrails, and wellheads. Thick slabs of rust replaced the orange paint on the pylons, bracing and lower supports.

The wellhead topped with the production tree stood ten feet above the main deck. A white, navigation warning light mounted on the handrail and powered by a bank of batteries charged with solar panels clicked off and on. The incessant rhythm of that click was only slightly less irritating than the foghorn's repeated, piercing blare. The faint hum of gas streamed through the piping, like water from a faucet, and spanned the gap between the horn's blasts.

Meshach climbed the small work platform and checked the gauge on the wing valve —

just shy of 1500psi.

"Helloooo!" Shanteel yelled from the boat tied to the landing below. "Are we going to stay here all day? Baby, drink a beer with me. You haven't had one yet. I'm lonely." The last statement sounded like a reminder.

Three hours earlier, she'd twisted the top off the first beer and hadn't shut up since. Her mouth outran the boat at ninety-nine questions an hour. After the first thirty seconds and ten questions, he regretted he'd opted for the displeasure of her company.

Platforms dotted the ocean surface in every direction. Too many to number without losing count. He didn't loathe the sight, as did some of the more ardent earth-first believers he knew. Those morons didn't know their ideal world would take mankind back into the fifth century. Meshach liked his toys and the convenience of world travel at a moment's notice.

"Darling, I mean it." Her voice turned shrill and grated like fingernails on a chalkboard. Now, she was mad. He could see she was the foot-stomping type if she didn't get her way.

He put his hand on the key to the boat in his pants pocket and felt better about leaving her alone.

She'd already proved valuable. Maybe he

should keep her around, just in case.

"I want to go home!" she yelled.

Then again, maybe not.

Late afternoon cooled into a nice evening. The sunset painted lazy white clouds in shades of red and yellow. A slight breeze broke the ocean surface except for a few glassy patches in the distance that had to be slicks. Crude oil leaks weren't always to blame. A passing vessel pumping out the bilge, lube oil leaking from propeller shaft seals, or the oil and biological debris from fish feeding on other fish caused the same effect.

He turned the handle of the wing valve on the production tree. One round, two rounds, three, four . . . the humming intensified as the gate inside of the valve-body made the opening smaller and smaller, pinching off the flow of gas. A final *swoosh* then silence. Seventeen turns to the right. The gauge pressure rose gradually and stabilized at twenty-eight fifty. Next to the wing valve, upstream, closest to the tree, was another barrier, a failsafe-closed valve with an actuator that used the well pressure and the natural gas produced to hold the gate in the open position. He punched the red emergency shutdown button.

There was a reason for the no smoking

sign at the bottom of the stairs. The expulsion of gas as the valve closed was strong and substantial.

Several hours would pass before the pressure in the line dropped enough to be noticed, but someone, somewhere, at the production facility where the line he'd just closed ended, would soon wonder what happened to the line pressure. The field hand sent to investigate would see right away the failsafe had tripped, but he might take a while to think to check the manual valve. After all, who would close it?

Small thorns caused the most powerful elephant to limp. A man just had to know where to stick them.

He descended the work platform and made his way down the steps to the boat. Shanteel had finally consumed enough beer to douse her fire. She slept curled up on the seat, exposed to what sun remained. Passed out more likely. Despite her tan, she looked cooked. As he took off his shirt and put it on her, he wondered why he cared.

A ragdoll had more life.

An hour later, the camp house came into view. The fancy boat was still gone, but the other two sat in their slips.

A cop walked down the dock from the parking area behind the house Shanteel had appeared from that morning.

Meshach motored past the row of houses, like all was normal. He just hadn't arrived at his intended destination. Another group of houses a mile distant gave the ploy credibility.

The cop paced the dock once before planting himself at the head of the narrow slip where he stood erect, arms behind his back, like a poster-boy for a police recruiting drive. The man looked everywhere but at Meshach. His cruiser sat next to the red Audi, Shanteel's car. His lips and cheeks worked from grimace to pout and back. He did not look happy.

Meshach eased the throttle forward a touch. If Shanteel woke and sat up, she'd be visible. He'd bet money the cop was her ex-something, or even worse, her current something. In either case, past or present, he didn't want to find out.

If the situation soured, the backpack held his way out. One in the chamber and six in the mag.

Meshach didn't care if Shanteel didn't want to talk. He didn't want to either. She woke up sore as a bad tooth, no doubt hung over and visibly sunburnt. Her supply of show-girl smiles had run out.

The night closed in thick when he turned the key and the running lights clicked off. The boat settled against the rubber bumpers. Water lapped. Voices drifted through the windows of the end house to the east, where the late-night bunch stayed. Sounded like they'd gotten a second wind. No lights shone from Shanteel's house, a good sign. He couldn't see anyone lurking, but lights from an occupied house made shadows darker, more distinct and easier to hide in.

She didn't wait for him to moor the boat. She stepped ashore and padded off into the night. After a minute, a door slammed. One light came on — a bright one toward the back of the house. Then it dimmed as another door slammed.

He felt a sting in the middle of his back and another on his neck. Mosquitoes reminded him she'd run off with his shirt.

The cooler held plenty of food, as well as water and ice for another outing. Gas would be a problem soon. He should have filled up at the marina on the way in, but he didn't want to be seen by the local population with a woman he knew nothing about and who was passed out in the boat. This proved to be a good call with the cop wandering around. Shanteel had to be a local, someone everyone knew, and from the way she acted, more than casually.

He grabbed his gear and stepped onto the dock. Halfway up the steps to his house he paused. The deck stood fifteen feet tall. The railing around it added another forty inches. He set down the bag and trotted back to the boat. In the forward compartment lay the anchor and tied to its crown, one hundred feet of good-quality, braided nylon rope. He untied the end attached to the bow of the boat, grabbed both, and trotted back to the east side of the house, in the deep shadow of the empty house next door.

The anchor weighed ten, maybe fifteen pounds and was made of galvanized-steel, eighteen inches wide and twenty-four long. He shook it. The thing clanked, but that could be fixed with cloth to dampen the metal-on-metal ring. He shook out several loops of rope, grabbed the end of the anchor and heaved, letting the loops of rope peel off his hand as the anchor and chain sailed over the handrail onto the deck above. Might as well have thrown the thing through the front window. It had the same effect when it landed on the glass tabletop. He cringed and looked into the night, but there was nothing to see. The buzz from the marsh quieted for a second then continued. After a pause, he pulled on the rope and dragged the anchor and the patio table frame across the wooden deck until the rope tugged tight. He pulled himself halfway up, hand over hand, then slid down. The rope was slick, but knots two feet apart would cure that.

Sometimes, the right tools lay at your fingertips.

12

Wednesday morning

Wes's eyes opened; he sat up and looked at his watch. Seemed he could never sleep past five no matter where he was. Like his internal clock changed time zones when his cell phone did.

He took a hot shower, dressed, grabbed the *USA Today* off the carpet outside his door, and headed downstairs. As he passed the front desk, he took a copy of the *Times-Picayune.* A few early risers filed into the restaurant. Good Cajun coffee came only one way: strong and black. He got a cup and found a chair in a quiet corner where he could read the news, go over his notes again and check e-mails.

Cole hadn't replied to his update. Nothing from Lisa. Should he send her an e-mail or a text? Texting was the more personal of the two. Afternoon would be a good time.

Monique had a new follower: Lamech.

Maybe Sullivan wasn't involved, but time would tell. Nothing new from Meshach.

Jessica entered the lobby from outside, striding across the marble floor in yellow running shoes with orange soles, wearing modest blue jogging pants and a matching pullover. She removed the band holding her ponytail, raked her fingers through the mop on her head, gathering a few errant dark strands, and bound the tresses back. She glanced his way and changed course.

He checked his watch, 6:20. Reminded him of the Marine Corps and five miles before breakfast. Much too early for a run in his book.

"Good morning." She pulled out the opposite chair and plopped down. Small beads of sweat covered the smooth skin above her upper lip.

"Good morning. How was your run?"

"The humidity is horrible. There's no place to jog except down the edge of the street. It's nerve racking. Men honk. I need some water. I'll be right back." She stood and walked toward the front counter.

Her comment about honking came out with a little venom. She was gorgeous and some men had no respect. She returned with a bottle of water and sat. Before crossing her legs at the knees, she peeled off her bottoms, revealing blue shorts. She'd had knee surgery, an athlete's injury.

"I won't be wearing these again." She held out the bottoms.

Wes said, "The humidity is normal for Louisiana. It's only going to get worse. There's a gym here."

"I hate treadmills. Boring." She drew out the *r.*

"Nice shoes."

She straightened her leg and wiggled her foot. "I like them. They're comfortable . . . and colorful. I assume the color scheme is what you were referring to."

"It is."

"I've been thinking. Oleos isn't a person's name. Our guy is trying to harm a man who owns an oil company. That's the reference, oil."

"Yes, ma'am, I believe you're correct."

"Hmm, I'd like to change the subject. I apologize for the way I acted last night. Tony and I talked. Again, I'm sorry. My track record with men is, well, I assumed when I shouldn't have."

"You never said a word."

"Did I have to?" She took another drink, looked at him over the bottle and raised her eyebrows.

He shook his head.

She capped the bottle. "What's his name?"

"Whose?"

"Your son-in-law's."

He had to think a second. Not about the name, but why she would ask. "Josh, Joshua Bell."

She nodded.

He stared.

Coffee cups clinked on saucers. Silverware scraped plates. Muted greetings and conversations mixed with the rustle of newspapers. The wail of a distant siren followed someone through the front door.

Then, he got it — bluebonnets. Her eyes were as beautiful as the Texas countryside in the morning sun.

For someone who claimed to have a bad record with men, she had an easy way about her. No wasted motion. No fidgeting under his gaze. He realized she was comfortable without dialogue. As he was. He felt like he'd known her longer than two days.

He had to be crazy.

She stood and took a step to stand next to him, looked toward the door and let her hand rest on his forearm. "Wes, we don't know each other, so I hope you don't think I'm forward. Don't chase your daughter. I pushed my dad away until it was too late. Don't be my dad. He's gone now. We were

119

never friends." She walked toward the elevator.

As one elevator door closed on Jessica, the other one opened, and Tony stepped out. He walked like he was on a mission — breakfast. He waved. "Morning." Tony returned with a plate of melon. Then he doused every cube with pepper. He took a bite of honeydew. "Question. Is patience a name? Why the question mark? Why two of them?"

"Well, I knew a girl in high school named Patience. She was slow too, poor thing. You had to have patience with Patience. As for the question marks, who knows?"

"That's funny. Have you seen Jess? She's an early bird. Runs every morning."

"We talked. You just missed her."

Tony's head bobbed. He was thinking. Puffed cheeks gave him away every time. He'd have been a terrible poker player. "Did she say anything?"

"Do me a favor. Don't ask me a thousand questions when one will do."

"I only asked one, but I'll get to the point. Did she apologize?"

"Yes, but she didn't elaborate. She mentioned her dad had passed away. They must not have had a relationship."

Tony finished his bite then used the fork

to point over his shoulder. "Dude, I told you her ex was a wife beater. I think her dad made the ex look like a pacifist."

13

Wednesday, 11:00 AM

Teenagers didn't own the patent on texting and driving. Wes had fought the urge to type one himself since leaving the rental car place down the street from the hotel. Jessica was right about not pushing himself on Lisa — as hard as it was for him to do. That's why he'd let her alone the past five years. He'd already composed a polite message in his head. Something he might send an old friend after a chance meeting. He would wish his daughter the best, say it had been good to see her, and leave it at that. Besides, she might need some time to cool her heels since he'd opened his mouth and inadvertently blabbed about his covert queries into her life.

Downtown New Orleans came into view as Interstate 10 veered southward. The most obvious landmark, the Mercedes-Benz Dome, home of the football team, The

Saints, dwarfed the buildings around it. In the far view, the gray steel hulk of the Crescent City Bridge spanned the Mississippi River, connecting New Orleans and the cities of Gretna and Belle Chasse.

He checked his watch, 11:05, then slid the arrow across the bottom of his phone with his thumb and opened *Maps.* The closest exit dumped out onto Poydras Street, next to the football stadium. He took it, drove up Poydras, and found a spot to park the Malibu on St. Charles Avenue, one block from the Federal District Courthouse.

Frank "Bubba" Broussard was the craziest, life-loving man Wes had ever met. He grew up on the bayou. After four years in the Corps, he took advantage of the G.I. Bill, sold crawfish on the side, and put himself through law school at LSU. He ran traps before and after classes, sorted and bagged them, and marketed the end product. Pure determination.

Bubba was a federal prosecutor and a friend. He counted on the man's workaholic habits to have him planted behind his desk in his office. Wes wanted to surprise him.

He dialed Bubba's office number. It rang twice. "Mr. Broussard's office. This is Vanessa."

He thought about keeping the tone formal, but the Mister-mister stuff might not get him in the door. "Could I speak to Bubba, please? This is Wes Hansen, an old associate who'd like to touch base."

"One moment, Mr. Hansen."

Elevator music had changed over the years. The tune in the background picked up Adele singing "Rolling in the Deep." A good song. He had it on his phone.

The music stopped. "Who dat, Wes? Brother, where are you?"

His long-time friend made Wes smile. A crawfish-and-cornbread-fed Cajun through and through, and he sounded like it, but honest and sharp as a tack. "I'm sitting in a rental car two hundred yards from your office."

"You're kiddin' me. What da world brought you down here, work or pleasure?"

"Cole Blackwell. I wanted to express my appreciation for the reference."

"Well, what do you know 'bout dat. Cole asked me if I knew a PI. I told him I knew a sorry Marine who couldn't find a starving dog on the streets of Bagdad using a side of beef for bait." Bubba spoke eloquently when he had to, but around friends, he could slip into a bayou brogue of *dis* and *dats.*

"If you're trying to get my goat, you'll have to get up earlier in the morning. What's your day look like? Have you got time for lunch?"

"Dern, wish you'd called earlier. Can't do it, not this week. Got BP in my hair. After the Deepwater Horizon burned and sank, killing eleven men and making the mess the oil caused, dat means big problems, not British Petroleum. How long are you going to be here?"

There was a loaded question. He hoped for Cole and his daughter's sake, not long. He wanted to get his guy and go home. "I don't know yet. Can I pester you for a favor?"

"You know better than that. What can I do for you?"

"I need to look at recent air travelers and check the more obvious things, like parking and traffic violations. Still have my e-mail address?"

"Yep, got it. I'll have you a contact before six. My cell phone number is in my signature if you don't still have it. Call me some evening. We'll make plans for dinner. Rae would love to see you. I've got nothing Saturday. We'd like to see you at the house."

"I'll do it, thanks. Hey, one more thing. Point me to some good food. Local cuisine."

"Dragos for oysters, Red Fish Grill if you hit Bourbon Street. Ruth's Chris for steaks,

Copland's —"

"Whoa, thanks, that's enough. I hope we're not here long enough to eat at all of those."

"There's a hundred more."

"No, that's good for now."

"OK then. Hey, for me. Cole didn't give me the details, but I know you're not looking for a runaway, and you didn't fly down here to thank me for a job reference."

"You're right. I don't know much now, but when I do, I promise I won't leave you out of the loop. It's bigger than the NOPD."

"What kind of big?"

"My gut tells me it's about the size of the BP in your hair right now."

14

Wes drove the long way back to the Hilton, crossing the bridge into Gretna, circling west to Boutte, then back into the west side of town to the hotel. Why he'd gone downtown instead of calling to see if Bubba was available aggravated him. He had to do something, and sitting in another hotel room was doing nothing.

Chasing a criminal through cyberspace was like pursuing the wicked witch through a nightmare. Meshach existed and he had mass. He breathed, walked the earth, slept, and ate, but where? What in the world was he up to?

As he parked, Jordan called to tell him he was on the way to New Orleans in the jet. He sounded better.

He heard Tony and Jessica bantering before he opened the door to his room. The team's office. They sat with their computers at the small table next to the window. Tony held up one finger. A sign. Wait a second or I got it? Hard to determine. Wes waited.

Jessica smiled over the top of her computer screen.

"Got a new chirper. Sullivan finally commented," Tony said.

"Chirping and now Chirper. Did you just come up with that? And he didn't chirp." Jessica shook her head and gave one school-marm *tsk*. "Lamech passed the message along. 'Luck Sullivan.' "

"Semantics, semantics." Tony rolled his eyes and pulled at the hoodie. "OK, a new player." He eyed Wes. "Your hunch was right. How was your trip?"

"My contact had other business, but I talked to him. He's on board. In fact, let me look." He opened his laptop. The thing ran like cold molasses sometimes. "Yep, I'm going to forward this to both of you." He went through the process and passed along the message from Bubba.

Their employer wrote one word in a reply to his update — *thanks.* There was nothing else of interest.

Nothing from Lisa.

Tony spoke up. "This e-mail you forwarded — who's this Risa Richard? What a name."

"It's French. We're in Cajun country. The

last syllable is pronounced 'shard,' like a piece of broken vase, Re-shard," Jessica said.

"You're kidding me." Tony tapped at the keyboard like a woodpecker on meth.

"I wouldn't do that. We've been together too long." Jessica gave Tony a playful nudge with her elbow.

"Two days. Feels like years," Tony jabbed back.

Wes liked it. The banter meant they got along. He also liked the twitch at the corners of Jessica's mouth as she suppressed a smile and the gleam in her eyes. She caught him staring again and winked.

"I don't know who Risa works for, but my buddy, Bubba, is a Fed. She's his contact. Introduce yourselves and pick her brain. Look at traffic violations and parking tickets. Stick with nonresidents. Get Meshach's name out there. Give Risa a rundown on the definitions. She'll be another set of eyes. Another computer."

"What timeframe?" Tony said.

"Three days. Start Sunday." Wes looked at his watch to confirm the day's date, the ninth. "Meshach indicated he was here, in Joan, Sunday evening. If he is here, I think he flew in. That would put him in the air, possibly, that morning. Risa will be able to get passenger lists. If she can't, let me know, and I'll contact Bubba again."

"Hotels and rental cars too," Jessica added.

Tony held up both hands, palms out. "Stop, stop, stop. All good ideas. Now, tell me again who we're looking for? Height, weight, hair, eyes, and better yet, give me a social security number."

Tony was right. They had no physical description, no real name, nothing to go on. "OK, we're done for the day. It's five and Risa is probably off work anyway." Wes snapped the laptop closed. "I'm hungry, and I'm buying. What will it be? Cajun, steaks, Italian, what?"

Jessica and Tony looked at each other, then Jessica said, "We're in Cajun country, not Italy, and I can have a steak at home. I vote for the local fare."

Tony nodded. "I can do that."

Wes rubbed his hands together. "It's settled, back to your rooms, both of you. I'm going to shower and change. Let's meet in the lobby in an hour and go downtown to the Redfish Grill."

Jessica raised both arms with clenched fists. "Shotgun!"

Wes's peripheral vision seemed more acute than ever with Jessica in it. A pang of guilt gripped his heart again. How could he feel guilty about looking at another woman after so many years? Never mind that the one sitting in the car next to him as he drove through heavy traffic was more distracting than typing a text.

"Did your daughter respond?" she asked, watching him.

"I haven't sent her anything. I started to text her this morning, then again this afternoon, but didn't. I know what I want to say. Just haven't said it yet."

"I don't know your daughter, of course, but I suspect she's anxious to hear from you. Daughters need their dads more than they'll ever admit. You're her rock. The one who slept in the room down the hall, only a yell away, when her imagination played with shadows and night noises."

He'd have to think about whether or not Lisa needed him. She'd already mentioned she had Josh and didn't want his help.

"Didn't she contact you?" Raised eyebrows begged for a response.

Good point. Lisa had made the first move. He hadn't thought of that.

Jessica adjusted her shoulder belt. If men had any sense, they would declare women the first wonders of the world. He was sure Adam thought that about Eve.

He left her comment unanswered and concentrated on his driving. I-10 inbound through the downtown area moved at near normal speeds, unlike the stifled lanes full of the city's workforce on the way home on the other side of the concrete median. According to *Maps,* the Redfish Grill wasn't far from where he'd been that morning.

He took the same exit onto Poydras Street, wove his way across to Canal, and parked near Harrah's Casino. He led his entourage two blocks to Bourbon Street and one block right to the restaurant. The place was made for servicing volume. Roomy with lots of simple tables and chairs. Stools lined the bar against the far wall. Dozens of waiters, waitresses, and busboys worked the tables. Tonight, the restaurant buzzed.

The hostess led them to a table toward the middle of the room. "Brit will be your waitress. Enjoy your meal."

Wes pulled out a chair for Jessica then sat and opened the menu. He saw immediately what he wanted. "I'm having the namesake, blackened red fish."

"Me too." Jessica folded the menu and placed it on the table.

He eyed Tony who gave the list of fare a cursory glance and folded his menu. "Tony?"

"I haven't decided yet. Maybe a burger."

Jessica grabbed her menu again and opened it like she'd missed the Happy Meal section. "You are not serious. A burger? Oh, look, they have them." She tapped the page.

Tony shrugged. "I like a good burger."

A young woman placed three glasses of water on the table. "Hi, I'm Brit. I'll be your server tonight. Can I start you out with drinks?" Wes stayed with water, Jessica cranberry juice, and Tony opted for diet coke.

When the waitress left, Wes addressed Jessica. "Well, what do you think about our project? Is being a private eye what you expected?"

"Different. That's for sure."

"It may seem like we're at a dead end, but this job is like an archeological dig. If we excavate long enough, deep enough, and sift enough dirt, sooner or later something will turn up. I call it PR work. Patience required."

Tony chimed in. "Running background checks on air travelers won't take long. Eliminating women, kids, doctors, lawyers, and conventioneers will narrow the list down to two or three hundred suspects. A couple of days maybe."

Jessica stood. "If you two will excuse me a

minute?"

Wes nodded as she edged between the tables and headed toward the ladies' room.

Tony held out his phone for Wes to see. "A Jean Cooper is following Lamech now. Her bio is complete. She lives in Kansas. Her avatar is that of a middle-aged dishwater blonde. I'll do a little research on her, but I can tell you, if she's involved, she's the dumb one."

"I think he'll mess up, if he hasn't already." Wes moved his menu as the waitress returned and set the drinks on the table. "Criminals think they're smart. Our prisons are full of the most intelligent people in the world. This Meshach character will be no different."

Jessica returned. She sat, situated her chair, eyed Wes and Tony, and smiled. If Wes didn't know better he'd say she looked smug. To reinforce his thoughts, she shrugged and clasped her hands together. She looked like a teenager who'd just answered the extra point question on the big algebra test. "I have a little surprise for you guys. You won't believe what I overheard in the ladies' room." She glanced over her shoulder toward the restrooms and the bar.

Another waitress approached. She was already tall, but the blonde hair piled on top of her head and the heels she wore stood her over six feet. Jessica pushed out the fourth chair for the lady. She sat and folded her hands in her lap.

Wes was stumped. Long lost cousin, the sister Jessica didn't know she had, what?

Jessica indicated Wes. "This is my boss, the investigator, Wes Hansen. Tell him what you told me."

The lady glanced at Tony before she focused her green eyes on Wes. "I think I met him," she said.

"You think you met who?" Wes said.

"Meshach. Last night."

Now Wes was more than stumped. How in the world?

She continued. "Isn't that a strange name? I met a guy next door at a bar where I hold a second job. He said his name was Meshach."

No wonder Jessica looked smug.

Tony's mouth hung open.

Wes gathered his thoughts. This was exactly the kind of chance meeting that broke cases wide open.

"Ma'am." He looked at her nametag. "Paula, tell us what you can remember about him."

She looked hesitant and suddenly wary.

"It's important." He nodded at Jessica.

"She told you I'm an investigator. This is my team."

Paula nodded and wrung her hands.

Wes was an investigator and this was his team. What Paula didn't know about his lack of legal standing might help them get the answers they needed.

She scooted forward onto the edge of the chair. "Look, I just, well, I hit him up and tried to flirt. He was gorgeous, movie-star dreamy. But it's like . . . like he doesn't like women." She hesitated and looked between them. "I can see him, uh, dark brown hair, cut close, a shadow of a beard, like he shaved it that way, with defined lines on his cheeks and below his neck. Strong jaw and nose."

"Tall?" Wes asked.

"Six two, maybe more. Muscular, real strong." She looked at Jessica. "This sounds childish, but he looked inviting, confident, safe. You know, like he was a hunk, but . . ."

"But? But what?" Jessica asked.

"After we talked and he walked off, I got the creeps. Like he looked right through me. Not the undressing type of look." She glanced at Tony then focused on Jessica again. "You know what I mean. How men can make you feel naked. Not like that, but like he didn't like me. He was clipped and short when he told me his name, and he whispered, raspy like. Then he stared at me until I felt stupid and wondered what to say or do next."

"What color were his eyes?" Tony typed notes into his phone with his thumbs.

She stood. "That's the strange part. I don't know. He wore sunglasses, inside the bar, at night. Look, I, I have to get back to work. I hope I've helped."

Wes could have hugged her. Hopefully, she'd just given them what they needed to find Meshach's true identity.

Jessica was still smiling. She shrugged. "I heard her mention his name."

Tony leaned over and held out his hand for her to give him a high five. "You need to go to the ladies' room more often."

She slapped his hand. "Speaking of, I didn't. I'll be back."

"Wait, here, give her my info just in case she remembers more details." Wes handed over a business card.

She stood then leaned over and tapped the table with a long, glossed nail. "I'm just speculating here, but who wears sunglasses at night? Self-esteem issues? Sensitive eyes cause headaches. Immaturity? A Mr. Cool syndrome? Or vision problems? I'll bet he only has one eye. That's the avatar, the orb."

15

Wednesday, Venice

Meshach sat at the bar tying knots in the anchor rope, using the width of the back on a second barstool to measure the spacing. The rope wasn't ideal for what he had planned, but it would suffice. He had no doubts about his ability to scale it with ease when the time came.

A warm, musty breeze coursed through the camp house. The French doors stood open. All the windows were up. He sipped tap water and ate raisins from the box. Whitecaps covered the distant bay. The Gulf would be worse with seas three to five feet, maybe less, but enough to make a trip in a small boat rough and wet.

He'd positioned himself next to the French doors, inside far enough that wandering eyes wouldn't see him and watched Shanteel's place. If the cop who had paced the dock had the woman in mind, which seemed likely, and returned to snoop, he wanted to know.

He finished with the rope and unfurled a blue, flat bed sheet. The only dark-colored one he could find in the house. He tore it into four-inch-wide strips and laid the narrow pieces across the tabletop. He wove strips between the stabilizer and the anchor flukes, careful not to use too much. The cloth would cushion the metal-to-metal impact, but the flukes had to rotate on the stabilizer so it wouldn't matter how the anchor landed. He had one attempt. The anchor had to catch on the handrail. No ifs.

Better options were available for purchase. Like the grapples law enforcement used to dredge water for bodies. Again, he could not afford questions.

Shanteel emerged from her place carrying a small sport bag. Had he not just seen her walk out of the house, he wouldn't have recognized her. She had on clothes. Tan skin-tight slacks and a white blouse, white tennis shoes, hair loose in the wind.

He glanced at the time on his computer — lunchtime. He'd be surprised if she didn't have a hangover.

She padded out to her car and tossed the bag into the backseat. Shading her eyes, she peered into the distance, toward the highway, then planted both hands on her hips. A white Sheriff's cruiser sped down the gravel road toward her. Had to be the same cop. He got out in the cloud of dust just as his car skidded to a stop and started in on her. Too far away to hear the exchange. The deputy pointed. She pointed then stomped a foot. He threw his arms out to his sides. She stomped again. He stuck his face in hers, then took an I'm-a-cop-and-a-man stance, arms back, chest out, like an *I dare you.* She flipped him off, and he slapped her hard enough to make her stumble then looked around. No doubt to see if anyone saw what he'd done.

Shanteel recovered quickly and launched a foot toward the man's groin that missed the intended target, but not by much. Her shoe marred the leg of his creased uniform. When she stormed away, he didn't follow.

The girl had spunk.

A heavy knock sounded at the front door. Meshach did a quick survey of the room, grabbed the anchor, the rope, what was left of the sheet and put them in the bedroom closet. After one more quick check, he pulled the Kimber from his belt and stuffed it behind the center cushion on the couch.

Some guy stood at the door. A gray T-shirt hung on boney shoulders and covered about half of his black shorts. He reached for the jamb with a closed fist. Meshach jerked the door open. "What do you want?" Meshach took a step back but didn't open the screen door.

"Um." The man moved up his sunglasses, astraddle the bill of his red ball cap. "I'm, Scott Breaux."

"Am I supposed to know you, Scott?"

"Well . . . this is my place. Just thought I'd check on you, see how you're getting along with my boat. I see it's still in one piece." He chuckled at what he must have thought was a joke.

Meshach knew the man periodically came by to check on the house. He probably wasn't used to leaving his renters un-escorted.

Scott reached for the doorknob. "Do you mind?"

Meshach flipped the latch, walked into the kitchen, and leaned against the counter.

Scott followed and did a quick scan of the living room. His yellow Crocs squeaked on the floor when he walked. "Something wrong with the air-conditioning?"

"I shut it off."

"That's a first."

"Air-conditioning makes men soft."

"You don't look like you've spent much

time indoors, then."

The guy wanted to make small talk. Meshach didn't like talk. Period. If he engaged the man in conversation, he might stay longer and he'd already overstayed his welcome. Meshach stared at him and crossed his arms over his chest.

Scott looked away and moved toward the deck. He spun and pointed outside. "What happened to my table? The glass top is shattered. You didn't even clean it up."

Nothing like a little righteous indignation to embolden a man.

Enough was enough. "Here, Scott, come here." Meshach pulled a wad of bills from his front pants pocket.

Scott eyed the cash and shifted his weight from one foot to the other but remained where he was.

Meshach cocked his head. "Didn't you make an agreement with the man who rented this place from you? Privacy. I like my privacy. I know he told you that, and I know you've been paid handsomely too. You're not upholding your end of the bargain. Your tabletop is broken. Here's two grand for a new one." He counted out two stacks of one-hundred-dollar bills, twenty in each stack. "And another two grand to leave me alone. Let's call it a bonus. Take the cash and go. Or don't and I'll go." Meshach pocketed the dozen or so bills left, turned his back on the unwanted visitor, and walked into the bedroom. The moment he rounded the corner out of sight, he spun and crouched next to the open doorway.

Meshach followed Scott's movements by the squeak of his shoes. Four rapid steps to the counter followed by a long sigh. A long squeak as he spun on the ball of his foot and turned toward the door. The screen door bumped the jamb, sounding his exit.

Meshach moved back into the kitchen and watched from the living room window as Scott descended the steps.

As he suspected, Scott had taken the bait. A good stack of C-notes worked every time.

Scott walked to the end of the slip and boarded a Skeeter Bay Boat. He lit a cigarette and watched the camp house. He puffed rapidly then pulled a long drag and blew the smoke from pursed lips.

Meshach knew Scott stewed, weighing his options: keep the cash, or return it and evict his client — his wealthy, albeit eccentric, money-throwing client.

Shanteel drew Scott's attention as she pulled out of her space onto the gravel road and sped away. He flipped the cigarette into the water, untied his boat and motored into the marsh.

Meshach closed and relocked the front door. At his computer, he opened the Automatic Identification System. He entered the user name and password into the AIS. A broad view of the Gulf of Mexico popped up. He narrowed the display down to twenty-five miles around the Venice area. Dozens of small, bullet-shaped icons, each one representing a ship or boat, appeared on a blue background. The Mississippi River was obvious, displayed as a narrow blue field between bumpers of green, representing dry land or marsh.

He clicked on one of the icons and a small inset window appeared — a Candies boat, Miss Munroe, speed: six knots, course: 105 degrees.

Now, he needed to find the right vessel moving in the right direction.

Darkness settled in and quieted the gulls. Mosquitoes woke. The marsh came alive slowly with the croak of toads and chirp of crickets. The only lights in the house glowed blue on the satellite receiver, green on the computer's charging adapter and red on the coffeemaker.

Meshach glanced at the orange fluorescent hands on his watch — 10:25 — gathered the anchor and rope and walked out.

He stored the anchor and retied the loose end of the rope onto the bow. The Yamaha purred when he turned the key. He backed out of the slip and eased into the channel before he flipped on the running lights. *The Lowrance* displayed his previous track. He followed the line on the screen, out of the marsh and into the Gulf. The wind had died down. The boat bucked and bounced across the top of the small swells the wind had left in its wake. Obstruction lights on a thousand platforms flashed over and over, like fireflies drifting through the night.

The GPS took him directly to the platform he'd sabotaged the day before. He bumped the throttle into neutral. A drift test confirmed the current came from the south. He moved around to the north, tied up to a cross member, and let the boat drift back twenty feet before killing the engine. He didn't want to be directly under the structure. With the anchor wrapped in a dark cloth, if he missed and the hunk of steel fell back into the boat, at night, he could end up with a headache.

To the rhythmic, shrill blare of the foghorn, he gathered loops of the knotted rope in his left hand, grabbed the anchor, tested his footing on the flat area on the bow of the boat, and heaved. The hunk of steel disappeared into the darkness above. The obstruction light flashed just in time for him to see the anchor clear the handrail. He pulled on the rope, one, two, three lengths before it pulled taut. Whether the flukes caught a handrail or not didn't matter. There was plenty of piping for it to hang-up on. He secured the loose end to a forward cleat mounted on the side rail of the boat, grabbed the rope, and pulled himself hand over hand twenty feet straight up to the main deck. He went down in the same manner, suspended over the water, then scaled the rope again. The second time he pulled himself onto the platform, loosed the anchor from a pipe laid along the deck, and dropped it into the sea next to the boat.

The hum of gas flowing through the pipes meant they'd sent someone to check on the problem and open the line he'd closed the day before. Another glance at the gauge on the wellhead tempted him, but he left the valves alone this time. He climbed the handrail and placed a foot on the wellhead behind him to keep his balance. If his employer saw him now, he'd think Meshach was off his rocker and scream about him risking an injury and jeopardizing the operation. The man might be right too, on all counts, but he would never understand the rush of doing something no one else would ever consider.

Meshach launched himself over the side, into the deep, cold waters of the Gulf, and swam to the boat. He retrieved the anchor, cranked up, and headed for camp. By the time he moored the boat, midnight had come and gone. The anchor was back in its compartment in the bow, proven and ready to go.

The chill of wet clothes felt good for the first fifteen minutes of the return trip. Now, he looked forward to a hot shower. In the house, he turned on the light under the microwave and punched the button to wake up his computer.

Chirp. A start up garnering little to no attention. A perfect tool for him and his clients. Untraceable.

Lamech left him a morsel. *akando check paris's antics west*

That was off the wall. He had to think. Some of the text was outside the code they'd agreed to use. His code. *Paris, Paris . . . antics. Paris. A place? No, possessive. Paris's antics. Paris Hilton was always in trouble. Oh, a hotel. There was no way. Who could know and how had they found out?*

Gasoline for the boat would have to wait.

16

Thursday morning

Meshach had left the camp house at four, after a shower and a three-hour nap. He passed the airport on the right. To his left was the only Hilton on the west side of New Orleans, a couple of off-airport parking businesses, and a Days Inn with an IHOP attached to it.

Using the short-term lot at the airport was out of the question. Too many cameras for his liking. And he didn't want to park in front of the hotel. He flipped a U-turn at the next light and picked a spot in front of the IHOP, a short one-hundred-yard walk from the Hilton. He exited the car and locked it.

He entered the hotel and grabbed a newspaper off the counter on the way by the front desk. The receptionist talked to an old couple and didn't seem to notice him. He took a seat on a tan sofa toward the back of the reception area, near the unlit bar. Perfect, a view of the elevators and front entry just over the top of the paper. Several people sat in the restaurant. No one else stirred.

The paper was simply part of his cover, like the white shirt, dark tie, and polished black shoes he loathed to wear. The boogieman never looked so refined. If they, he, whomever, had any sort of description of him, the get-up would throw off wandering eyes.

He had to admit, Lamech had connections. Somehow, he'd gotten wind of an investigation — someone snooping into their affairs — and passed along the warning. The plan was in place. He had his orders, but word to move hadn't been issued yet. He knew the longer they delayed, the greater the odds of failure.

At least he had something to do. Find out who was digging around, assess the threat, and if he had to, neutralize it. Could be fun.

The code word for police wasn't used, so who? Cole Blackwell? This job and oilman were linked by an industry, but totally unrelated in purpose. The visit he paid Cole's daughter wasn't personal. A job was a job. Money was money. The people who paid him for that visit hated big oil. And

149

their coffers were full. He didn't care who paid the bills as long as the money was in the bank on time. If Cole hired someone to find him, and they stumbled onto the scene . . .

Someone else might find irony in the coincidence. Meshach did not.

The elevator door opened, and a looker stepped out dressed in blue shorts, a loose white pullover, and colorful running shoes. Toned. Not skinny. She checked her watch as she exited the front door.

He checked his — 6:02.

A waitress walked down the short set of marble steps from the restaurant area and spotted him. She approached and straightened her apron. "Sir, could I get you something? A cup of coffee? The buffet is open if you'd like to eat. Or you can order from the menu."

He smiled. "Black coffee will be fine."

"OK, dear." She spun and hustled back into the serving area.

A tall man stepped from the elevator. Big hands, solid arms and shoulders, straight back. Sharp jaw and light brown hair. Even lines on his face showed he shaved regularly. He'd be near forty if Meshach had to guess. The guy wore jeans and a tan, short-sleeved shirt. His arms were white, like they hadn't seen the sun in a while, a contrast to his tanned face and hands. He didn't look like the suit and tie type, so he'd traveled from a colder climate. Maybe. Purpose rode in his step as he strode to the desk and picked up a newspaper. After a quick glance at the front page, he tucked the edition under his arm with another paper and headed into the restaurant where he chose a four-place table against the wall and sat facing the entrance. He glanced Meshach's way once.

Meshach knew the type, ex-military, probably a jarhead judging from the haircut. Still in good shape but middle-aged and waning. Not as dangerous, but not to be underestimated either.

Could be his man. Time. Just a little more time.

Meshach kept the paper up, turning the page every so often, but he never read a word. The elevators went up empty and returned with people who checked out and left or hit the breakfast buffet before tending to their bills.

The old man kept busy with his reading.

The waitress approached and placed a cup of coffee on the low table in front of Meshach. He nodded. His eyes remained fixed on the paper.

"Anything else, you just wave at me,

sweetie." She left.

Sweetie, honey pie, darling, baby, the list of endearments he'd heard since he arrived in Louisiana went on. Reminded him of his doting mother.

The looker walked in from outside. Her flushed face cried jogger. She glanced into the restaurant then walked up the steps straight to the old guy. She took the chair he slid out for her and sat facing him.

Husband and wife or girlfriend?

They talked, but about what? She looked at him. He looked at her. She patted his hand.

Too timid. Not married. Not lovers.

The man shifted his gaze from the woman to the elevators. A chubby guy in a black hoodie, black pants, and black-and-white checkered shoes stepped out. They nodded at each other.

Had to be who Meshach was looking for. The woman exercised. Early too. Something to remember. No bags with them, so they had additional business. The old man was the boss. What could the fat guy and the woman bring to the table?

As hoodie walked up to them, an iPhone appeared in his hands. That was his role, the computer guy. The woman stood, walked to the elevator and got on. Her quick glance made Meshach look away, a first for him. She had the bluest, most penetrating eyes he'd ever seen.

The waitress glanced Meshach's direction. He waved her off. No more conversations with gushing women.

The phone disappeared from the chubby boy's hand into a hoodie pocket as he stood and walked toward the buffet.

Meshach rose, dropped a five on the table for the coffee and tip and walked across the lobby. The key to disrupting this little team was the woman. The old man would sacrifice himself for her. Even if they weren't lovey-dovey, a soldier's protective instincts were innate.

Meshach counted on it.

The conference room the hotel provided seated over one hundred at the many tables arranged evenly throughout the room. It was much too big for Wes and his team, but better than a cramped room.

He set up his computer and laid out a legal pad. As soon as the computer booted, he typed out an e-mail to Cole, giving him a rundown of events during the previous evening and the rough description of Meshach the waitress had given them.

Tony and Jess walked in. Jess looked

showered and refreshed. She wore black slacks and a red top. Her hair was tied back in a ponytail. Tony had on the trademark hoodie and black, baggy pants. The checkered shoes were a new addition. Like Op art, Wes was sure if he stared at them long enough he'd either see an elephant or get vertigo and fall down. Wes had always thought the bags Tony dragged everywhere he went, the anchors he'd called them, held computer equipment. Wes had never asked. Tony had on a different ensemble every day. Those cases were full of clothes. Had to be.

Tony's iPhone had his attention. He sat across the table, next to Jessica. "Just got some info from Risa. It's early, barely eight o'clock. She's on the ball."

"Probably a computer nerd," Wes said.

Tony glanced up and smiled. "That's real funny."

"I thought so. Anything interesting?"

"Not at first glance. We've got inbound flights for the last couple of days. Speeding tickets, parking tickets, illegal lane change, indecent exposure, you name it, must be a couple thousand of them. An overview of robberies and murders, domestic abuse, sexual assaults and animal assaults. Drive-by shootings. You can't make this stuff up. Lots of info, but license and social security numbers have been redacted. Risa is good. I'd like to meet this girl."

"Pass it on to me and Jess."

"I got it," she said.

His computer booted. The list of e-mails popped up one by one, he slid the bar across his phone, opened messages, and typed a text to Lisa. *good 2 c u. looked happy.* He started to type *keep in touch,* but people who made that statement didn't intend on doing likewise. *am proud. can't wait to meet levi and josh. love always.*

He reread the text twice, hesitated one deep breath, and pushed send. As the *whoosh* sounded from the phone, indicating the text had been sent, he wished he could look down and find the stamp required for a letter he'd have mailed ten years earlier stuck to his thumb. How come it was always so hard to talk to loved ones? Had he said the right things?

Jessica looked at him and nodded. She knew the *whoosh* and the intended recipient. He was glad she did.

The info Bubba's girl sent was extensive. They'd be a week looking through so much data.

"No one named Meshach in this stuff," Tony said. "Caucasians matching anything close to his description are too old, too short, too heavy. Once you weed out the residents for traffic violations, there isn't much to look at under that subject line."

"How did you get through all of this so fast?" Wes said.

"Word searches. Keywords. Put in dark hair, eye or eyes we don't have, pun intended, weight based on the height the waitress gave us, a name that's a pseudonym, and you get what I got, nothing, zero, and zilch. That doesn't mean he's not here somewhere. The cops would have better computer resources."

"I know. Whether he's done anything illegal or not, only God would know. We have to look. For now, concentrate on the events downtown. That's where the waitress said she'd met our man. Start there and work outward."

Wes liked books. He liked to turn a real page, not a virtual one on an iPad or a Kindle. He needed a printer and a highlighter so he could print the lists, go though and eliminate each suspect one by one and cross out a name. He needed a map. "I'll be right back."

He left the hotel for the Shell Station next door and purchased a city map. It was a touristy thing highlighted with area restaurants, golf courses and museums, but it would work for what Wes had in mind. Returning to the conference room, he spread it out on a table. "All right, let's do it by the book. Street by street."

"What first?" Jess said.

Wes had to think about it a minute. "People walk downtown. As in park and walk, like we did, or they take a taxi and walk. Leave out traffic violations. Except parking tickets. It's easy to get one with so many red zones and meters. If we find a parking violation, we'll have Risa run the plates to see if it's a rental. Jess, take the even numbered pages, Tony the odd. I'll give you the street names to look for. Then we'll mark the map."

He'd reached for a pencil and a Sharpie when he realized Jess was staring at him. Her blue eyes held something that made him pause. *What?*

"I assume you want to start with Bourbon Street, so here's an arrest for fighting, three guys, Tuesday night. Not our guy. These were locals." Tony broke the spell.

Wes marked the map and made a short notation. "For now, we'll record every incident. Then we'll talk about them afterward. You never know."

Jess studied her screen.

Tony added another offense. "Purse

157

snatcher, north of the intersection with Conti Street. Didn't catch the perp. Description vague."

"Here's shoplifting," Jess said. "Looks like a local too. Another one for dealing drugs, but it's a black man. That's about it for my pages."

"Me too. Pick another street," Tony said.

Wes crossed Canal with his finger. "Carondelet."

Both techies typed then shook their heads.

"Baronne. Baronne and Royal Streets." If the pickings were slim, he'd give them more territory to look at.

"A murder, on Baronne, near Union." Jess typed. "A guy from Las Vegas. Lane Woodard, age twenty-five, white man. Throat cut. Possible robbery. No wallet found. Just a cell phone. Suspect in custody."

Wes marked the map. "They nabbed a robbery suspect who'd cut a man's throat for his wallet? That's a terrible price to pay for credit cards and cash. If someone gave me an either/or ultimatum, I'd hand over the wallet. It's not easy to cut another man's throat either. And he took the man's wallet, but not his cell. What's the timeframe?"

"They found the body at nine thirty and made the arrest at eleven-o-five," Tony said.

"Where? The arrest. What street?" Wes said.

"On Decatur and Iberville," Jess said.

Wes studied the map. One location lay south of Canal, the other north. Easy walking distance but something smelled. He could feel it in his gut. There were two hotels within a whisper of each other shown on the map on Baronne. Lots of people roamed the streets in the French Quarter at nine thirty at night. That's a desperate move on a crowded street. Had to be witnesses. "Monday night? How did the NOPD find the man and link him so quickly."

Jessica nodded. "Yes, Monday night. A notation on the report says an anonymous tip led police to the suspect."

"That's it." He picked up his cell. "Tony, give me Risa's number, at the bottom of her e-mail." He dialed as Tony read the digits. The phone rang twice.

"Risa Richard."

"Risa, my name is Wes Hansen. I'm Bubba's friend."

"Hi, Mr. Hansen. What can I do for you?"

"Lane Woodard's murder. Is there anything not in the report you sent me that you could let me have?"

"One moment."

Seconds turned into a minute. "NOPD

159

has a guy in custody. He had the knife on him. Has a long record, but he's never been violent. He's a drunk. One bust for petty theft."

"Did he have a story to tell?"

"Oh yes, denies everything."

"What about blood? Was the suspect covered in the victim's blood? Any cuts on his hands?"

"I'd have to check with the arresting officers. I don't see a reference to either in their notes," she said.

"The report says you've got a cell phone. Anything there?"

"Let's see. The usual calls. He wasn't married. Business, one sec, he worked for a company catering to the casinos. He was here on business. This isn't backburner, but it is a new case, and we have many of those, more every night in this crazy town."

Tony mouthed *text,* held his phone up and poked at it with his finger.

"What about texts?"

"Yep, just before eight, to a Marlin Sands of Las Vegas. Let's see, 'never guess who I saw?' No reply. A couple more texts but earlier in the day, before noon. Looks like business associates arranging lunch."

"Do you mind sharing Marlin's cell number?"

"I don't see why not. I'll send it your way."

"Risa, thank you."

"You're welcome."

The phone clicked off in his ear. "Jess, any reason why you can't fly to Las Vegas with me today?"

"I can't think of one."

"Good. As soon as I can get in touch with Jordan, we're gone."

"He's over the bug? That was quick," Tony said. "You two will like the bird he flies."

"I need to pack. If you gentlemen will excuse me." Jess reached over and pinched Tony's cheek. "See you when I get back, sweetie." She stood and gathered up her computer and accessories. "Wes, just call my room when you're ready. I won't be long."

Wes nodded.

The moment she rounded the corner into the hall, Tony sat up in his chair and put his computer on the table. He whispered, "Boss, write this down, *akando check paris's antics west.*"

"What's that, another post?" He wrote it on the pad. "Akando . . . with a k?"

"Yes. Lamech sent it. I saw it earlier, but it took me a bit to figure out the meaning. Then, I didn't want to alarm Jessica."

"What, why? Tony, talk to me."

"I think someone is on to us. *Akando* is Native American for ambush. 'Paris's antics' has to be a reference to Paris Hilton. She's always pulling something off the wall to get her face on the evening news. We're on the west side of New Orleans, in a Hilton."

Wes glanced at the door for Jess. "I don't know about keeping things from that girl. She's apt to poke you on the nose. Besides, she'll check their messages for herself sometime or another. What time was that posted?"

"Just after midnight."

Wes jumped to his feet. "Are you kidding me? How'd we miss that? He could be onto us right here and now." He began gathering his things. "I'm going to check on Jess and warn her, now. I have to call Jordan to see if I can bum a ride to Nevada too. You mind a little downtime working with Risa until we get back?" He shoved his computer into the shoulder bag.

"No, I don't. But wait. You know what else this means, don't you?"

Wes nodded. "I do."

Now he had to figure out if the leak came from Bubba or one of his sources.

17

By the time Wes reached their rooms, the feeling of urgency had eased. He put his ear to Jess's door. Voices on the television, but too low to hear what played. He raised his hand to knock then heard the familiar screech of the hotel's cheap ironing board either being stowed or unfolded. Satisfied she was OK, he moved down a door, swiped the key card and entered his room.

He called Jordan to arrange a flight and started packing at the same time. The unlimited use of a private plane was a luxury few people had the privilege of experiencing. This was a first for Wes. The availability made his job easier.

He hung up and punched Tony's number. It rang once. "This is Tony."

"Hey, Jordan is expecting me and Jess within the hour. I want you to book another room somewhere. In another part of town. If this maniac is on to us and he's killed before, you're not safe. Until we find the leak, keep your location private. That means from Risa too."

"Where do you want me?"

"I don't care. Just let me know when you've settled in."

"You talk to Jess about Meshach?"

"Not yet, but I will. Ride with us to the airport. You can take the car and get another hotel after we're gone."

"I'm not packed."

"That's OK. Come back, but I mean it. You get out of here this morning."

"Got it."

"Be ready in ten." Wes clicked off then dialed the front desk, checked him and Jess out, and informed them of Tony's late departure.

His employees stood in the hallway when he answered the light tap on the door a few minutes later. Jess looked smart in the same black-and-red outfit. If Tony ever appeared dressed in something other than the hoodie, Wes didn't think he'd recognize him.

"Are you ready?" Wes tapped the iPhone in his shirt pocket and the wallet in his hip pocket. After another quick check to make sure he had everything, he grabbed his bags and stepped out.

"Ready as I'll ever be," Tony said, a big

dose of whine in his tone. He smiled.

Wes squeezed Tony's neck. "Not you."

Jess reached and flipped up Tony's hood. "You poor darling. Late Saturday, or early Sunday. Two days, and we'll be back. You won't be alone for long."

Wes led them to the elevator. "Tony, you've got plenty to do. We'll only be a text or call away."

"I know. Just razzing you two. I don't need to go to Las Vegas anyway."

"Are you a gambler?" Jess said.

"Nope, but I might be tempted into thinking the odds are in my favor when I know they're not."

Made sense to Wes.

"I saw an interesting chirp, as you call it Tony," Jess said. "I know y'all have seen it."

"We have," Wes said. "Tony saw it this morning."

"He's on to us, isn't he?" she said.

This lady was sharp. "I believe he is," Wes said. "We're going to assume he is, for our safety."

"Jessica, I saw Lamech's warning before you left to pack. My bad. I should have said something," Tony said.

She nodded. Her eyes wandered the elevator door.

Wes knew he should've knocked on her

door. He was responsible for her safety, if not legally, then morally. But then another part of his being wanted to keep her from worrying.

They made the short trip down two floors to the lobby. Wes scanned the area when he stepped out of the elevator. Looked like business as usual. Mostly cleaning up, preparing for the next rush of overnighters. No one seemed to pay particular attention to his team. Meshach's general description eliminated most men, but Wes didn't know for sure if Meshach worked alone. He could have his own team on the ground with him, other than the online connections.

Although, in Wes's experience, men like Meshach worked solo.

As they walked across the parking lot to the rental car, he made another sweep of the area. The place was swamped with automobiles. Off-airport parking businesses surrounded the Hilton. Cars waited in line at every pump at the nearby Shell station. The short and long-term airport lots were directly across the street. Meshach could be sitting in any of a thousand cars.

They loaded their bags. Jess got in the shotgun seat.

Wes closed the trunk lid, then took Tony by the elbow and handed him a thousand dollars. "Take this. Get receipts. Account for every penny. Let me know where you go. Don't get a room downtown where you have to walk everywhere. Don't play into his hands. I believe this guy is very dangerous."

"You think he's really watching us? Like now?" Tony glanced over the top of the car and stuffed the grand in his hoodie pocket.

Wes cringed. "It's going to be hard to get receipts for that cash if you lose it."

"I won't. I promise."

"Look, I don't think we're in imminent danger, but be aware of your surroundings. Lay low until we get back."

They got into the Malibu and Wes cranked it up. He backed out, but instead of turning left to exit the lot onto Airline Boulevard, he veered right and looped around the center two rows of parked cars.

Jess glanced back at Tony then focused on Wes. "I wear big girl panties. Don't ever keep me in the dark again."

Meshach changed parking lots. He picked a space on the far west side of the hotel's lot where he could see the front door in a side mirror.

His mom liked oldies, late 60s and 70s, even disco. His dad liked country music:

steel guitars and the whining, dying, drinking stuff. Meshach hated both and he despised rap. That left gospel, Cajun, and some moron spouting opinion on talk radio. He lowered all four windows an inch. He'd as soon listen to the traffic on the roadway and the planes taking off and landing.

He caught sight of them leaving the hotel and eased lower into the seat. The old man pulled one bag and carried another. The woman did the same. Why not the fat boy? They walked up to a silver Malibu. Looked like a rental from the stickers on the back window. The woman got in the front passenger side. The other two loaded the bags and talked. Dad handed Hoodie something. If Meshach had to guess, a wad of cash. Spending money. He was staying put.

Mom and Dad were taking a trip. Where?

They got in.

Go or don't go? Like gambling: nothing in, nothing out. This had to be who he was looking for. He liked the odds.

The Malibu backed out and drove toward the exit. A white tag in the upper right corner of the back glass would make tailing them easier. Meshach hesitated and the seconds paid off. The car made a right just as he lifted his foot to step on the brake and start the engine. They disappeared behind the line of parked cars.

Coincidence? Did one of them forget something so they had to stop by the front entrance again? He refused to believe it. He slid lower in the seat, below the windows, and counted, *one thousand one, one thousand two* . . . He watched for a reflection in the windshield. They passed on fourteen. He gave them another ten count then sat up, started the car, and sped to the nearest exit. The Malibu had turned right, away from the airport and had just passed the Shell station. He followed, two cars back.

At the second light, the target turned left and travelled a four-lane road along the right side of the airport's perimeter fence, next to a north/south runway. General Aviation, a medium size blue building, came into view on the left, off the end of the runway. Three small private jets and two helicopters were arrayed on the tarmac in front of the place. None of the birds had identifying logos other than tail numbers. If Cole Blackwell hired them and the one-percenter supplied the transportation, this was where they'd go.

Then, in a moment, the old man slowed from forty-five miles an hour to fifteen, forcing everyone following him in the right lane to pass him on the left.

Now what? Pass or stop and blow his cover? He might be blown anyway. Meshach didn't have a choice.

He flipped on the left blinker, moved over and put his bumper within ten feet of the pickup in front of him. As he passed the trio, he'd looked left at the United Airlines jet lined up for takeoff. Just ahead, the road forked, the ramp onto I-10 to the left, Veterans Boulevard to the right.

Meshach had found who he was looking for, and they were not amateurs.

He knew the old man would take the same ramp he did.

Wes watched the mirror as he pulled onto Airline and maneuvered into the left lane. A black sedan pulled out of the driveway behind them. "Notice anyone walk out of the hotel as we passed through the parking lot?"

Jess glanced at him then looked back. "The black car?"

"That's a Chrysler 300 with a Hemi. I own one in matte black," Tony said. "I saw it when we left, but I didn't see anyone in it."

Wes saw one occupied car in the middle row, toward the end, a white Taurus. Could he have missed the driver in the 300? How long would it take someone to stroll from the hotel, get into an automobile, and leave the parking lot? One minute, two at the least? That fact made the appearance of the Chrysler more interesting.

General Aviation, their destination, was on airport property, but the entrance was located off of Veterans Boulevard a mile away. He made a left, north, along the edge of a runway, and accelerated to forty-five miles an hour.

The black car followed.

Wes glanced at Jess's seatbelt to make sure she was buckled in. "Tony, do you have on your seatbelt?"

"Yep."

He had two options: drive, play the unsuspecting rabbit and use the map application on his cell phone to lead their tail into a trap and confront him, or force his hand. Identify him and shake him. If he wasn't careful and Meshach was the driver of the 300, the first option could get someone killed. Wes glanced at Jess and Tony again and picked door number two. "You guys hang on."

Instead of applying the brakes, he shifted the transmission into low gear. The Malibu's engine screamed at the sudden change, slowing the car to a crawl in a matter of seconds.

"Dude," Tony said. "That was slick. He's moving over." Tony craned his head around. "He's going to pass. It's a man, but he's looking west. He has on sunglasses too. Got to be him!"

"Can you get a license plate number?" Wes watched in the side mirror as the cars shuffled to avoid him.

"I'll try to get a front plate, but he's tailgating the pickup. Only forty-eight, the last two numbers," Tony said.

The Chrysler passed and moved farther left. A car behind him obscured the rear plate.

Ideally, he'd move over right behind the subject car as it passed and put pressure on the driver, tailgating him to get a reaction, see what cards he held. This time, he couldn't, too much traffic.

Wes stepped on the gas pedal then moved rapidly through the gears using the car's manual Techtronic transmission. "The rear plate's dirty. Clean car, dirty plate. This reeks."

One hundred yards ahead, the car turned right to exit onto Veterans.

The Malibu's speedometer needle passed sixty before catching up with the two cars following the Chrysler.

Wes braked hard.

Jess pushed against the deceleration, arms stiff, clutching the sides of the seat. "He's going right. Watch it. Traffic to the west. No way."

She was correct. They were stymied. He braked to a stop. They'd gone from prey to predator to stifled by traffic in less than thirty seconds. "You see him. Watch for him. This isn't over yet. Here we go." He pulled in front of a red car and waved a quick *sorry* to the driver for the offense. "You got him?"

"I don't. He's gone. Too much traffic," Jess said. "Tony?"

"Nope. Lost him."

They sped through the light on Williams just as it turned red. A black car turned in behind them from the right. Wes knew. "There he is, far lane. That's enough."

Veterans Boulevard spanned six lanes, three each direction, with a wide, grass-covered median. They'd just passed a U-turn access. The guy was thirty yards back, two lanes over, behind two cars. A delivery truck and three cars were lined up in the center lane. From the light on Williams, far to the rear, it looked like the start of a NASCAR event speeding their way. It was going to be close. He stood on the brakes, put the Malibu in reverse, and hit

173

the gas. In a second, they were traveling backward at forty miles an hour.

The Chrysler went by on the other side of the delivery truck.

As they came even with the U-turn lane, Wes made the same move in reverse. Once moving forward, he veered left and made the turn, headed in the opposite direction.

If it *was* Meshach, there was nothing he could do.

Tony sat quiet as a titmouse.

Jess smiled. "Nice driving."

18

Thursday, 1:00 PM

Meshach parked his car on the lot of the Crowne Plaza Hotel at the corner of Williams and Veterans.

He was aggravated. The little exercise in driving the old man displayed nearly turned into a disaster. He'd pulled two good ones without hesitation. Meshach had underestimated him. His car had to go now.

One thing for sure, after this morning, they knew each other existed. But how did the guy know Meshach was at the Hilton? Had they guessed? Gut feeling? Had Lamech rolled over on him? Seemed unlikely because Lamech had posted the warning.

Without a doubt, the game was on.

A brown SUV taxi double-parked next to the entrance into the hotel caught his attention. *New Orleans Limousine Service* written in fancy script lined the edge of the hood. Right. Should say *Taxi.* A misnomer.

He approached. The driver's window was down. "Hey, I need a ride, no problem?"

A bearded man looked up. "No got problem. Please, sit, other side."

No got problem? A foreigner. No speakie Enguish. Meshach walked around, opened the front passenger's door and got in. The thing smelled like a mix of Mr. Clean and incense.

The driver sported a hefty black beard that draped to the start of his ample belly. He wore brown suit pants, silk maybe, and a white dress shirt. "Where you go?" He spoke fast. English didn't fit his tongue well. He started the meter mounted on the dashboard, put the SUV in gear and eased to the exit.

Meshach pointed right. "About two miles up here, on the left, are two small used car dealers. Drop me off at the first one."

"No need downtown?"

"No need downtown," Meshach said. "Go right, two lights ahead, on the left, at Airline Drive. That's all I need."

"I go Hyatt, New Orleans. You go too. Good place walk Bourbon Street."

"Got the T-shirt. You're not listening. Up here on the left."

The meter clicked over $8.50 as they pulled in and stopped. Meshach dropped a ten on the console and got out.

The car dealership looked like a condemned fast food place. Still had the drive-up window. The sign on the awning read *D'Jay's* and advertised used cars. The building looked like someone got a deal on yellow paint.

Meshach eyed a white Altima parked between a yellow Beetle and a faded blue, seventy-something Cadillac. The right front fender had some damage. A jagged crack in the windshield stretched from the upper corner on the passenger's side, across the black shoe polished *Red Tagged $1799,* to the center of the dashboard.

A tall, thin black man strolled out of the building. White belt, red slacks, and yellow shirt. He had to be colorblind. "You lookin' for a car?" he said.

Meshach stopped and held out his hands, palms up. "What do you think?"

"Well, you lookin' at 'em, so. . . ." He slapped the hood. "This'n here would look good on you. Where you stay at?"

Meshach opened the driver's door and pulled the hood latch. "Where do I stay at?"

"Yeah, like live. You don't stay 'round here none."

The man backed up a step as Meshach walked to the front of the car, tripped the safety latch, and raised the hood. "You got a rag?"

"A what?"

"Never mind." Meshach pulled the dipstick and checked the oil. It was full and looked clean. He slid the thin rod back into the motor, slammed the hood closed, and took another survey of the car. Still had good tread on a set of Michelins, none of them low. "How many miles?"

"One-twenny-five. Old engine is in good shape. Don't use no oil."

"Let's go inside and talk."

"Now, 'fore we do." He opened his left hand and tapped the palm with his right hand, like *put her here.* "I gots ta tell ya, we likes cash 'round here. Franklins 'n such. Especially for folks we don't know. You feelin' me?"

Meshach nodded. "I'm feeling you."

Thursday, 1:30 PM, somewhere over southeast Texas

Wes gazed out of the small window next to his seat. The land below looked like a playroom floor strewn with building blocks. Square plowed areas mixed with grass and trees and lakes crossed with rivers and highways. The view gave little evidence to

178

indicate mankind had any sense of organization.

Jordan turned around in his seat at the controls of the jet. "You guys comfortable? Too hot or too cold? Let me know. We should have a good ride all the way. Thunderstorms are building in west Texas, but we'll skirt 'em to the south with little delay."

Jess said, "How far is it?"

"Just a smidgen over seventeen-hundred miles. I've got the cruise set on three-eighty. We'd make better time with a tailwind, but we won't be blessed with one this trip."

"Thanks, Jordan," Wes said.

"Make yourselves at home. You know where the drinks and the snacks are."

"Thanks, again," Jess said.

Cole said he owned two jets. If this aircraft set the example, jetsetters would be sorely disappointed. The bird was a five-foot-diameter culvert with wings and seating for six in leather chairs. A small refrigerator, coffee bar, and lavatory took up the back of the plane. The four chairs in the front of the cabin unlocked and swiveled for inflight comfort, like posh lounge chairs with seatbelts. A small table affixed to the floor between the two seats on the left side served as a desk.

An oil tycoon's work truck.

Jess's demeanor baffled him. Granted, she had a point about his failure to pass on his suspicions regarding Lamech's warning post.

The million-dollar question: did he think they were in danger? At the time: no. Now: possibly. If they got closer to the real reason the man was in Louisiana: definitely.

Neither employee asked him why he ended the chase. They had Meshach. Wes could have run him down. He'd stepped into harm's way many times. That was different than risking the lives of Jess and Tony or some bystander.

He glanced at Jess. She still had her back to him, facing the window. Her statement about the kind of panties she wore tickled him. She'd waited long enough. Like a large pot of cold water on a small flame, she took a while to boil over, but boil she did. His mom had that fortitude. All woman, but tough emotionally, and she spoke her mind, as Jess had.

She scratched the top of her head and raked her fingers through the dark tresses.

He knew better than to assume what a woman thought. A lesson he'd learned early in life.

Then, as if reading his mind, she unbuckled her seatbelt and moved to the chair behind him. "Can we talk?"

That question was never good. Not coming from a woman.

He unlocked the chair and swiveled around to face her across the table. Wasn't too many years ago a gaze so intense would have made him squirm in his seat.

She took an audible breath, held it a heartbeat, and let it out. "I want to apologize, Wes. I, well . . ." She looked at the ceiling and back. "It's not your fault, but calling me Jess kind of caught me off guard. It's been a long time since a man called me that."

Ooh! Shortening her name? The apology disarmed him. He was the one who should apologize. "I didn't realize. It just came out. I didn't mean to be presumptuous, if that's the right word."

"You couldn't know." She gazed out of the window as if the portal gave her a look back at troubled times.

"I grew up in turmoil. Dad drank. Beer he handled fine, but whisky, whisky made him mean and vengeful. No one was safe around him. Mom and I lived on the edge, one bottle to the next. Then, at eighteen, I ran from my abusive father straight into the arms of an abusive husband. I stayed because that's what Christian women do. For

181

better or worse. More worse than better, I'll tell you. A liar, unfaithful, mean." She laughed without mirth. "Dad called me Jess when he wanted his little girl back, my ex when he wanted . . ."

Her eyes grew wide. She looked at Wes as if the thought of what she was about to say broke the trance. "I left ten years ago. I haven't dated twice since. I swore off men. Even wore my wedding ring for three years after we divorced so guys would leave me alone. Got to where the ring didn't matter. No morals anymore. Just added to the mistrust I felt for every man who looked at me."

She smiled suddenly, flashing straight white teeth. "Now, I need to apologize again for rambling."

"No, you don't." It was his turn to look out the window. He had a thousand questions he wanted to ask her. Kids? No kids? What happened to her dad? Though he could guess. Where's her ex? "So, I suppose we need to communicate more. I need to apologize too, for not warning you about Meshach. I started to knock on your door but didn't want to worry you for nothing. Turns out I should have. Meshach isn't a figment of our imaginations."

She nodded. "What's Tony going to do?"

"I told him to change hotels. I need to send him an e-mail and remind him to check rental dealers for Meshach's car and see if we can get a real name. I don't think our guy is dumb enough to use his real name, but you never know. I'd like him to visit Avis and Hertz, all of them, and see if someone recognizes Meshach's description."

Jessica pulled out her iPhone. "I'll send him a text, but I'll bet you he's already looked for records. I'll mention a visit to the rental car places."

Wes agreed. Tony didn't miss much. Wes had reservations about hiring his computer tech, but his doubts didn't last long. Tony was good. "You're right. He'd have called by now if he'd found anything. I had another thought. He needs to get a different car. We didn't see a plate number on the Chrysler. That doesn't mean Meshach didn't see ours."

"I'll mention that too. What's our plan for this afternoon?"

"We can start right now by getting a rental car reserved and a place to stay."

Jessica leaned over and grabbed her computer case. "I can do that. How long? What kind of car?"

He removed his credit card from his wallet and handed it to her. "I like a Malibu. Lots of room inside and it has a big trunk. If one isn't available, then get something of comparable size. Two nights should be plenty. I suspect Lane's address is a house. The search only turned up one contact for Woodard. Either way, he hasn't been deceased long, and he was murdered. His parents won't have closure until the murderer is found and convicted. That's a plus for you and me. They'll want to talk to us and do anything to help."

"So, what's a good time of day to call on them?"

A good question. "No time is perfect, but some are better than others. I like afternoons. The husband may be at work, or both of them will be. We'll have to see. But normal working hours, otherwise, they're apt to be wary, guarded. I don't like to pop in during mealtimes. It's rude. I always pop in. Never call. People screen calls now more than ever with the flood of telemarketers looking for victims. People like to see who they're talking with, and they'll be more comfortable."

"Tony sent us a note." She read for a moment. "He's already moved to a Days Inn in Mandeville. Where's that?"

"Across Lake Pontchartrain. Louisianan's

call the area the North Shore." The location was perfect. Bubba lived on that side of the lake, east of Abita Springs.

Wes leaned back in the chair. Jessica worked at her computer. This mode of transportation was really the only way to fly.

"What else, Jessica?"

She glanced up and said, "Please, call me Jess," then focused on the screen again.

He gazed out the portal. Looked like foothills into the snowcapped mountains of eastern New Mexico below. Clear skies as far as he could see.

The woman was three, five-hundred-piece jigsaw puzzles mixed up in the same box.

19

Thursday evening

Wes eased the brown Malibu to the curb across the street from the address they had for Lane Woodard. If he had to guess, the house, like all of them in the area, dated back to the fifties. Red brick extended to the eaves of a nearly flat, hot-mopped tar and graveled roof. Fixed narrow windows along the front of the house reached from the foundation to the eaves. Instead of a garage, the roof extended across a narrow slab of concrete to form a carport on the left side of the structure where a blue station wagon sat. The yard consisted of natural, no-maintenance desert, like the southern Nevada and Arizona countryside. Every plant looked like a pincushion or a chainsaw.

He glanced at his watch. "It's five ten. We're cutting it close, but this needs doing."

"Looks empty," Jess said.

"Let's find out." Wes opened the door and stepped out.

Jess exited and came around the car. They crossed the street.

Jess pointed toward the side of the house. "Look. What are they?"

Four birds sprinted for the backyard, like trailers tied together. Follow the leader. "Look like quail. I forget what kind. Not bobwhites or blues, but like blues. We'll have to ask someone who lives here."

The place looked empty, but not vacant. A clay pot full of red flowers on the porch looked healthy. The Chevy wagon under the carport was old but in good shape, like the house. It had been washed recently. Someone lived in the home.

He rapped on the jamb of the white storm door.

Seconds passed. Jess smoothed her red blouse with a swipe of her hands. She glanced at Wes. "I'm nervous."

"Don't be. You're lovely. You'll put them at ease." He squeezed her elbow. "I'll start. Just be yourself."

The deadbolt clicked and the main wooden door opened. If the lady who answered stood five feet tall, he'd be surprised. Gray, short hair hung loose around her face. She was petite, frail even. She opened the storm door a crack. "Can I help you?" she asked in a weak voice.

"Ma'am, I'm Wes Hansen, a private investigator. This is my associate, Jessica Wahl. We hoped we might speak to Mr. and Mrs. Woodard, Lane's mother and father."

It was then Wes noticed the assorted bouquets and vases of yellow, white, and red roses scattered around the living room behind the woman. The type of flowers friends and family would send after a tragedy. They were at the right house, but the woman looked too old to have a son twenty-five.

"I'm Miss Woodard. I've already talked to the police. A detective from New Orleans came here this morning and asked a bunch of questions. I had few answers for him, and he didn't have a one for me. He didn't even know when they're going to send my son home to me."

The title struck Wes. She didn't say *Miss* with emphasis like a feminist trying to make a point. *Divorced? Widowed?* She was spent. She looked like she hadn't slept or showered in a couple of days. Her voice was low, resigned to whatever. He regretted the visit in the first place, but especially so soon. "Yes, ma'am, I'm sorry, but could you spare a moment for us? We'd like to see if you recognize the description of a man we suspect of involvement."

She inched the door open and turned away. Wes took the move as an invitation and held the door for Jess.

The woman walked to a green chair, next to a well-used upright piano, and plopped down. "Please, have a seat." She indicated a matching green couch against the wall to their right. "You'll have to forgive me. I'd offer you something to drink, but frankly, I just can't go anymore."

"That's OK," Jess said, sitting closest to the lady and folding her hands in her lap. Wes sat next to Jess.

Pictures of young and old, couples, groups and singles covered the walls. A music book titled *Songs for the Ages* sat in the holder on top of the piano. The interior of the house took him back to his childhood. Wall-to-wall shag carpet in a greenish-yellow he couldn't describe without using the word hideous and a textured ceiling flecked with glitter.

The place looked clean. For a family man in the nineteen-sixties the house would have been a move up.

She leaned over and offered her hand. "I'm Elizabeth. Call me Liz."

Wes didn't reach for her but nodded.

Jess took the shaking hand in hers. "Very nice to meet you. We're so sorry for your loss."

Tears flowed from the woman's eyes. She fell back in the chair, her head down, arms on the cushioned rests to each side. She cried. Not a sound. Just tears. A flood of them poured down her cheeks.

Jess matched her tear for silent tear.

An oak grandfather clock in the corner of the room next to the doorway into the kitchen ticked with the rhythm of its pendulum. It clicked off seconds but seemed too slow and grew louder in the silence. Despite his efforts, Wes couldn't keep his tears in check.

He didn't know Lane, but he knew death. He knew what it felt like to have a broken heart and to cry until the well dried. No words could ease the pain.

After a minute, Liz stood. As she rounded the corner into the hallway out of sight, Wes put his hand on Jess's shoulder and gave it one light squeeze. She leaned her head and raised her shoulder to press his hand between the two. Her tears wet the back of his hand. She straightened and removed a tissue from her purse to wipe her eyes and nose.

The big clock chimed on the half hour, eight minutes fast.

Liz returned and sat, clutching a white tissue. "I lost Lane's daddy to colon cancer fifteen years ago. Lane had just turned ten." She held her hands out as if to say *help me.* "Lane was my life. He still lived here, with me. He was going to marry this August. I don't know what I'll do now."

"Miss Woodard . . . Liz," Wes said. "I am sorry for the intrusion. I know there's no good time to ask questions, but we wouldn't be here if I didn't think it was important. What we find out from you, about your son, his friends, may save lives."

The woman seemed to rein in her emotions and focus. She sat up and inched forward onto the edge of the chair. "Please, what can I do to help?"

Starting was the hard part. No place like the beginning. "I was hired to find a man who assaulted a woman in Lubbock, Texas. My investigation led me, us, my team, to New Orleans. I think our guy and your son's murderer is the same man. I think a chance meeting got Lane killed. I believe he knew his assailant."

"You said you had a description. No name?"

"Tall," Jess said. "Around six-two, dark

hair. Very attractive, masculine and strong, but with one distinguished flaw, we think he's blind in one eye. He wears sunglasses day and night. The eye or the area around it could be damaged enough to put people off at first glance."

Liz looked between them, then at the ceiling and shook her head. "I can think of a couple of Lane's friends who are tall, but no one who has one eye. Everyone is tall to me, young lady." A faint smile crossed her lips.

He didn't want to say it, but they weren't looking for a friend. *A friend doesn't cut his friend's throat.* "Meshach is the only name we have."

Liz looked between them again. "Really, like the man from the fire? Strange name for this day and time anyway. I don't believe I've ever heard of that name outside of the Scriptures."

"Was your son in the armed services? Law enforcement? Did his current job have security risks he might have mentioned?" Wes said.

She shook her head at each question. "He worked on slot machines."

Wes went through the info in his mind. "Does the name Marlin Sands ring a bell? Lane sent him a text just before, well, that evening."

"Yes, Lane went to school with Marlin. The detective mentioned Marlin this morning, but he didn't say anything about a text. Like I told him, I believe Marlin runs a pawnshop for his father, off the strip, or casino alley if you will, on the north side. What kind of text?"

"He typed 'never guess who I saw?' That's why I think Lane knew the man in question."

"Where did Lane go to high school?" Jess said.

"Canyon Springs. Not far from here."

"Could we look at yearbooks, old photos, baseball and football team pictures? That type of thing," Wes asked.

"Well," Liz stood. "Lane didn't play sports because of me, or his dad, actually. He took a job working for a local landscaping company when he got old enough to drive. As you can see, we don't have much. I never remarried and would have never made it without Lane. Come on. You're welcome to look at anything I've got if it will help catch the man who murdered my son."

They followed the woman down a short hallway into a small bedroom. A single bed covered with a blue comforter sat under the only window opposite of the door. A six-drawer chest made of oak stood to the left. On top of the chest, closest to the head of the bed, sat a small wooden box full of change, two Titleist golf balls, and one red tee. In the corner, a metal desk held an older model computer with a huge, bulky monitor. The floor was tiled in brown linoleum. An area rug with a bright southwest theme covered the center of the room.

Wes stroked the top of the oak chest. Smooth. Well-built.

"Lane made that in shop when he was a senior. He loved woodworking." Liz turned and pointed at a corkboard on the wall between the door and the computer. "That's a picture of Lane and his girl, Olivia. She sure loved my son. Poor thing is a wreck."

Lane looked his youth, blond hair and lots of it, high cheekbones and green eyes. The girl looked of Spanish descent, eyes as black as her long hair. The picture caught a great moment. Her chin was raised, eyes bright and fixed upon the man she obviously loved.

What would it be like to have a woman look at him like that?

Liz opened the bi-fold door to the closet. The usual line of shirts and pants hung from the bar. A set of golf clubs rested against the wall to one side. An assortment of shoes and boots lined the wall on the floor. She pointed to the shelf. "I can't reach them, but help yourself."

Wes grabbed a stack of three yearbooks and one photo album.

Liz tapped Wes's elbow and pointed again. "Grab that shoebox too. It's full of old pictures. You can take any or all if you must, but I want them back."

Wes complied, grabbing the items, and placed everything on the bed. "No, ma'am, all we need to do is take pictures. These new iPhones have great lenses."

"Well, you help yourself then. I'm going to sit this out if you don't mind." She walked to the doorway and stopped. "I wonder why the New Orleans detective didn't ask to look at pictures?"

"Well," Wes said, "I don't think they've put all the pieces together yet. I promise you we'll be communicating anything we find with them when the time comes."

Jess watched her walk away then turned to Wes. "Poor woman is heart-broken."

"I know. Let's get this done and go."

Jess scanned through the yearbooks.

Wes sorted the pictures. Lane on a tricycle, holding a small catfish, standing next to a black and white pony, on the golf course leaning on a driver next to another kid. Most of the pictures included the man who had to be his father. They looked alike.

The photos could be stacked, thumbed like a deck of cards, and the sequence would take the viewer through Lane's life, from toddler into manhood. About halfway through, the poses with fish, ponies, and dad abruptly stopped. Cancer took the male influence.

Not a dozen pictures depicted kids other than Lane. Two were poor snaps of a Cub Scout or Webelo Troop on an outing in the desert.

Wes wrapped up his end of the project and placed the shoebox back on the shelf. "Not much here."

Jess used her iPhone and took pictures, turning pages in a yearbook one by one. "Not in these either. No one stands out at first glance. Meshach is over six feet tall and could have been full-grown or close to it by the time he was a senior, but none of the athletes in any sport fit his description. I'm just taking pictures of groups of kids. I had an idea too. Several websites exist where you can search for old school mates. Might be a good place for Tony's skills. Look in the yearbooks of other local schools."

"Yes, you're correct. We'll give him a call tonight. You done?"

"I am." She closed the last book and

handed it to Wes. "Lane was typical. Not many pictures of him. Looked like a happy kid, though. He wasn't a jock or a nerd. Just there."

Wes replaced the books and turned off the light on the way out. He remembered kids he went to school with who were there, in the background. He talked to them, liked them, but outside of class, if they didn't have something to do with sports, they didn't hang out. Just the way it was.

They found Liz in the green chair, sitting in silence, legs pulled up and arms wrapped around her knees.

"Liz, we've got what we need. I'm going to leave my card for you, in case you remember something. I'll call if I have news. Anything we find we'll turn over to the authorities of course." He held his business card so she could see it and placed it on the piano top.

The evening sun shone bright, but the room sat in a pall of unlit gloom. The poor woman was on the edge of losing it.

Jess knelt in front of her. "Can we do something for you? Do you have someone who can stay with you?"

When she didn't reply, Jess looked at Wes. "I'm not leaving. I'll call you in the morning."

20

Thursday afternoon, Venice

Meshach locked his new ride and surveyed the area as he walked down the narrow path onto the cypress landing toward his camp house. Shanteel's place appeared to be vacant. No car. His boat sat in the slip next to the other three. Two men stood on the deck of the first camp. Smoke billowed from a black barbeque grill. It was that time of the day.

Too far for conversation, one guy waved by raising his glass of whatever. Meshach nodded then ignored him. He didn't want a spur-of-the-moment invitation to decline.

As he ascended the stairs to his house, he noticed a smudge on the toe of each wooden step. Not a smudge, but a slight scuff exposing un-weathered wood. Something narrow and heavy had been dragged on the stairs. He slowed, did another quick scan of the area, and reached around to the small of his back with his right hand to touch the .45 tucked in his belt.

At the door, he checked for the tattletale, a small length of blue thread from the sheet covering the anchor he'd trapped in the door when he left that morning. It was gone.

He palmed the pistol and thumbed back the hammer.

Opening the screen door, he turned the knob. Locked. No sign of forced entry. Both of the windows within sight were intact, but something didn't smell right. He tried to think. Was the object taken in or out of the house and if out, what weighed enough to cause the damage?

The key slid into the lock with little more than a click. He turned the knob and eased open the door.

The air conditioning hummed. Panes of glass in the French doors framed new patio furniture on the deck outside. Scott had pulled cardboard encased furniture up the steps into the house.

Meshach slammed the front door, secured the .45 and placed the pistol on the island next to the sink. He took a long deep breath then let it out. Scott's lucky he wasn't caught in the act. Since when does someone, owner or not, enter an occupied rental uninvited, other than a hotel room for cleaning?

He checked each room. Nothing looked out of place. His bed and backpack remained as he'd left them. Each cache of money was undisturbed.

Back in the kitchen, he turned on his computer and eyed the new patio additions. Scott used the cash Meshach gave him well. He'd up-graded to a slate-topped table and added two outdoor recliners to the mix. If the next tenant decided to throw an anchor on the table, it wouldn't make such a racket.

The broken glass from the previous piece had been swept up.

He logged on. Lamech hadn't posted squat.

What is he waiting for? The right time? Meshach thought all along Lamech was a go-between, not the boss. The longer this went on, the more convinced he was.

It wasn't Meshach's right time Lamech waited on. The job would be over if he had anything to say about it.

He typed *interesting trip to paris eye out appreciated paused* then reread it twice before posting it.

He checked the weather — forty percent chance of thunderstorms tonight, fifty Friday and sixty Saturday. In Louisiana, that meant rain, period. *That's about right.* He'd bet money Lamech would give him the go-ahead when the weather beat its worst.

He hated waiting.

Someone knocked on the front door. He grabbed the .45 and peeked around the corner. He had to look twice. Hair in a tight bun, white blouse, and modest black shorts gave Shanteel a schoolteacher look.

The woman was like waking up from a bad dream only to lay back, close your eyes, and discover the nightmare had only paused and continued to play.

Where had she come from? He glanced behind her house again, no car.

She knocked a second time, but more persistent. "Helloooo."

He'd heard that croon before. She knew he was home.

He opened the door.

"Hi," she said, shifting her weight from one foot to the other.

"Hi, back."

She held up two bottles of beer and looked toward her house and back. "I saw you drive up. What happened to your car?"

"Traded it. Where's yours?"

"Having it detailed. Too bad about your ride. The one out back looks used."

"It is," he said.

"I only meant . . . I don't know. Are you going to invite me in or what?" She held up the beer again, as though the suds would sweeten the offer.

He thought *or what* sounded good, but he nudged open the screen door with his foot.

Her walk looked choreographed. Moving that many body parts in sync over and over with every step took effort and practice.

She passed him a beer on the way in and took a survey of the room. "Looks like our place. The layout I mean." She pulled out a barstool and made herself at home at the island across from him.

"Shanteel, what can I do for you?"

"You can start by opening this." She slid her beer across the counter and propped her chin on her fists, elbows on the table.

He twisted off the top and handed the lukewarm bottle back. Cold beer wasn't his favorite. Warm beer didn't rank anywhere on the chart.

"So?" she said, taking a sip.

"So what?" He laid the .45 on the counter and set his unopened beer down next to it.

She thumped her bottle down hard enough for the beer to foam and ooze over the snout. She eyed the pistol. "You're so exasperating."

"Look . . . Shanteel . . . you knocked on

my door. Let me demonstrate how this works. Start a knock-knock joke."

She stared, blinked. "Excuse me. Start one?"

"Shanteel. You start it. Go ahead. Say knock-knock."

A sigh accompanied rolled eyes. "Knock-knock."

"Who's there?"

"You're not funny." After another noisy sip at the foam, she used the bottle to indicate the .45. "I've got one just like it. My . . . a friend gave it to me."

"The cop?" Meshach leaned against the counter.

She couldn't talk without another sip of beer first. "How do you know about him?"

"I saw him slap you."

"And you just watched?" Now she was huffy.

Meshach laughed at her. "Quite the show. Besides, it looked to me like Barney is the one who needed to be rescued. What's he to you anyway?"

This time she threw her head back and took a big drink. Her eyes rapidly scanned the ceiling. He knew the exercise. She was busy searching each quadrant of her brain for the best lie to tell. He could see her thinking about the answer that would better her chances of what, a one-night stand or a happy-ever-after with her big hunk?

Wasn't happening.

She pinched off the flow of beer with the smack of her lips and gave a satisfied sigh. "What happened to your eye?"

She could change the subject without blinking.

"My dad knocked it out for me."

"No, he didn't."

"OK, he didn't."

"Did he really?" Her eyes narrowed, furrowing the dark, painted brows.

"You said he didn't."

Now she was stumped.

Meshach pushed off the counter and stepped to the sink. "Look, you believe what you want to. I don't care one way or the other. I told you he did, and you said he didn't."

She eyed him and took a sip. "I don't think I like you."

Now they were getting somewhere.

With one swift motion, she flung the beer bottle at him.

Before she'd finished the move, Meshach grabbed her by the front of her white shirt and jerked her out of the chair. He held her on her back, stretched out on top of the island.

"Listen."

She kicked and screamed, and he shook her once, hard enough to make her quit thrashing. Then he leaned over her, breath to hot breath. Her blazing eyes searched his face and focused on his good eye. Her lips curled, baring teeth he had no doubt she'd sink into him if given the chance.

He moved slowly, deliberately, rubbing his unshaved-cheek against hers. Her chest rose and fell. With each rapid pant came the odor of cheap beer. Her heart pounded like a trapped rabbit's. His lips touched her lips, her chin and cheek, then, floating on his hot breath, he skimmed the softness of her neck to the peach fuzz on her bare earlobe.

A quick tremor rippled through her.

He turned loose of her throat and dragged the back of his hand across her thin shoulder, down the sleeve and onto the goose bumps covering her arm.

"I don't like you either," he whispered for her ears only.

He released her and stood.

She took one deep breath, squalled, flipped to her stomach like a feral cat and grabbed his .45. Before he could blink, she had the hammer back. The muzzle came up only inches from his face. He jerked his head right, out of the line of fire, and swept his right hand left for the automatic. As he gripped the pistol, thrusting it toward the ceiling, pain seared the end of his little finger.

Shanteel spun off the countertop and darted for the entryway. She scooted through the screen door and down the steps at a run.

Meshach eased the hammer back to release his lacerated and bloody fingertip.

He'd looked at death many times. How exhilarating.

21

Thursday night

Meshach sat in the dark living room watching Shanteel's house through the open patio doors. His backpack at his feet contained the computer, the cash, all of it. Just in case.

Lightning flashed offshore. A gust moved the curtains. The thunderstorms had arrived. Weather was as unpredictable as the broad who'd stuck his own pistol in his face. She'd nearly killed him. Only a finger's width away. He grinned at that thought. She'd never know.

Headlights topped the levee — an unrelated vehicle, someone returning her car, or the poster boy cop? A glimpse at the bridge of lights mounted on top of the car told him the latter. A man exited the cruiser and walked toward Shanteel's. He was off duty, dressed in civilian clothes, but no doubt still armed.

He trotted up the stairs to the front door

and entered without knocking. The door slammed. Another light came on.

Meshach glanced at his watch: 11:07. He'd like to hear that conversation. He'd bet money it was one-sided.

Lightning illuminated heavy, menacing clouds. The smell of rain rode on a cooler wind. Wouldn't be long reaching the area now.

Minutes passed: 11:21. The front door opened. The cop stepped out and slammed the door behind him. He walked with authority and determination. Either the wildcat had tried to emasculate him again, and he was fleeing for his life, or he was out to avenge the slight she'd suffered. He trotted down the steps. As he reached the walkway that would take him back to his car, another quick flash of lightning flared almost on top of them. The thunderous crack stopped him in his tracks.

Hard to tell what direction he looked, but Meshach could guess. Another bolt arced cloud to cloud. The guy stood with his hands planted on his hips, staring toward Meshach.

Could he see Meshach staring back from just inside the door? Meshach hoped he could.

In a second, the distance between them

filled with a torrent. Wind blew rain sideways through the doors into the living room. Lightning split the night in half, revealing emptiness where the cop had stood.

Thursday night, Las Vegas
Wes's cell phone chirped as he walked through the door of the Hampton Inn, not far from the Woodard residence. He glanced at the display and answered. "Mr. Blackwell, good evening."

"How's the desert sun treating you?"

Wes moved to one side of the door and shed his shoulder bag. "It's hot compared to what I'm used to for this time of year it is."

"You've been busy."

"I have. My apologies for not letting you know my intended destination this morning."

"Don't worry about that. I approved the flight. Besides, I hired a professional. I expect him to do his job and I leave him alone. What's the news?"

Wes walked up to a display like those he'd seen in the lobby of a hundred other hotels. This one held fliers and ads for day-trips to Hoover Dam, casino specials, golf courses, rental cars, nightclubs and live shows. "I'm trying to think about my last update. I told

209

you we actually got a description of our man from an unlikely source the other night. We still don't know his real name."

"Any further cyber postings?"

"Yes, and we believe there's a third player involved now, a Sullivan."

"Yeah, you mentioned him. What're your thoughts on my daughter's security?"

Wes took a deep breath. He knew he was right, but to voice it held risks if he wasn't. "I believe Meshach's mission has changed altogether, and you, the Blackwell family, your daughter, in particular, are no longer in the crosshairs. I think they, not he, have something planned, something big, maybe aimed at your Gulf interests or at the industry as a whole. What? I haven't got a clue. Not yet."

Female voices in the background on Cole's end dimmed the silence. Wes gave the man time to think. Wes's phone beeped in his ear. He gave the face a quick glance. Tony.

"What leads you to that line of thinking?"

"A feeling more than proof. At least three people are involved that we know of. Meshach is a long way from your neck of the woods. I hate to say it, but after I called Bubba and asked for a local contact in law enforcement so we could check flight manifests, hotels, rental cars, that type of thing, Lamech sent a warning about our investigation."

This time the line went dead quiet. Wes glanced at his phone again — still connected. He waited, looking at the display of fliers without seeing them, distracted, his concentration on Cole's lack of response. He continued, "I'm sure we had contact with our guy this morning in New Orleans. He tailed us out of the hotel parking lot. I had to lose him in traffic. Unfortunately, we didn't get a good look at him, nor did we get a complete plate number of the car he drove."

"Then we've got bigger problems, as a whole, and you have a personal problem. I know Bubba's your friend, but this is some kind of conspiracy. Is he involved? How did an assault on a woman in Texas morph into — into the Lord knows what?"

"I can't answer those questions right now, but we are getting closer."

"You have to set him up."

"Who?" Wes knew whom Cole referred to, but he asked anyway.

"Bubba." A sigh traveled the connection. "You've been to war as a Marine. Now you're a private investigator. You weren't born last night. You know the dangers. Keep them in mind. Don't let an old friendship impair your judgment. I know him and like him too, but think it over, hard. The moment you have the evidence, hand it over to the police and let them sort it out. If it's as big as you believe, we'll get the FBI involved, or DHS. I have personal dealings with the Secretary of Homeland Security. I went to school with him. Interfering with oil production has national security implications, not to mention lives are at stake. And the environment."

"Yes, sir, I will, and I know what you're saying about Bubba. I've got it to do, and I know it."

"What took you to Las Vegas? And don't tell me my airplane."

Albeit dry, Cole had a sense of humor. "A New Orleans murder and a text. May be a tie to our guy. If so, we could find out his true identity."

"A text?"

"Yes, sir."

"Well, I'm not into publishing details about private life or opinions for the world to read, but I exchange texts with my wife and daughter. All right. Hang on." Papers ruffled. "You said he tailed you."

Cole was no dummy, and from what Wes

had just heard, he took notes. "I believe he did."

"But you didn't engage him?"

"I did not."

Again time lapsed. "Your people with you?"

"Jess and Tony, yes, they were."

"Smart move. Need some money?"

The man didn't banter words. "I'll bill you when this nut's behind bars."

"Good night, then. Godspeed."

The line went dead.

Wes pocketed his phone and stared out the window into the parking lot. The lights from casino row lit the sky. Traffic on the highway looked like rush hour volume, and it was after ten o'clock. His eyes burned. He was tired.

Wes had been working for Cole less than a week. He liked him. Confronting his long-time friend would not be easy. He found it hard just to contemplate the idea.

He dialed Tony back. "Hey, you rang."

"Yeah, just checking in. Did you visit with the Woodards? Get anything out of it?"

"Not at first glance. Cancer killed his dad. His mom isn't well. She's an older woman. We got pics of pics to look at, but nothing concrete. Still have to talk to Marlin. We'll do that in the morning."

"Meshach conveyed his thanks to Lamech for the warning. Said he had a good trip to Paris. Dude, I'm telling you."

Wes looked down at the display again, and Tony's comments never registered. His focus fixed on a flier in the middle of the mix. He slid the folded slip from its holder and held it up. The words Liz uttered at the mention of the name Meshach echoed through his thoughts. The man from fire she'd called him.

"Unbelievable."

22

Friday morning

Except to make coffee and get a cupful when it was done, Meshach had not moved from his vantage point in the chair just inside the open French doors. After the storm passed, he'd catnapped through the remainder of the night, more awake than asleep.

Darkness edged to gray. White wisps of fog drifted over the waters between the canebreaks giving life to the morning. Reminded him of Dracula movies his mom used to watch late at night. The thunderstorms added to the humidity. The temperature had cooled.

A black beetle trekked through the water beaded on the floor in front of the couch. Meshach could imagine Scott's outrage at the sight.

No one stirred in the cabins next to him, but he knew the fishermen would be along as soon as the sun rose.

He caressed the smooth steel action and wooden grip of the .45 in his lap. The Kimber had a majestic feel and look he valued more than the lithe figure of a woman. He leaned over, opened his backpack, and removed a cleaning kit. Gun oil had a unique aroma, like the smell of leather seats in a new car or a fresh stack of banded Franklins straight out of the vault. His attention wandered the marsh and nearby cabins as he broke down the pistol with practiced precision. Two gulls bickered over a scrap on the dock below. The loser squawked louder as the victor flitted off with the prize. He looked through the barrel of the pistol at them wondering if they were the same two birds he'd seen going at it the first morning. He wiped every piece with loving care, then put the automatic back together and shoved home the clip.

A growing list of questions nagged him. Where had the Hilton trio come from? Who hired them? He could probably guess — Cole Blackwell. What really bugged him was how fast they'd found his location.

Lamech hired him, but would the man pay the million-dollar fee one day and spring a trap the next? He answered that question as fast as the thought formed. Lamech had made all the arrangements for the job — the car, the gun, the cash and the cabin, all of it. If he wanted to give up Meshach, all he had to do was call the police and leave them a tip.

And the plan was Lamech's idea to begin with. It was bold. Could one man take down a ship in the river? Unheard of. Meshach wished he'd thought of it.

He woke up his computer. Nothing. Too quiet. This was one instance when he hated silence. Time to push. He started to type then stopped. *Patience. Where had his cool, unflappable patience gone? Take a minute and think.* He closed the laptop and the doors leading onto the deck and headed for his boat.

Friday morning

Wes opened his eyes. Something woke him. He'd heard what? A hint of light glowed from around the blinds covering the window. A chirp sounded to his left. He grabbed his phone. "Hello."

"Good morning."

"Good morning, Jess. You're up early."

"No, I think you've overslept."

"What time is it?"

"Eight fifteen."

Wes swung his legs out from under the

217

covers and sat up. "You're kidding?"

"Nope." She laughed. "You must have needed the rest."

"I guess so." He turned on the light. "How's Miss Woodard?"

"She's better. Some sleep helped. Her sister will be here this afternoon from Seattle. That will go a long way."

Wes stood and walked into the bathroom. "Well, good. You ready to go? I'll be ready in a few minutes."

"I am. Take your time."

"Give me half an hour." He disconnected.

After a quick shower, he dressed and drove to the Woodard's. Before he could get out of the car, Jess walked out of the house. She had bounce in her step and a smile on her face.

Wes's bounce was more like a deflated basketball. He'd slept too long.

She tossed her bag into the backseat, got in, and closed the door. "Good morning, again." She clipped her seatbelt.

"And to you." Wes pulled away from the curb and made a right on the first cross street. "You're looking spry. Have you had breakfast?"

"I cooked eggs and toast for Liz and me. You haven't had time to eat."

"No, I haven't eaten, but no worries." At

the entrance onto Interstate 15, instead of turning right toward downtown and their hotel, he made a left, north. "Are you up for a little excursion?"

"I am. Where to?" She looked at him, eyebrows raised, bluebonnet-eyes intense.

Then, just like the perfect timing of every clue they'd received since taking the job, he saw a large brown sign typical of a state's recreation department just beyond the on-ramp. He pointed.

Valley of Fire State Park
55 Miles

Jess looked at the sign, at Wes, then back at the sign until they passed it, then shook her head like she couldn't comprehend what she saw. He handed her the flier. "I noticed this in the hotel last night. I couldn't believe it either."

"Well, praise God. That's all I can say."

"Meshach was one of the men who walked out of the fiery furnace. 'The man from fire' Liz said last night. Her comment is what struck a chord when I saw the flier. Makes little sense as yet, but it could be another piece to the puzzle . . . if we're correct in our assumption."

"What else can it be?"

Wes canted his head, yes and no. Some leads turned into dead ends. This one might be one of them, but he had the warm and fuzzy about it. He didn't get that feeling often.

He set the cruise and settled back in the seat. "I talked to Tony last night. No hits on Meshach at the rental car outlets or on flight manifests. Seven Chrysler 300s from Avis, Hertz, and Budget were on the street yesterday. Two of those were black and both were rented to older businessmen. One man is from El Paso and the other is from Atlanta. Nothing fishy about their profiles."

Jess nodded. "Did you get a chance to send him the pictures you took? I didn't."

"Too tired. After talking to Cole and Tony, I turned in."

"You see Meshach's last post?"

"Tony mentioned it. Looks like we met our man."

"I think we did," she said. "He was warned too."

Wes's phone vibrated and dinged. He pulled it out of his shirt pocket and handed it to her. "Check the text for me, please."

She took the phone and thumbed the unlock bar. "Password?"

"One, two, three, four."

"Original."

He smiled. "It's easy to remember."

It's from your daughter." She held out the

phone for him to take back.

"I'm driving. Please, read it for me."

"You don't mind?"

"Of course not."

" 'Dad, sorry so long to get back. Dropped phone water. One day to get replaced. Thanks for note. Levi kicking up a storm. Love Lisa.' " She handed him the phone.

"Thanks." He put it in the cup holder in the console. "That has been a long time coming."

The desert bloomed with cactus and wild flowers in every color. Alive. He felt alive for the first time in years.

"What happened?" Jess asked. "Sorry. That was a little direct."

He knew what she referred to, the relationship with his daughter. And his late wife, or ex-wife, though, the divorce wasn't final when she passed. "That's all right. I like direct. Her name was Teri, Lisa's mother. She overdosed on meds. The coroner ruled it suicide."

"Oh my, Wes. I'm sorry I asked."

"No, that's all right. We were separated but not by my choice. Lisa blamed me. Just a big mess all around. I loved Teri, but she wasn't the same anymore."

Jess turned sideways, facing him, left arm on the seatback, knee up, and tucked her left foot under her right knee.

"The Corps owned me. Being at Uncle Sam's beck and call, doing the only thing I knew how to do at the time wasn't all Teri thought it would be. When the day-to-day of married life set in without me, she realized she didn't share my sense of sacrifice. I think she loved and married the idea of me, the Marine. Then, after Lisa was born, I didn't know Teri anymore. Like something, someone else took over her mind and soul. I used to shake my head at her moods. It's not something men, in general, understand. The changes in a woman's body during and after childbirth are very real. Today, they call it postpartum depression. I don't think she knew who she was anymore either. She struggled with it for years before a doctor put her on antidepressants. Then she started hearing voices." He shook his head. "Her mom found her. Not good."

Wes felt a sort of relief wash over him. He'd just told a woman, an employee and a new one at that, things he'd never uttered to another person. It felt right.

Now that the door was open . . . "What about you? Kids?"

"Oh no. I knew better. Ben — Benjamin — Lord forbid I ever called him Ben, wanted children. No way." She shook her head, then turned, placed both feet on the floorboard, and waved her right hand as if sweeping the thought aside. "It's terrible to say, but I married him to get away from my dad and ended up with the same mentality. My therapist, whom I don't see any longer, thank you very much, told me that subconsciously, I had looked for someone just like my father. Whatever."

She took a deep breath and smiled. "Then I gave my life to Christ. I had hope for the first time I could remember. Ben mocked me until the day I left him. Hell itself would flood before he would father my children."

Wes had done that long ago, been saved, as a kid in Bible school one summer. He hadn't thought about those days in a while. He'd thought about God a million times, especially in Iraq. He'd asked for His help. No atheists in foxholes as the adage goes. After Teri killed herself, he'd asked Him why. Never got an answer.

Five miles of hot pavement passed under them. They exchanged glances.

He held out his fist. She smiled and tapped it with hers.

The last twenty miles to the park entrance went by in a flash.

Wes had his doubts about the location of

223

the state park. The countryside didn't look much different than what he'd seen in Iraq, except for the colorful display of wild flowers and cactus as far as he could see. Orange, red, yellow, green, and blue, a random mix scattered across the desert. Nevada had vegetation going for it. Southern Iraq was as barren as Mars.

Over the next few miles, he changed his mind. Red sandstone rock formations showed promise. He could see the draw.

He stopped at the pay station, deposited the ten-dollar entry fee, picked up a quick-reference map, and continued into the park. He handed the map to Jess. "Would you navigate, please?"

"I can do that." She unfolded the display. "Where to?"

"You tell me." He turned left at the first crossroad.

"Well, you've found the visitor's center on your own. Are you stopping?"

"Nope. Let's drive and look. Just get a feel."

She folded the map in half. "This road dead-ends five miles ahead, at White Dome, whatever that is. There's a trail. Looks interesting. Who would have thought this was out here?"

"I don't know what I expected. Houses, a

subdivision, something more substantial. An abode for the man from fire."

"Maybe he got lost out here or something." She looked at him. He looked at her. "OK." She laughed and shook her head. "So maybe not."

"Maybe we're wasting our time. I had a good feeling about this, but now, I'm not so sure."

"Not many visitors." She turned the map over. "This says there's a car show here next month."

"School is still in session, and it's a weekday. Won't be long and the temperature will be one-ten in the shade around here too. I'll bet it hits ninety today."

The roadway meandered across a sandy desert floor between towering wind and water-etched red sandstone walls. Narrow washes ended in shaded box canyons strewn with boulders. He parked in the designated gravel lot at White Dome two spaces from the only other car, a white SUV.

"Let's go for a walk?" he said.

"I'm ready."

Wes shut off the car. They exited. He locked it.

The sweet smell of flowers accented pure, clear air. The day warmed quickly.

A wooden post with a sign "Pack it in,

pack it out" and a small arrow pointed them up a well-beaten path. The trail took a gradual, user-friendly route around a rock outcrop.

Wes let Jess take the lead. She stepped out at a brisk pace. Before they'd walked a hundred yards, he'd made up his mind to hit the gym more often. The girl was killing him. Sweat rolled. He was melting.

A quarter of a mile later, they topped a rise and stopped. The reason for the name White Dome lay ahead. The red sandstone hills in front of them looked like God had accidentally picked up the white when he mixed the shades of red then just left it as it was, like two different colored taffies twisted together.

Jess took a deep breath and let it out. "Isn't this beautiful?"

"I can't disagree. It's a wonder."

She stood on a rock at the edge of the trail, gathered her hair behind her head and slipped on a tie to hold it in a ponytail. They were eye to eye now. "What's next? For us I mean. In Las Vegas."

"We need to locate the pawnshop and interview Marlin. After that, unless Marlin has a revelation, back to New Orleans. Let Tony do his thing. Look at the pictures we took. I'd like to talk to the NOPD detective who talked to Liz. It's time to bring them in. And Bubba. I have to figure out a few things there."

"You think he had something to do with Meshach finding us?"

Jess scanned the scenery and didn't catch him looking at her. Or she knew and didn't care. The beads of sweat on the smooth skin above her lip glistened in the light. She seemed to relish the heat.

She knew something was fishy with Bubba but didn't mention her concerns. Smart and perceptive.

A young couple walked by holding hands, giving him an excuse to delay his answer a minute. Or not answer. Wes nodded at them. Jess and the girl said hi. As before, he didn't want to think about Bubba, but Cole was right too. It had to be done. He prayed there was a simple answer.

He watched the guy and his girl until they rounded the corner in the trail fifty yards away. When he looked back, Jess stared at him.

"You like campfires?" he said.

"That's off the wall, but yes, why?"

He feigned disbelief. "Didn't anyone ever tell you it's not wise to tell your boss he's off the wall? It's not conducive to career advancement, salary increases, that type of thing."

She rolled her eyes and let a sly "Nope" slip out.

"Well, as to my question. People stare at campfires, at the glow, the pulse of heat, the flicker of light and flames. It's the warmth, a draw they can't help but gaze into."

"And?" she said.

"Your eyes are like a campfire." He stared. She stared back. Her cheeks flushed. *Oh yeah, he got her. A wordsmith lost for words.* He loved it.

She looked away.

He smiled.

Wes had more questions in mind, but the time wasn't right, not yet. He gave her a playful slap on the shoulder with the back of his hand. "Come on, girl. Let's get to work."

He led the way back to the car.

23

Wes approached the counter of Easy Pawn. Another man stood there, hands on top of a glass display case full of watches, peering at an open doorway of an office and the source of a mumbled conversation from an unseen party. Wes nodded when they made eye contact.

A man's voice drifted out of the office, one side of a phone conversation.

Jess stood at Wes's side a second then strolled around the store. Guitars, amplifiers, one set of drums, hand and power tools, watches, cameras, rings, knives, guns, name it, anything and everything was stacked against the wall, displayed behind glass or hung from the ceiling.

The merchandise ranged from junk to Rolexes. It looked like most of the store's goods leaned heavily toward the former.

Stickers and signs advertising payday

loans with no credit check, offers to buy and trade coins, cash paychecks, and brand name cameras and watches splattered the front windows. He'd seen an episode of Pawn Stars once. This wasn't the place.

Jess stopped her window shopping and leaned forward, hands on her knees, and squinted from the guitar rack, past Wes. Wes did a double take when he looked back. The guy who walked out of the cubbyhole looked like the gas tank on the Harley parked on the concrete walk just outside. Or his head did. It was shaved and tattooed with bright yellow and red flames.

The flames seemed to fit on the black gas tank of the motorcycle.

Wes stepped away to let the customer barter and finish his business in private. He winked at Jess. She rolled her eyes.

Flame held up a gold ring. He told the man the price the store would pay and stuck to his guns when the owner countered. The guy accepted, took his money, and left. Flame placed the ring in a small case and set it just inside the office door.

"What do you need?" He addressed Wes.

"I'm looking for Marlin Sands. Does he work here?"

Flame's eyes narrowed over his hawk nose. The tats on his head dominated his looks and could not have been more distracting than if he'd stepped out of the office in his underwear. "I'm Marlin. What do you want?" If the direct question wasn't enough, the reply had a defensive edge to it.

Jess moved to the counter. Marlin gave her an appreciative and obvious onceover. Wes knew the look was anything but welcomed. She smiled back at him, but her eyes told a different story.

Wes tried a conversational tone. "My name's Wes Hansen. This is Jessica Wahl. I'm an investigator. If you have a minute, we'd like to ask you a few questions about Lane Woodard."

Marlin shook his head, looked down, then back up and locked on Wes. "I'll tell you just like I told a New Orleans cop yesterday, I don't talk to the fuzz. You might as well take your babe and find someone else to bother."

Wes matched Marlin's stare. He was a punk and spoiled rotten. The Marine DI's he knew loved to get their hands on guys like this. "I'm a private investigator, not a cop."

"I don't care. Same thing in my book." Marlin looked away first and waved off Wes. "I'm busy. Get lost."

Wes stood his ground a long moment. "We

understood you and Lane were friends. He sent you a text just before someone cut his throat. He knew his assailant, and we believe you know him too."

Marlin messed with an item in one of the cases and never looked up. "I haven't seen Lane in years. Suddenly I get a text from him. Big whoop. Can't help you. Beat it."

Wes nodded at the exit, hinting to Jess. He thumbed a business card from his shirt pocket, tossed it on the counter, and followed her out into the bright sunlight. He stopped next to the motorcycle. Apehanger handlebars, leather strings dangling from the grips . . . and flames on the gas tank. "Marlin just boosted my ego. Suddenly, I feel . . . normal."

Jess eyed the bike, studied the tank, and then glanced at the tinted front glass of the store before looking back. "They did a better job of painting the bike. I wonder if the gas tank influenced the tats, or the other way around?" Jess shaded her eyes and peered down the street. "Well, we went nowhere fast with him. What's next?"

Wes turned and looked at the madhouse of cars and people on the main thoroughfare a block away — casino-generated chaos. "First, fast-food, I'm starved. Then back to New Orleans. Time to arrange a dinner out with a federal prosecutor."

Jess nodded. "Yeah, and see if the match-head inside and our man from fire have a connection."

Friday afternoon

Meshach stood on the bow of the boat, facing a stiff southerly breeze. He'd motored into a little cove in the cane breaks to get out of the waves. The low-pressure system and associated thunderstorms stirred the shallow Gulf and inland waters into a muddy mess. No one had a line in the water today, no matter how avid the fisherman.

He faced the marina two miles away. He needed gasoline, but was hesitant to enter a public area to buy it. What were the odds of meeting Scott, Shanteel, or the cop? A gambler who fanned open his hand one card at a time and uncovered the ten, jack, and queen of spades wouldn't go all in before he checked if the next two were the king and ace of spades.

Too many coincidences had piled up on the wrong side of the scales lately.

It all started with the decision to gamble at Harrah's. Then bumping into Lane. Really too bad about him. Meshach remembered a scrawny, buck-toothed boy. At least he'd grown into his teeth like a dog grows into his paws. A strange feeling he'd only experienced a couple of times in his life tugged at his soul. If he didn't know better, he'd call it guilt. He did know better. Guilt held no meaning for him. He never had the urge to apologize for anything he'd done, ever.

The Hilton trio still had him baffled. He'd push that issue just for fun if the time dragged out. He'd love to see how far the old man would go to protect the blue-eyed looker.

Two short, deep, blasts of a ship's horn followed by two high-pitched toots fought the wind for dominance. Two vessels signaled each other that they'd pass portside to portside on the Mississippi a mile away. Part of *Rules of the Road* for ship traffic that dated back to a time when a bell was the only means of making noise.

A tanker headed upstream. Little or no load on her and riding high in the water. In a couple of days, she'd be loaded and traveling back out to sea. If Lamech would give him the word, she'd be a perfect candidate. Not too big to board at sea and a smaller crew to contend with.

The needle hovered just under the halfway mark on the fuel gauge and presented a conundrum. Go or don't go. Toward the north lay other options to fill his gas needs, but they held the same risks as bumping into Scott or the cop at the marina. Though, he wasn't so sure the cop would recognize him. He wasn't going to take the chance.

Then the northern option wouldn't put Meshach in a public venue, and he'd be in complete control. If he had to, he'd trade boats with an unsuspecting fisherman.

Then again, maybe he had enough gas.

He started the boat motor and headed back to the camp house.

24

Saturday morning, Mandeville, Louisiana
Wes selected the Broken Egg Restaurant, an old house-turned-eatery, located one block off the northern shore of Lake Pontchartrain. The residential neighborhood dated back to the turn of the twentieth century. Now, some of the more unique houses had been transformed into a mix of Cajun bistros, small eateries, and formal restaurants. Residents preserved their southern heritage with fine cuisine served in refurbished, well-aged but unique architecture. The result drew a fair tourist following.

Paved trails led bikers and hikers along the lakeshore under some of the largest oak trees he'd ever seen. The lake provided a wide array of watersports ranging from the Yacht Club to Bubba's Jet-skis. Fishing charters and bicycle rentals ranked somewhere in between.

He parked the car Tony had rented when

the techie left New Orleans, and got out. He pointed the fob at it, pressed the lock button, and shook his head. He'd never driven a Chrysler 300, much less one painted canary yellow. The thing looked like the pants Tony wore to pick him and Jess up at the airport last night.

The morning sun laid out a perfect setting for a table on the veranda. He sat down with his pad and cell phone and requested a cup of coffee from his waitress. When she brought his coffee, she quizzed him about breakfast. His stomach ordered for him. He didn't need the calories in a side of pancakes along with eggs, hash browns and sausage, but he was hungry.

Wes hoped the air travel ceased for the near future. The past few days reminded him of his frequent trips during his stint in the Corps. Except for the speed and comfort of his current mode of transportation. To find a similarity between a wooden bench in a lumbering C-130 and luxury seats in a swift corporate jet took imagination. Either way, it seemed like the older he got the harder it was for him to adjust to time changes and jet lag.

They didn't arrive at the hotel until a little after one, but this morning, somehow, he was wide-eyed and ready to go by six.

He unlocked his phone and sent a text to Tony — *going to be out awhile this morning. if jess sleeps in, let her. look over pix. see what you can find. any news???*

Evidence of the late evening thunderstorms covered the city. Broken tree branches littered yards and high water from substantial rainfall left its mark in a line of leaves, pine straw and manmade debris. The cool, humid morning generated a layer of low fog over the lake.

He grabbed his pad and pencil. Jotting down his thoughts was something he'd done since high school. Looking at his written ideas evoked more ideas and sometimes, game changing revelations.

Tony replied to his text as the waitress placed his meal in front of him. Wes thanked her and checked the message. *no problem. no news. found connection n posts — 2 spaces before code words (names) or so it appears. jess & i in a small meeting room on the 2nd floor. call when u get back 4 direction.*

Spaces, that was different. Meshach thought he was smart. Jess and Tony had unraveled his childish code in no time. Though the conversation with his daughter had set the ball rolling in their direction. Speaking of. He needed to touch base with her again. Maybe the first of the week.

A sudden thought about Levi gave him a good fatherly feeling. If Jess knew the Bible well enough to recite the story about the namesake, then maybe Lisa did too. He prayed his daughter had made some soul-changing decisions.

His phone buzzed again. Tony. *spaces might b fat fingers texting 2. do it all the time. we'll c.* Wes put his phone aside. He hoped they'd see sooner than later.

Over the next hour, he managed to drink four cups of coffee, eat his breakfast, and scribble three pages of notes on the legal pad. Then, he sat back in the chair, with the warm sun on his face, and studied each item again. Meshach's cryptic messages, Lane and his mom, pictures, Marlin, Cole and his daughter, Bubba and lastly, Jess. Though, he didn't have notes written about her.

Only thoughts . . . lots of them.

She was definitely her own person. A self-starter. On the flight back, she'd pored over the pictures they'd taken at Liz's house. She kept her own notes. She took the job seriously, and all personal feelings he was beginning to develop aside, she earned every dime he paid her.

Somewhere over Texas, he'd looked up, and she'd nodded off to sleep, her head back against the chair. A lock of dark hair had fallen across one eye and cheek. She was, she was . . .

He flipped the page on the pad. *Concentrate.*

Bubba weighed heavy on his mind and his heart. He'd about decided to tell his friend what happened. Wes could let his imagination run wild and assume the worst. Look into a dark alley for the boogieman, or shine a light and see who or what lies in wait. Communication was the best tool. His gut told him Bubba had nothing to do with the leak. His gut had never lied to him. At least not yet.

He'd know soon enough, he hoped. Last night he'd sent Bubba a query about getting together for dinner. So far, no reply.

His phone chirped. Tony. He answered. "Hey, what you got?"

"Dude, where are you?" He sounded excited.

"Near the lake. Sitting. Thinking. What's up?"

"Come to the hotel. Jess might have found our man."

Wes entered the small conference room, more the size of a large office. Something the hotel would use for intra-company meetings. One long, black Formica-topped table with a dozen rolling chairs took all the available space.

Tony stood behind Jess, hands in the pockets of his black hoodie, looking over her shoulder at her computer. Two broad smiles greeted him. "All right," he said, sitting next to Jess and pulling himself up to the table. "Let's see what you've found."

She turned her computer toward him. "See what you think about this picture."

The image was one from out of the shoebox of old photos of the Scout Troop he'd taken at Liz's. "What am I looking at?"

Jess reached up and touched the computer screen with a glossed nail. "The kid in the back, in the middle. With his head canted to one side."

The kid looked like the other eleven squint-eyed boys in the picture — blue short-sleeve shirt, blue cap, tan shorts, tan arms and face and knobby knees. The picture was in color, but pixilated and of poor quality. The desert around them was bare. Obviously hot with all the canteens visible. The kid in question was a little taller than the rest of the boys. He wore a pair of binoculars around his neck and wore mirrored, aviator sunglasses, but then three other kids had on sunglasses too.

Wes looked at Jess. "OK, if this is a stump-the-boss conspiracy between you two, it's working. What am I missing?"

"Look at the kid's binoculars," Jess said.

Wes did, again. They were black and looked like they weighed ten pounds. Then he saw what she meant. "Un . . . believable. There's only one lens cap open, the right one."

Jess nodded. "Came to me the same way. Like wow, so obvious, but, but, it just hit me. The other cap is either broken off, he hasn't opened it yet, or this kid can only see out of one eye and flipping down the cap just doesn't make sense."

Wes sat back and took a deep breath. Then he turned to Jess. "Great job. What a catch." He held up his fist for her and Tony to tap. "Now, before we get too confident, we have to put a name to him and confirm whether or not he's blind in one eye. So far, we've assumed he has vision problems. We have to put the two together."

Tony sat down at his computer and nodded. "We're fixing to catch this dude."

Wes had the warm and fuzzy again, but then he cautioned himself. "We need a name. Liz has already said she didn't know anyone who fits the description, and Marlin won't talk to us."

"I think I'll call Liz anyway," Jess said. "I want to see how she's doing. I'll ask her to check the picture. Maybe someone wrote all the names on the back. You know, front row, middle row, that type of thing."

Wes tried to think. He didn't remember looking at the backs of the pictures. Good idea. He really hoped he didn't have to fly back to Las Vegas.

His phone chirped, an unknown number. "This is Wes."

"Hey, brother. This is Bubba." The Cajun accent ran thick.

The second Wes heard Bubba's voice he remembered Cole's warning. *Don't let a friendship cloud your judgment.* "Good morning. How are you?"

"All well, all well. You up for a shrimp boil today?"

"I am. What time? Can I bring a couple of friends?" Wes eyed Tony and Jess.

"About three. We'll get an early start on the evening. Bring your friends. You remember how to get here?"

"I do. We'll see you this afternoon."

"Wait. How's your manhunt coming? Did Risa provide what you needed? I expected to hear from you the last couple days."

"She did and it's a saga. We had to run out to Vegas, and I know you're busy. I'll fill you in when we get there."

"Sounds good. See ya then."

Wes disconnected and looked at the time on his phone. He had five hours to either work out a scheme with Tony and Jess or go with his gut and be straight up.

"Bubba?" Jess said, eyebrows raised.

He nodded. "It was. I hope you two like shrimp."

"I like shrimps, plural." Tony grinned and rubbed his hands together.

Jess held her facial expression, brows arched in question, and Wes knew why.

25

Saturday afternoon

Jess sat in front, Tony in the back. Jess looked smart in flats, jeans, and a loose-fitting, white blouse. She'd left her hair down. The dark tresses framed her face and flowed around her neck to her shoulders. Tony sported the usual odd mix of colors with black on top, red tennis shoes, and yellow pants.

Wes had been to Bubba's years ago. If he remembered correctly, he should turn right onto the first lane just past a small bridge. He hoped he recognized the bridge.

To the unsuspecting eye, the forest on both sides of the two-lane blacktop northeast of Abita Springs looked uninhabitable. The roadway cut through pines, hardwoods, and undergrowth thick enough to hide a herd of elephants. A stranger would never guess hundreds of small family acreages lay just out of sight, on both sides of the road, and for just that reason. These people liked their privacy.

The bridge was as he remembered. Bubba had hidden his place well back off the highway. The gravel drive wound through thick growth and timber for a good four hundred yards before opening up to what looked like at least five spacious acres of impressively manicured grass scattered with just enough oaks and pines to shade the entire area. A beautiful ranch-style home constructed of dark, natural wood accented by a towering roof covered with galvanized metal stood as the centerpiece.

He remembered a smaller house.

Both garage doors were closed. Three red four-wheelers sat willy-nilly next to a swing set.

He parked on the edge of the circle drive, and they got out. A lazy breeze whispered through the treetops. Just enough wind to cool an afternoon get together.

"Tony," Wes said as they walked around the front of the car. "When Bubba shakes your hand, grab ahold and squeeze back hard. The man's a beast. Don't take any lip about your britches and shoes." Wes winked at Jess when Tony looked down at his own feet.

Tony gave Jess a look that said, "Great."

The front door burst open, and a stocky barefoot boy jumped out onto the concrete porch for a gawk at the arriving guests. "Mom, they're here!" he screamed without looking back into the house to focus the effort on its intended target.

All six foot four, two hundred and fifty pounds of Bubba's frame filled the doorway. His wife, Rae, peeked around his waist like a bashful kid. She stood a foot shorter and weighed a third as much, but when she pushed, he moved. She gave him a playful whack with the white hand-towel she held. "Big ox, get out the doorway. Hey y'all." She waved with the towel and led Bubba off the porch.

"Big ox is right." Wes said. He kissed Rae on the forehead, gave her a hug, and then turned to face Bubba. Wes would like to think they stood eye-to-eye, but Bubba had him by two inches. No obvious changes in the big man, other than a smattering of gray in his curly black hair. Wes's gaze slowly moved down the large frame to his feet. "White shirt, blue shorts, and orange boat shoes?"

"Brother, I'm jus' trying to stay fashionable."

They shook hands. Wes hugged his friend's neck and Bubba hugged back. 'Nuff said.

"Well." Bubba turned toward Tony and Jess. "My name's Frank. You can call me Bubba. This here is Rae, and the overgrown young'n there, that's Little Frankie. He's ten. His sister, Rae Lee, and brother, Jake, are around here somewhere. Probably out back playing in the mud."

Rae swatted the towel at her husband again. "Why no, they ain't either. Quit your fooling. Rae Lee's in the house primping, and Jake's in the shower. They'll be out."

Jess stepped forward and held out her hand to Bubba then Rae. "I'm Jessica Wahl. So nice to meet you." The girls touched cheeks.

Tony held back, but Bubba stepped toward him. "What's your handle?"

"Sorry, I'm Tony Moran." They shook. Tony's jaw clenched with the effort he gave his grip.

Rae grabbed Jess's hand. "You are so cute. Just look at your eyes. Come in here with me. I'm getting a few things together. You can keep me company." She tugged Jess toward the front door.

Jess smiled back over her shoulder at Wes.

Little Frankie padded off the porch straight to Tony. "Wanna see my four-wheeler? Come on. We can ride 'em if you want." He took off across the yard at a run.

248

Tony looked like he faded four shades then followed him.

Bubba clapped Wes on the shoulder. "Bro, let's go around back."

They followed Frankie and Tony. As they passed the ATVs, Frankie looked like he was in full form, giving Tony the rundown on the ins and outs of four-wheeling.

The roofline shading the patio extended off the back of the house. Bubba opened the screen door and held it for Wes. "Welcome to my man cave, my man."

Wes looked around. Open ceiling, twenty-by-thirty-foot concrete floor, and two big ceiling fans above a twelve-place patio furniture set. "It's huge and screened-in to boot. I'm impressed."

Bubba let the door close and walked across the room. "You forget. If it wasn't for their beak, you'd confuse the skeeters with the chickens around here."

"No, I didn't forget." Wes followed him to a cooking area that would make most women jealous. Pellet-fed smoker, three big gas burners, sink, and a preparation block made from laminated oak, all set in a base of stonework.

Bubba pointed back toward the house at a huge flat-screen television mounted above the sliding door. "That's what this old man likes. I can sit out here and watch the Saints and LSU play."

"What a place. When did you build this house? This is not quite what I remember."

"As you'll recall, my ma passed when we were overseas, so Dad had the old place where I was raised up, and he left it to me. Rae and I grew tired of the bayou living in Cutoff. Lost two houses to hurricanes in twelve years. Got to where it takes a millionaire to afford the insurance. That's why we moved up here to start with. I sold what Dad left me in his will. Built a new house and cleared a bit more land to make it airy. A humid summer day in these woods will smother a man."

"Beautiful place. You've done well. Sorry to hear about your dad."

"Yep, well, we've all got it to do. Die I mean. It's a good thing Dad didn't have to bury me after all that stuff we went through over in that desert. Your mom and dad too."

They turned toward the sound as a four-wheeler zoomed by. Little Frankie had his ears pinned back, shifting through gears like a pro. Tony trailed him at a more leisurely pace, yellow pants, red shoes and all. "You know," Wes said. "If you don't quit watering that boy there, you're going to have to change his name."

Bubba grinned and nodded. "I believe you're right. *Little* isn't the right adjective, is it? How about a drink? What can I get you?" He raised the lid on a cold-water cooler built into the end of the bar.

Wes looked into the swirling water — three brands of beer, two flavors of wine coolers, an assortment of sodas and the pure non-alcohol type. "I'm going for the clear stuff today." Wes grabbed a plastic bottle of water and twisted off the top. He wasn't against drinking a beer now and then, but alcohol made him sleepy, and the day was early.

Bubba grabbed a bottle of beer, popped the top, and held it out. "Here's to ya. Good to see you again. It's been too long." They tapped drinks.

Rae Lee opened the slider. "Dad, Emma's up." A little girl about four years old held her hand.

"Come out here, girl."

Rae Lee had grown into the mirror of her mom. Petite, sharp features and raven black hair. She wore red shorts, heel-slapping flip-flops, and a bright purple and gold LSU T-shirt. "Emma wants you, Dad."

The little barefoot girl pulled away from Rae Lee and ran for Bubba. He scooped her up and held her close. She wrapped her arms around his neck. A skinny, blond-headed kid didn't fit the darker Cajun mold.

"Hi, Mr. Hansen."

"Hi, Rae Lee. You've grown up. What grade are you in now?" He gave her a hug.

"Going to be in the tenth." She looked at her dad like maybe he needed to hear how old she was as well. She sounded like her mom.

Bubba carried Emma and sat down in a cushioned metal chair. "What's your ma up to?"

Rae Lee turned and walked to the slider. "Doing what she does best."

"Mind your manners, girl," Bubba said. "Is she ready for me to put on the shrimp?"

"Yes, sir. The shrimp, no, sir, not yet." She rolled her eyes.

"You come tell me when she is, you hear? So you can take Emma, and I can cook."

She nodded, said, "Yes, sir," then disappeared into the house.

Wes watched the exchange with amusement. Nothing like family. He missed it. "What's Rae doing best?"

Bubba situated Emma with her legs across his lap and her head resting on his chest. "Talking. The Lord knows she can talk. Rae Lee was being sassy." He brushed the hair out of Emma's face and whispered to her.

Too low to hear what. He glanced up then gave the girl a gentle squeeze. "My new addition. Not mine, but will be as soon as the adoption goes through."

The drone of revving four-wheeler engines reached the patio. Bubba cocked his head. "Sounds like Frankie rubbed off on your man. Tony, is it?"

Wes nodded. "He's my techie. Smart guy, real smart."

Emma reached up with her right hand and stroked Bubba's cheek. He didn't seem to notice. "And Jessica? She's striking. Alluring eyes. Bet it's hard to sit still when she locks onto you with those things. I noticed she was prone to do that too. Lock onto you, I mean."

Wes smiled. Bubba had hit the cord with that note.

Bubba took a sip of beer. "My niece, my sister's kid, she's a meth head. She had this young'n and then dragged her around in hell for three years. The whole bunch is about sorry as worm dirt. Hate to say, and I still love her, but my sister too. The woman knew Emma was at the mercy of the Lord-only-knows-what and never said a word. She's in denial about my niece."

He looked down at the girl on his lap. "She's not right, this little one. Don't talk, just points. Got the same look in her eyes as those little kids we seen in Iraq. Like they seen the devil himself, and it scared the sanity out of them. I don't know if she got poisoned living in the same house where them crazies cooked drugs, or she's just seen too much. We've been praying that she'll grow out of it. It's going to be a long road."

The four-wheeler noise grew louder, moving toward the house. Bubba smiled and squeezed Emma again. "She's my darling. I represent the law of the land. I'm its voice, or one of them, but I'll tell you this here and now, I'll become a felon before I let this girl go back to hell. All who are responsible know it too."

The little hand still wandered Bubba's dark face. As the fingers passed over his mouth, he kissed them. She turned her head and looked at Wes. Just a quick glance, but long enough for him to see the light was missing from her pale blue eyes.

Wes made up his mind. A man with Bubba's heart would not be involved with Meshach. No way. "Brother, we need to talk."

Wes started the account at his conversation with his daughter about the possible names for his grandson. When he got to the chance meeting with the waitress in the restaurant on Bourbon Street and obtaining their first description of Meshach, Rae Lee edged through the slider to take Emma into the house and to tell her dad to put on the shrimp to boil.

Bubba listened without comment and added seasoning to a stainless pot full of water. He sipped at one beer, then a second, between occasional glances in Wes's direction.

Wes thought about omitting the warning Lamech sent Meshach from his rendition, but nixed the idea. After all, that detail pointed the accusing finger of doubt in Bubba's direction in the first place. He continued, revealing every twist and turn, right down to this morning and Jess's discovery of the kid with the binoculars around his neck and the one-open-lens-cap/one-eye scenario.

Bubba sat in his chair. He focused on Wes then searched the ceiling before coming back to Wes. The wheels were churning.

Wes took a big drink of water from the bottle. He felt like he told the story with one breath. It dawned on him that both Tony and Jess had been unusually scarce since their arrival. More than likely it was a joint-effort to give him time with Bubba.

His friend stood, checked the shrimp, and then turned back to Wes. "You put a name to this cat yet?"

"No, we haven't, but we're hoping someone scribbled the boys' names on the back of the original picture. It's in a shoebox in Las Vegas. We tried to call the victim's mother this morning to ask her to check the pic for us. She's grieving and has company. May take time. We'll keep trying."

Bubba took a deep breath. "OK, first, I don't believe I've ever heard a longer list of coincidences strung together on one case in all my life. Either you or Cole or both of you must be living right. Second, you need to bring the authorities in on this. I'm going to finish these shrimp, which won't take another five minutes. The water is boiling. Then, I'm going to make a phone call. I've got an FBI agent in mind."

"What are we looking at, Monday?"

"Oh, no, tomorrow, a meeting bright and early in the morning in New Orleans. The sooner the better because if Risa or I didn't warn Meshach, and we didn't, I can promise you that whoever did has access to some high level databases." Bubba turned his attention back to the steaming pot on the stove.

Wes had made the right decision being open with Bubba. His friend was in the clear, but he felt a sense of foreboding instead of relief.

Who could monitor private web exchanges, phone calls and e-mails, find out who looked for whom, and pinpoint their location right down to the hotel they stayed in? He answered the question as quickly as it formed. Only four agencies he could think of had the ability: the Department of Homeland Security, the NSA, the CIA, and the people Bubba wanted Wes to meet with in the morning.

26

Saturday evening

Meshach circled the room, past the sofa and chair, into the kitchen, and around the island and back. Twenty-seven paces, over and over he made the loop. He carried the .45, first in one hand then the other. Reminded him of the leopard he'd seen at the zoo when he was a kid. Back and forth the cat paced across the front of the cage. Huge claws rasped the concrete floor every time the animal pivoted. Its long tail twitched and its golden eyes threw darts at the staring faces but never fixed upon any one thing or person. He'd told his mom he wished he could open the door to the cage. She thought he wanted to set the animal free, to send the big cat back to the jungle. She'd been partially correct. He did want to let it out, but so he could see what the claws would do to human flesh.

The woman doted and bragged about her

son who could do no wrong. In the end, the disappointment she felt was the product of her own blindness. He knew who he was. One couldn't make good from bad. The ingredients just weren't there.

He'd been cooped up in the house twenty-four hours, biding his time. No news about the operation. He was stuck on pause, and he didn't like it.

He stopped in front of the French doors. They stood open. All of the doors and windows were open. His boat sat in front of him, the open ocean just beyond that. His car was parked not far away. He wasn't caged, not yet. So why couldn't he escape?

Shanteel . . . he should have left her marooned on the platform the day he met her. The cop would never admit it, but that would have done him a favor as well.

His phone rang and he stepped to the island to glance at the number. *Again!* He stared at it. After six rings the caller would be connected to a voice mailbox that wasn't set up. It went silent but rang again within thirty seconds. He snatched it up. "What in the —"

"You did something stupid. What was it? You're blown."

"I'm not blown."

Lamech took a deep breath. "Now, you're

the one who's not listening. Have I not yet proven the extent of my connections? The warning about those at the Hilton, your car, the cash, the weapon, and your very handsome deposit were not enough? Somehow, a PI has figured you out, and he's talking. We're done. You're a liability. The job is cancelled."

The looker with the blue eyes flashed in his mind. The jarhead seated across from her in the hotel restaurant as she'd patted his hand in a way that said, "good boy." Not lovers then, but now? "You can't cancel. We have a deal."

"That's funny. There's no honor among thieves, or have you never heard that quote before?"

Meshach suppressed the urge to unload the .45 into the ceiling.

"Meshach, or whomever you are, for some reason I felt the need to warn you. So maybe there is one thread of loyalty among us. I'd tell you to run, but I don't think any sense of self-preservation exists in you. I feel one day soon I'll read of your demise in the morning paper and not even recognize that it's you. Good-bye."

"Wait! Wait!" Meshach yelled into the phone. The connection remained open but silent. "A name. Give me a name and location." The lull lasted a minute.

"Hansen, Wes Hansen. The Days Inn in Mandeville."

And so the game would continue, advantage Meshach.

"Lamech. Now you listen to me. Watch the papers and the news. After I'm finished with the PI, I'm going to do your job pro bono."

He hurled the phone against the wall.

Sunday morning

The hotel advertised continental breakfast as a selling point. Whatever that meant. One thing was for sure: it had nothing to do with home-cooked or fresh. Honey buns, muffins, donuts, packaged waffles and sugary cereal lined the counter. As soon as Wes's crew got up, he'd let them sample the fare at the Broken Egg.

He poured a cup of coffee and took a seat at a table with the Sunday paper and his legal pad. He had a lot of info to give the FBI, none of which would convict Meshach of jaywalking in a court of law.

Jess walked in, dressed for a jog. "Good morning." She twisted the top off a bottle of water.

"Good morning. You're up early. It's barely five thirty, and you're off for a run already. I don't see how you do it."

"It's easy for me." She raked her hair back into a ponytail with her fingers and put on a band to hold it. "Starts my day off right. Makes me feel better if I run early. Wakes me up and gets the motor running."

"I guess," he said. "To each his own, or her own." He rolled his eyes at her and smiled.

She pulled out a chair and sat. "So, you don't see the draw?"

"I do not. The Marine Corps cured any desire I might have once held for running before noon. Though, I don't ever remember having the desire, so maybe it wasn't there to start with." Wes indicated her colorful shoes. "Looks like you wandered off the beaten path into the mud."

She looked at her feet. "I went for a walk last night after we got back and stepped into a hole up the street, in that area of road construction. The mud is bright red and sticky. I should have washed it off when it was still wet. I forgot." She took a sip of water. "Well, we have a meeting this morning. What would you like me to do?"

"Attend, all of us. It would help if we could contact Liz and get a name beforehand. After the meeting, we'll have to see. I think we're winding down. Unless Cole wants me to continue, and frankly, I don't see the point. This is a job for law enforcement."

She nodded and shifted in her chair. "Nevada is Pacific time. I'll try Liz again at eight her time, ten ours." She stood. "Well, OK then. I'm going to make this quick so I can be ready when you are. Again, I really enjoyed your friends. I like Rae. She's a talker, but at least, you know where she stands. I'm glad you and Bubba could talk. I was very happy to hear what he had to say."

"Yeah, me too." Wes watched her a moment. As she turned away, he said, "Jess, one minute."

She faced him and locked onto him with her bluebonnet stare. "Yes, sir?"

He took a deep breath. "If this meeting doesn't drag out, would you like to have dinner with me tonight? Just you and me?" He found himself wringing his hands and fidgeting like a kid.

Her gaze remained. He had hope in the light he saw there, but she was taking a long time to answer. "Are you asking me out, Wes? Like on a date?"

"Yes, ma'am. I am."

"I'm sorry, but I have a rule about dating my boss. Too complicated. As they say, I've got the T-shirt."

"Well," Wes said. "I'm just the man who can fix that."

"You are? How?"

"You're fired."

She held out her fist for him to tap and smiled. "Perfect. 'Bout seven then?" She turned and exited through the sliding glass doors.

She was killing him. He wanted to chase her. What a girl.

He jerked his thoughts back to business and sent Cole a quick e-mail update. The main topic: the leak did not originate with Bubba.

Tony strolled in from down the hall. "Morning, boss," he said and pulled out a chair. He grimaced as he eased himself down on the seat.

"What's the matter with you this morning?"

"That little Frankie kid just about killed me. I'm so sore from riding the four-wheeler I can hardly move. I've had leg cramps all night."

"Fun though, eh?"

"Loved it. I'm going to buy one. Seen Jess? She out for a run already?"

"She is." Wes glanced at his watch. "She's been gone five minutes. She said she was going to make it fast." He wondered what fast meant to her. "We'll go out for breakfast when she gets back."

Tony shook his head. "Running for five minutes would seem like an eternity to me. I don't see how she does it."

"Nor I. What's the news? Anything from Meshach?"

"Not a peep out of him. Nothing. Eerily quiet. Do you think he's gone?"

Wes thought about the question a second. "It's been my experience that once a plan is in place and a tee time is set, the team goes dark, radio silent."

"That's scary. I hope we can contact Liz this morning and that there's a name on the back of that pic. What time's our meeting?"

"Bubba said before noon, but I'm sure I won't hear from him for a bit. Most people with any sort of normal lifestyle are in bed asleep this time Sunday morning."

"You're saying we're not normal? Huh, I think I just answered my own question with the question." Tony pulled at the hem of his hoodie. "Could I have the car keys? I left my phone charger in the backseat."

Wes slid the key fob across the table. "Let's go over some of this info when you get back."

"I'll only be a minute." Tony pushed out

of the chair and limped toward the door.

The legal pad held twenty pages of notes. Wes scanned them one by one. Did he really need to rehash everything again? The pad held all he had to offer. The FBI was going to think he was a doozy with this stack of evidence.

Tony entered, moving like he'd found a new set of legs. "Has Jess come in?"

"No, why?"

Tony flipped a business card on the table, then turned toward the corridor, moving like Wes had never seen before. "I found that under the wiper blade on the car. I'll check her room. Then we have to make a round in the car."

The business card lay face up on the tabletop. The orb stared at him.

27

Wes sat at a table on one side of the breakfast area in the hotel. Two hours and ten minutes had passed since Jess walked out the door for her jog. He'd beat himself up every second since. Meshach or his handler had found them once. What made Wes think the man couldn't find them again? Changing cities had not minimized the risk one degree. He'd lost his edge and made a critical mistake. He'd let Jess down.

He and Tony had searched for her. First in a methodical circular pattern, expanding outward from the hotel, street-by-street, then lineal, across the grid, north to south and east to west. They hoped and prayed, but they both knew the notation on the back of the card, in pencil, in the same block letters as on the cards Cole had received, meant she was in deep trouble. *Come get her* was an obvious indication of what had transpired on a dark street not far away and a personal invitation Wes had every intention of accepting . . . if he could find the man.

Bubba, FBI Special Agent, Trent Carr, and two Mandeville police officers conversed near the hotel's front desk.

Like the evening before with Bubba, Wes's account of his investigation took little time to relate. The agent had jotted notes on a pad but never said a word. Wes wondered if the guy's mother knew her son's whereabouts so early on a Sunday morning. He looked like he should be home studying his spelling words. His lack of questions, especially with what little evidence Wes had to offer, did little to bolster that lack of confidence. Did the guy grasp the thread linking a single suspect to the string of coincidences, as Bubba called them? Was he convinced to act?

Someone in the FBI thought he rated a badge, and they'd backed it up by issuing him a gun, so maybe.

The city police seemed more interested in Jess's status than Meshach's, and Wes appreciated the fact. The second Wes finished with the descriptions of Meshach and Jessica, one of the officers relayed the info to their dispatcher. Wes's gut told him Meshach had ditched the Chrysler 300 they'd seen him driving in New Orleans, but he gave them a description of it anyway.

There was only one problem with the entire episode: by the time Wes met with them, she'd been gone close to an hour and could have been in Mississippi.

Wes signaled Tony who stood at the counter doctoring a cup of coffee. "It's close to six in Nevada. Call Liz for me. Ask her to check the pic for a name. I'm sure she'll understand, but apologize for the early hour."

Tony nodded and walked away, poking at his cell phone.

Bubba lumbered to the table. "Can you think of anything else?"

"No, I can't. Tony's calling to inquire about a name on the picture." Wes's answer sounded more like a retort, but Bubba took it in stride. Wes nodded at the uniformed cops and the Fed. "What are their thoughts?"

"Jess isn't a child, and she hasn't been missing long, but they're onboard. It's obvious she hasn't disappeared of her own volition. Both agencies have issued alerts." Bubba thumbed the card Meshach had left on the car from his shirt pocket and gave it back to Wes. "This cat has made this personal. You've hit a nerve. Try to think of which one. That might be the key to finding Jessica."

Meshach had hit a nerve too, and the man was going to find out just how personal Wes was willing to make it.

Tony paced the sidewalk just outside the hotel's entrance. He was animated, but subtle, lacking his usual sharp hand movements. Looked promising. Bubba followed Wes's gaze then clapped him on the shoulder. "It's going to be fine. We'll find her. Keep a tactical mind, and don't be too hard on yourself."

Wes stood. "Too late."

Bubba shook his head yes and no. "Because that's the way you are, but I had to say it."

Tony shuffled through the door and raised clenched fists. "Got it. Elgin Fairchild."

Special Agent Trent didn't hesitate removing his phone from his pocket and dialed as he stepped away from the counter. One of the policemen moved the other direction before he spoke into his radio.

An iPhone held Tony's attention. Wes knew he was doing his own search. "Any meaning in the names?" Wes asked.

"I'll check right quick. You know the kid to the right of Meshach in the picture was Lane, Liz's boy. The guy killed a childhood

270

friend. Liz is still not good, by the way. She had questions about Meshach I couldn't, wouldn't answer."

Men like Meshach had people they used, not friends. "She needs closure, Tony, and she'll get it soon."

Tony took several more seconds. "His names, together, means high-minded, fair-haired child. Doesn't seem to fit, does it?"

"Sounds like the high-minded part is applicable." Bubba's quick reply matched Wes's first thought.

Trent approached. "Gentlemen, turns out we have some interest in visiting with Elgin Fairchild, your Mr. Meshach, late of Las Vegas. Most of his interests, until he dropped off the grid two years ago, slanted toward environmental concerns to the extreme. He's marketed himself as a hired gun. He's a suspect in the kidnapping and brutal beating of an Oregon man who owns a logging company."

Wes indicated his eye, and Trent's head bobbed once. "I can confirm he has only one eye, the right one."

"Looks like Las Vegas social services knew his parents well," Tony added. "Abusive father likely caused the loss of the eye. Both mother and father are deceased. No next of kin I can find. His record is full of offenses from public disobedience to animal cruelty. Ten years ago, he looked like a troubled, misguided teenager except for the animal link. The dude is sick."

Tony made a quick sleight-of-hand move to conceal his phone as Trent leaned to look at the techie's source of information. If Tony wasn't more discreet, he would find himself being interviewed by the FBI . . . and not for a job.

"Here's another interesting tidbit," Tony said. "Father and son took a weekend trip to the Valley of Fire State Park, outside of Vegas, and only the son returned. They never found dad's body. Meshach was twelve."

Eyebrows rose at that info.

"Bet I can guess what happened there," Tony whispered to no one in particular.

One of the city officers left. The other one had a short, quiet word with Trent and followed his partner.

Wes had enough. "Bubba, Trent, this is not only about Meshach or Elgin, whatever his name is. Special Agent, I hope I don't have to explain this. How did he find us, me, my team? Who's helping him? How did he find out about my investigation and my location in New Orleans, then again here? Someone other than Meshach stinks to high heaven, and you," Wes indicated the baby-faced agent, "might draw your paychecks from the same bank."

Bubba nodded at Trent. "Wes is right."

Wes had to pack, and he wanted to get Jess's things to take with him. They'd already had the hotel give them access to her room. She lived out of her bag instead of a hotel chest-of-drawers, so she was all but packed. They found the bathroom mat draped over the rim of the tub and a used towel hung from the shower curtain bar. She'd made the bed. He found himself wondering about things he knew shouldn't be on his mind. Things a proper mate wouldn't know about a person until after they were married. Would she approve of his thoughts, knowing he'd been given access to her personal items and space?

The only thing that disappointed Wes: her iPhone was plugged into a charger next to the television. It could have been tracked. Though now, Wes didn't believe Meshach would have overlooked a cell phone on her person.

The phone was password protected, so he couldn't check her contacts for like-named relatives. Tony had offered to work his magic, but Wes declined. He prayed no one would need to be contacted. He had to keep that mindset.

He regretted now that they hadn't talked more. He'd wanted to from the moment he met her, but as her employer . . . Just asking her out to dinner took all the courage he could muster.

"You've got something in mind," Bubba said. "I can see it in your eyes."

"I do. This guy is on the other side of the lake, south of here, 'in joan' he'd said. That's where we're going. I'm not sitting here another minute. You both have my and Tony's cell numbers. Call when you have something."

Bubba caught his elbow as he walked by. "Are you armed?" he whispered.

"Of course."

"Keep it handy, brother."

Sunday, noon
Meshach rubbed his watery eye. He had enough problems with inaccurate depth perception and dealing with dust and other pollutants without the broad trying to gouge it out. Who would have thought? She didn't weigh one-twenty, but she fought like a tiger. She went for his eye immediately, as if she knew he only had one.

Did she? No way.

He glanced in the rearview mirror and

wiped his eye again. Driving into a bright morning sun didn't help.

Twice in only a few days, he'd misjudged a female. He was going to drag Shanteel and this blue-eyed beast offshore and leave them there.

He screamed and shook the steering wheel, "Don't fall asleep back there." He grinned at the thought of her distress." We'll be home soon, sweetie. You're going to love your new digs."

Louisiana had plenty of sheriff deputies. He'd passed two-dozen marked cars since leaving New Orleans. They'd all missed their chance to be the hero and save the damsel. Oh, the secrets a man could possess.

Poor girl.

His car died. Quit at sixty-five miles an hour. The steering went dead and stiff, all the warning lights lit. The gas gauge hovered just above half. He herded the car to the right, onto the shoulder, then onto the grass, well off the roadway, near a lot where an old trailer house stood on concrete blocks. Once stopped, he slammed the transmission into park and punched the start/stop button. The dash lights went out. He stepped on the brake and hit the button again to restart it. Nothing. Then again —

button, brake, button. The starter whirled but the engine refused to respond.

Now what? A short in the electrical system, something mechanical, or dirty fuel? He could take the time and look, and he might find the problem, but not at eight o'clock in the morning, with a woman in the trunk. Granted, he'd trussed up the wildcat with a roll of three-inch-wide duct tape, but without background noise, she could stir around enough to rouse suspicion if someone took an interest in helping with his car.

He was a good two miles from his turnoff.

The car moved. She stirred.

He got out, locked the doors, then reached and gave the trunk lid a hard thump with his hand. "I'll be back for you, darling. It's going to be awhile though. Get a nap if you can. Save your energy. You'll need it to survive the heat today. Sure is sunny. When you and I get done, I'm going to make your boss wish he'd stayed out of my business. His family, all of them will know me." He laughed. "But not for long."

The trailer was neglected. Weeds and deep grass grew in the yard.

He jogged up the levee and looked offshore. Perfect. Tonight, he could get his boat within a quarter mile of where he stood.

He'd have to carry her. He knew she wouldn't go willingly. The one time he'd left his backpack and he needed his GPS. He marked the spot using a two-story, red brick house tucked back against the opposite levee across the highway for a landmark. That one he would be able to identify at night.

A black pickup and a small red car appeared rounding the corner on the highway in the distance. He trotted back to the blacktop, waved, and a guy in the Dodge pickup shut it down and pulled over. Mississippi plates, oversized front bumper, and not a scratch on the paint.

Meshach opened the door and hopped in.

"Where you headed? Going to a heliport?" the guy said. He quickly ran the pickup through the manual gears to seventy-five, ten over the limit and too fast for Meshach's liking.

"No," Meshach said, taking in the man's camouflaged cap, jeans, Duck something T-shirt, and the smell of smoke from a pungent cigar of some kind. He was a bull. Hairy arms and hands like a catcher's mitt. A Globe and Anchor tattoo on his forearm screamed jarhead. The interior of the pickup was clean. The guy liked his ride. He dipped snuff. A peppermint something, from the smell of it, filled his lip and pointed to the purpose for the cup on the seat between his legs. "You can drop me off up the road. It's not far. Are you going to a heliport?"

"Yeah, I'm headed to Boothville, to PHI. Going out to the Deepwater Nautilus for Shell." He raised the cup, gave it a quick, noisy squirt from between the noticeable gap in his teeth, and peeked at his watch. "I'd help with your car, but I'm running late."

Meshach leaned forward a little to look back in the side mirror. A semi rounded the corner a mile behind them. His Altima was out of sight. "Don't worry about me. I've got someone who can help. Up here on the right." He pointed. "You can let me out at the next power pole."

Meshach hopped out and scaled the driveway up the levee. He had a problem now: no wheels and sixty miles from New Orleans. He scanned the camp houses and empty parking area behind them.

First things first.

He eyed his boat as he walked to the house and let himself in. He gathered his things again, including the cash he'd replaced in their hiding places. After a hurried count, he stuffed thirty-eight grand and change into his backpack. He looked around. He'd missed something, but what? Pistol tucked into his belt, computer, phone, he was done. Then he saw Lane's wallet and I.D. on the table next to the couch. Those he stuffed into a pocket in the bag. He grabbed his gear and stepped to the door.

Unbelievable, Shanteel's cop, on the porch in front of the door, like *poof,* the elephant in the magic show. No use in wasting time wondering where he came from. He'd missed seeing or hearing the cruiser drive up.

Meshach walked straight toward the man. That obviously stumped him. The cop stepped back. Meshach reached behind his back and palmed the Kimber. The danger appeared in front of the cop, but he didn't move. The brain took a second to register what the eyes saw then another moment for a thought of disbelief before the body reacted. He moved quicker than Meshach would have believed, bringing a Glock to bear, centered on Meshach's chest.

Like a slow-motion replay, Meshach saw the flash and a small hole appeared in the screen in the door between them. The action on the service piece slid back, and the spent casing sailed up and away to the cop's right.

Meshach's .45 bucked a blink in time after

the cop's gun chambered the second round. He felt it, hard in the palm of his hand, but too hard. Something wasn't right.

28

Sunday morning

Wes exited Causeway Boulevard onto I-10 eastward. Tony had been occupied with his phone since they left the hotel, quiet as a titmouse, and just as well. Wes didn't know where he was going, but he had to go. Tony's queries about their destination would have been answered with a shrug.

Bubba said they'd hit a nerve. What nerve? Pride? Ego? He reached for Tony's shoulder and gave it a gentle squeeze. "What are we missing?"

"I don't know." Tony was quick to answer but slow to turn loose of what he was doing and look up. "I'm going over his posts and the names again. I'm worried, but I wonder too, why the note on the card? Bubba was right about him taking this personal. I think we'll hear from him and soon. He's arrogant. Like a bully who wants to fight but only on his terms."

Wes wasn't so sure. He knew people who reveled in the anguish of others. Meshach struck him as the type who didn't have to see his enemy fall or suffer. A mental image sufficed. He started to voice those thoughts when his phone chirped. "This is Wes."

"Agent Carr, here. Do you know how to get to Venice?"

A chopper parked on the top of the levee next to a couple of sheriff's department cruisers marked the spot. Wes punched the button on the window as he braked to a stop and addressed a tall, skinny deputy. "Wes Hansen and Tony Moran to see Agent Carr."

The man opened a metal clipboard, scanned the contents, and waved them through.

A crime scene van sat behind a row of bungalows, though that wasn't the right word because they were huge. Wes had been to Grand Isle fishing with Bubba long ago. He knew these men took pride in their fish camps. Local companies used them to cater to their clients. These looked very nice. More like second homes.

The middle one of the five places crawled with uniformed personnel.

Wes parked well back, out of the way, and

he and Tony got out. Agent Carr stood at the end of a long landing talking to a guy in yellow boat shoes, red shorts, and a green T-shirt. One bay boat was moored in the end slip.

Wes pulled Tony aside before they stepped onto the dock. "Let's hang back until he's finished with the guy. Not everyone likes to talk to the FBI in private — much less with others listening in."

"This doesn't look good, does it, Wes?"

"No, but don't think the worst. I don't believe Jess's status has changed. Bubba and Trent wouldn't have left us hanging if they had bad news to convey."

Tony faced the house and jammed his hands in the pockets of his hoodie. "Something bad happened here."

Agent Carr turned their direction and walked over. "Wes, Tony, thanks for coming."

"Oh, no need to thank us, Agent Carr," Wes said. "You couldn't keep us away. What happened?"

"A Parrish deputy recognized the suspect from the BOLO we issued this morning and tried to make an arrest on his own. Shots were fired. The officer is critical. Evidence indicates our suspect is wounded, though how badly is in question. We're still working the scene."

"Are you sure it's Meshach?" Tony asked.

"We are." He checked his note pad. "A Miss Shanteel Dupree gave a positive description of the man. She's been very enlightening. She spent time in a boat offshore with him. Through her, we know members of the Coast Guard have also met him. We're tracking that contact." He turned and pointed to the house.

"Wait, please," Wes said. "Any sign Jess has been here?"

Trent shook his head. "I'm sorry, no. It's the first thing we looked for. We know he has or had access to a boat and a white car, but we don't know the make and model. According to Miss Dupree, his present 'white car' is a replacement for a 'shiny black one.' The boat is similar to the one there. Neither are present on location."

Wes glanced offshore. He knew the shiny black one, the Chrysler. As he suspected, Meshach had changed cars, but something didn't make sense. Meshach didn't drive a boat to Mandeville to kidnap Jess. The man could get to Mandeville by boat, from here, but why go by water? The trip would take too long.

Tony produced his phone, swiped at it, and then held it out for them to see the time. "Hang on. Look, it's after one. From the time Jess disappeared until the time you called us was . . . what? Five hours and a bit? It takes two hours to drive here from the north shore. What time did the shooting occur, nine fifteen, nine thirty? Meshach didn't have much free time." His voice went up an octave. "It's broad daylight. What did he do with Jess?"

To that, Trent could only shake his head. "The man I talked to when you arrived owns this middle place where our suspect's been staying the past week. You were right about the handler. The owner received a sizable sum in advance for use of both the house and a bay boat. During one of their conversations the suspect referred to another party as 'the man who paid.' "

Wes didn't care about the handler. He was the FBI's problem now. "Look, Trent . . ." The whop-whop of helicopter blades penetrated the breeze. A yellow chopper banked left in the distance. ". . . no way he made the trip by boat, but if he's in it now, where's his car? What about the Coast Guard? Will they put a bird in the air?"

"Already there, two of them. We've asked for a full-scale search and rescue effort. We've issued an alert to shipping companies, oilfield boat companies, and local fishing guides to be on the lookout for both Miss Wahl and the suspect. Someone will spot him."

Wes hated the word *suspect,* and Trent wore it out with every sentence. Law enforcement could witness a murder, arrest a man on the spot, with the weapon, get a confession, throw him in the back of a squad car, then turn to a reporter and call him the alleged suspect. Political correctness drove him nuts.

A guy who didn't look much older than Trent bounded down the steps from the house in question. He carried a small black valise. "You wanted this? I'm done with it."

Trent took the case by the strap with one finger. "Give me a pair of gloves, please."

The other man complied and walked away. Trent held the rubber gloves out to Tony. "Put these on."

Tony looked between the agent and the case.

Trent offered both again. "Tony, get into his laptop for us."

Tony rubbed his hands together and took the gloves.

Sunday, evening, twenty miles northwest of Venice
Meshach knew he didn't have much time.

Every lawman in Louisiana would be looking for him by now. He weaved his way north through the many waterways in the marsh, toward a more populated area where he had a larger variety of options for shelter.

He glanced at the levee to his right. His car with ole blue-eyes in the back would be safe until he returned. She was the praying type. He heard her ask for His help earlier that morning. She'd be praying now, he'd venture. He'd always wondered if the words had to be spoken. With her mouth taped, could her God hear her thoughts?

Had he known beforehand, he would have bought the old blue Caddi instead of the white Altima. The trunk of that Caddi would be an oven with the sun shining on it.

He knew without looking that blood dripped at a steady rate from the T-shirt wrapped around his right hand. Time to find a place where he could take care of his wound. He had his eye on a lone house in the near distance. Occupied or not, he would stop.

A typical clapboard-sided structure occupied the only tiny piece of muddy ground above sea level for miles. It looked like the one he grew up in except for the stilts it sat on. A rickety dock jutted out from the steps leading to the front door. Toward the back of the place, just like a driveway, a narrow waterway, not much wider than his boat, led to a small shed. He flipped the boat around, backed in, and killed the engine.

The first aid kit under the seat in the boat held means for treating minor cuts and mishaps with fishhooks, not bullet wounds. He didn't have other options. He grabbed it and tucked it under his right arm. He carried the cop's 9mm in his left hand to accent the Kimber tucked into his belt.

He ascended the steps and kicked in the front door. Sunlight filtered through the cracks between the boards over the windows and streaked the walls. Not much for furniture. Old newspapers littered the floor. No electronics, no fridge, and the gray, tiled countertops were bare except for one mousetrap. Black mold crept across one corner of the wooden ceiling. He wondered why they bothered to lock the door.

It was hotter and more humid inside than outside. It smelled stagnant. He crossed the room and opened the back door to get a cross flow. Wasn't much, but soaked with sweat, he felt cooler immediately.

He pulled the only end table and metal kitchen chair to the door, into the sunlight, and placed the first aid kit and both pistols on the table.

Like the place he'd just left, the only walled rooms were in the back of the house — two bedrooms and one bath. He rummaged through the bathroom drawers and found nothing he could use. Back in the kitchen, he jerked open drawers one at a time — plastic lids, metal lids, miscellaneous junk, tidbits of cheap silverware, a rolling pin and a sieve. He slammed the last drawer, then opened it again.

Now, it looked like he would have to man-up, as his old man used to tell him. Scissors. Appropriate.

He carried them to the table at the door, sat in the chair, and carefully unwrapped the bloody rag from around his hand. His little finger fell to the side. The cop's bullet had severed the bone leaving a mess of skin with no structure. A doctor might save it, but he wasn't a doctor.

If he could snip it off and leave enough skin on the outside to fold over the bone . . . if the skin had adequate blood supply . . . if, if.

The laughter he heard came from his own lips. The scream that followed sounded just like his mother's.

29

Sunday evening

Five hours had passed since Tony sat at the bar with Meshach's computer in the end house. When he powered up the machine, Wes made his exit. There was no use pushing or asking unneeded questions. If the techie found evidence on the hard drive he thought would help locate Jess, he'd report.

Just like there was no use quizzing FBI-and-company about gaining access to the house Meshach used. Not until the crime lab finished their work. Though he wondered what the holdup was. They were taking their sweet time.

Did he want to have a look inside? In the worst way. Agent Carr knew he wanted in too.

Wes found a perch and watched the show. Now and then he looked in on Tony, more for something to do. Somewhere toward midafternoon, about the same time he considered calling his employer, another helicopter landed a stone's throw from the first one and kicked out two more Feds. One of them a young woman Agent Carr assigned to assist Tony. The second agent entered Meshach's house and hadn't been seen since.

The roadblock didn't stop the curiosity factor from drawing gawkers. Looked like anyone who owned a boat cruised by or stopped a distance away in the many water passages and buried their faces behind a pair of binoculars.

He wondered about Meshach. Wouldn't be the first time a criminal stood in a crowd of onlookers to admire his own handiwork. It was hard to call fifteen boats scattered over four hundred acres of marsh a crowd. Meshach wasn't that dumb.

Wes walked over to the bay boat. Three-hundred-horse Yamaha outboard, a bit over twenty feet long, center console, live-wells front and back, and absolutely spotless, pristine condition. A posh fishing vessel from what he was used to seeing. What did Meshach want with such a boat? A list of potential targets came to mind — refineries, oil storage facilities, ships, platforms, the Mississippi itself, as a conduit for commerce. Easy land access made the first two on the list unlikely prospects. Wes believed Meshach had his sights offshore.

Wes's conscience refused to let his mind rest. Images of Jess at the hands of Meshach sucker punched him when he least expected. Stay tactical. Keep the mind on the facts. Dig, look, think about the information, find the man, and don't let the imagination run wild. Hard to do.

He'd think about her with the maniac until the images became almost real, like fresh memories. One image his subconscious seemed particularly fond of: Meshach in the sights of his Springfield .45. He'd let that clip play until he realized he was grinding his teeth. Then he'd shake off the thought and walk.

It wasn't like Wes to wish someone dead, but in this case, he couldn't really care less what happened to the man.

He asked himself why he didn't call Cole and, again, answered the question in the same thought. He didn't know. He'd messed up and made rookie mistakes, maybe fatal ones, and he could look any man in the eye and voice it. So what was his excuse?

Then again, he didn't have a regular job with set hours where he performed measurable tasks. The man had hired him to find Meshach. Appears he had. Now, the authorities controlled the investigation. He'd done what he said he would.

The guy in the bright boat shoes Trent had been talking to when Wes and Tony first arrived exited a cruiser among many. Trent mentioned the man owned the house in question. The man strutted onto the dock and stopped a few feet away, staring toward his property.

"Takes time," Wes said.

"Excuse me." He gave Wes a quick annoyed look and planted his hands on his hips.

"Time, PR work, patience required. I want to get in there too."

"What for?" The man's tone turned defensive. "I've got a group coming tomorrow, from out of state, and lots to do. My place is trashed."

"I won't be long. Just need to look around for myself, get a feel for —"

"We'll see about that." He turned and walked away.

The fuse had been lit that morning and had slowly fizzled down until nothing was left to do but ignite the dynamite. Three quick steps cut him off. "Hey, what's your name?"

"Scott Breaux. I'm the owner."

His dark eyes locked onto Wes's for an

instant then darted away. He tried to turn again, but Wes moved into his airspace, close enough to smell the stench of cigarette smoke mixed with sweat and force the man to retreat a step. His gaze returned to Wes's chin, matching the difference in their height. Wes had his attention now and whispered hard, just for Scott. "You're worried about money when lives are at stake, one very dear to me in particular. Another man has been shot and may not survive. Your focus is blurred, so go sit in your boat and keep your mouth shut until someone asks you a question.

"For that matter," Wes held up his right hand and wiggled his index finger to indicate the house. "I'll be surprised if your place isn't covered in crime scene tape and sealed up for a month."

Scott's mouth hung open. He walked away, fumbling at his shirt pocket for his smokes.

Wes took a deep breath. He'd spoken the truth. The FBI could keep the place under wraps indefinitely. He didn't know if they would, but Scott should know of the possibility, even if the presentation lacked tact.

Someday, after the mess was over, he might look up Scott, apologize to him, and shake his hand. Until then . . . His mind tripped over another thought. Agent Carr mentioned the USCG had talked to Meshach. What did he do to attract their attention? The girl who spent time offshore with him did so why? Where did they go? Where was she now?

Wes started for the steps. Agent Carr would know. Wes wanted to talk to her, now.

Thirty feet away, shoulder to shoulder, stood Bubba and Cole Blackwell.

Meshach had no control over the shaking. Shock had a mind of its own. He could count his pulse with every surge of pain in a finger he'd snipped off and tossed out the back door. Didn't make sense.

He'd need water soon. No telling how much his body had shed. Heat and trauma took its toll. Didn't help that he had to close up the house to keep from giving away his presence. Until darkness grounded the choppers, he'd be forced to hold up, out of sight. A coastie bird in the air would be disturbing. They had infrared equipment. When a pilot wearing night-vision gear locked onto your position, your goose was cooked. He had no doubts about that possibility.

Sounded like another helicopter headed his way — the fourth one in the last hour to pass within earshot. The first three were heavy birds, the thump of their rotor blades distinct. This one was smaller, sounded more like a bumblebee and it would pass by closer. It was surprising someone hadn't dropped in for a personal visit already. He glanced at the pistols on the table next to him. He'd give anything for a high-powered rifle.

The chopper passed directly overhead and low, but its heading remained steady, due west into the last half of the setting sun. So far so good.

Didn't take a rocket scientist to know what the fuss was about. Birds headed for offshore locations had altitude restrictions just like airplanes in a flight-corridor, to reduce the risk of midair collisions. The birds he'd seen skirted the deck.

He'd made the big time now.

The little boat garage had come in handy. Right place, right time, like his gun hand and the Kimber. The cop's bullet would have hit him in the forehead if not for his little finger and the butt of the pistol. The .45, like him, suffered damage but remained operable.

Moron. He'd dropped his laptop. Somehow it slid out of the backpack during the firefight. Someone would be into that in a heartbeat. They wouldn't find much. No personal info, no photos, nothing. His Internet history wouldn't get them anywhere. Fingerprints would. They had to know his identity by now. He didn't care.

He raised his hand. The bleeding had slowed. Not the best job of applying a dressing he'd ever done, but he wasn't left handed. Stripping off tape and gauze and tying knots wasn't easy with one hand and his front teeth.

He dealt with the pain easily.

Thanks, for helping me get used to it, Dad.

He eased off the kitchen chair and moved to a south window. A dark veil lay eastward. Blinking strobe lights revealed the many platforms normally overlooked on a sunny day.

Time to take a hard look at his plan. Time to make a plan. He had options. Ease back to his car, retrieve ole blue-eyes from the trunk, and bait the PI. *Oh, that would be fun. The game of life, real time, up close and personal.* With that done, he'd do the job he came here for. Or forget the broad. Just do the Lamech deal and disappear. Or the other way around. Then, he could just do nothing, get out of the country, and start anew. He could live in Mexico or Costa Rica.

The only option he refused to consider: do nothing.

30

Wes stood on the landing at the top of the stairs, outside the yellow tape, waiting for the officer controlling the entrance into the crime scene to get Agent Carr's attention. He could kick himself for not thinking to ask sooner where Meshach and the woman had gone in the boat.

His phone chirped. A text from Tony — *stacy and i starving. something close????*

Stacy? First name? Looked like Tony and his new FBI computer-guru friend were getting along well.

He was right too. Meshach fouled up their plans for breakfast that morning. They had not eaten since.

The last orange of the sunset lingered on the horizon. Soon he'd need a flashlight to find his way to the car. Bubba and Cole talked and drifted back toward what had been a parking lot for patrol cars all day. The two parish cruisers remained at the entrance.

Dark stains dotted the deck near the door. The hum of flies drew his attention to a larger spot a few feet away. More than likely where the officer fell. If not for the gaps between the two-by-six decking, he had no doubt the bloodstain would have been much bigger.

Before long, a Hazmat team would move in behind the FBI and clean up the blood and other human waste, if any. Sad to think people made a living performing such tasks.

The half-closed screen door blocked his view into the house. From the looks of the kitchen area, the place where Tony worked mirrored this one. He focused in on three small holes at chest level in the screen itself. The pattern looked familiar, like the close grouping in a paper target at the pistol range.

How many rounds were fired? Just three, or did one or more streak through existing holes? How many came from Meshach? No other damage to the screen or surrounding woodwork stood out. The kitchen window remained intact.

A man's natural reactions made him duck or crouch, even when he stood in the open with nothing to hide behind. Meshach inside, the cop outside, each man looking down the barrel of his weapon at the other, squeezing off rounds until they were either wounded and unable to continue, saw their opponent fall, or ran out of ammo. This firefight happened fast. *Bang, bang, bang.* No time for thought. Surprised, both men exposed to the other's gunfire, with no time to take cover or run. Otherwise, the holes would have been scattered over a larger area as each shooter ducked and dodged looking for cover.

No way a man could shoot such a tight group when running for his life.

The officer took one in the neck early in the engagement. Like most cops anymore, the man carried a high-capacity semi-automatic. Wes bet money Meshach wielded a similar weapon. Only three holes, so neither man had emptied their handgun.

Why hadn't Meshach finished off the cop? He'd used a knife on his childhood friend. Maybe the officer had his own friends in heavenly places.

Agent Carr said evidence indicated Meshach had been hit, so at least one Meshach-seeking bullet passed through the screen. He stopped a chunk of lead high in the torso or outer shoulder area, maybe the face.

One could always hope.

Wasn't often a barrier between the shooters helped trace the path of each bullet for the investigators.

Agent Carr eased through the door wearing blue shoe covers and sidestepped around the blood splatter. "Wes, we're just about finished."

"I'm not here to pester you about getting a tour. I'm wondering about the lady who spent the day offshore with Meshach."

"Miss Shanteel."

"That's her. Did she say where they went?"

Trent removed his pad from his hip pocket and flipped through the pages. "A platform."

"What kind, where?"

"If you'll remember her description of the suspect's car, the 'shiny black one,' you'll understand why I don't have anything else written down. I'm sorry."

Wes tried to think. Why an offshore structure? "She left you a number where she could be reached, of course."

"She did, but . . . here." He held out his pad for Wes to see the numerals. "I have a feeling she's at the hospital with the wounded officer."

Wes punched in the numbers on his phone then glanced at Trent. "They related?"

The agent canted his head, raised his eyebrows, and rolled his eyes.

Wes thought of himself as naive and slow to understand people, but not this time. "You're kidding me? Meshach, this Shanteel woman, and the cop, a lover's triangle?"

"Looks like it."

Wes listened to the ringtone and said, "The cop a rookie?" Trent quickly raised his eyebrows again, indicating a negative. Then he looked away.

"Hello. This is Stacy Collins. May I help you?"

"Stacy Collins? As in FBI Stacy?"

"Yes, this is Agent Collins."

"Unbelievable. This is Wes. I'll be over in a minute." He hung up. "The woman gave you the number for that place." Wes pointed. "It's a long shot, but what does platform mean to Shanteel? Some are huge and fitted with self-contained living quarters. Maybe Meshach found an abandoned site and took Jess there. Could you have someone at the hospital check, and if Shanteel is there, get a uniform to ask her some more pointed questions?"

"Will do."

"Any headway with the Coast Guard members who met him?"

Trent shook his head. "Nothing yet."

"We need to know what Meshach did to draw their attention. I'm going for something to eat. I remember seeing a Subway not far from here. You have a preference?"

"Anything would be welcomed, thanks."

Wes bounded down the stairs, trotted across the dock, and up the steps to talk to Tony. He and Agent Collins looked up when Wes entered. "The Shanteel woman gave this number as a contact. We didn't realize she actually lived here. Find anything on Meshach's machine we can use?"

"No, sir. Sorry it's taken so long. I'm, we're, Stacy and I —"

"It's OK. I'll be on my cell. Going to Subway. I'll get one of everything." The last statement would give Tony the warm and fuzzies.

He met Bubba and Cole at the bottom of the steps and shook their hands in turn. "You two want to ride with me?" They changed direction. "Cole, I'm surprised to see you so soon. News travels fast."

"I wanted to make sure you have all the help you need to find Jessica. I've taken the liberty of hiring three helicopters. I got one from Bristow and two from PHI, all I could find at present. We can make them available to the FBI to use as they see fit, or you can line them out. They'll be spooled up and ready at sunup."

Bubba placed his huge mitt on Wes's

shoulder. "In case you're wondering, I called him."

"That's good," Wes said. "I should have called you this morning. Thanks, Mr. Blackwell." Wes offered his hand again, and they shook as they walked.

"No worries," Cole said. "You've done an unbelievable job finding the guy. Now we need to concentrate on your girl. I'm here to help."

His girl? Yeah, his girl.

Wes unlocked the doors to the Chrysler 300. He didn't know why, but he felt the urge to apologize for the car Tony had rented, effectively using Cole's money. It *was* a car, and roomy, but the yellow paint job didn't look the part. He let it go.

Cole crawled into the backseat, Bubba into the front.

Wes started up and sped down the gravel road to the exit.

Bubba said, "Where are we headed, brother?"

"Oh, my bad. Sandwich shop a few blocks over. It's the only place I know of. Everyone is starved. I thought we could talk along the way. It's not far. Get this, and I don't know all the details, but looks like jealousy got the officer shot. A woman named Shanteel who spent time with Meshach offshore

305

is connected to the wounded cop."

He steered across the two southbound lanes, over the grass median, and headed north. He pushed the gas pedal to the floor then eased up as the needle closed in on seventy miles an hour. He pulled the turning signal lever one time to dim the lights.

"I'll be the last man on earth to question his motives," Cole said from the backseat.

Wes knew he liked Cole. He empathized with the wounded officer's reasons for confronting a killer alone, however short-sighted they may have been.

Wes flashed the high beams at an oncoming car. The car flashed back twice. *I get it. Your lights are already on low, but they need adjusting.* Wes stepped on the brakes and stopped in the middle of the left lane. What had he just seen illuminated in the lights of the oncoming car, on the other side of the highway next to a brown trailer house? Just a white parked car. But there was something about it . . .

"Hey, bro, you OK?" Bubba asked. "There's a car coming up fast behind us."

Wes looked at his friend then back at Cole. *What was it? Think.*

"Oh Jess! The red mud on your shoes! Red mud on the car!" Wes spun the wheel and floored it. The backend of the Chrysler skid-

306

ded around and they shot across the grass median onto the blacktop, traveling the opposite direction. He hit the brakes again, punched the unlock button, and opened his door before the car stopped twenty feet from an Altima.

He palmed the automatic, chambered a round, then sidestepped in a semicircle, ten feet away. He leveled his pistol at the driver's window. Bright lights from the Chrysler outside made it impossible to see through tinted glass inside. He moved around to the front of the car and peered through the cracked windshield. Nothing.

Cole stood next to the rental car, forearms resting on top of the open door. Bubba moved between the Altima and the trailer house and scanned the night. Always a Marine, covering his teammate's back, even when unarmed.

As Wes stared at the front window, his dim reflection shook. He didn't move but the car did. "The trunk, Bubba, Cole. The trunk!" Wes moved to the driver's side and checked both doors.

Bubba checked the other side and shook his head.

Wes struck the driver's window with the butt of the Springfield and shattered the glass. The alarm went off. He reached inside and opened the door. Trunk release button — dashboard, glove box, driver's door, floor next to the seat — come on. The dash. He pushed and pulled at the button until the lid popped up.

Cole found his legs and ran to look inside the trunk. He yelled, "Glory! She's here."

Wes yelled, "Don't move her," and quickly shuffled to the rear of the Nissan. "Cole, would you turn on the emergency flashers on my car then do something with the alarm. Jerk the wires off the battery, something?

"Bubba, here, take this .45. Just in case. There's a round in the chute." He passed over the automatic to his friend.

She laid on her right side, across the back, head to the right, facing the dark emptiness behind the backseat. Her shoulders shook. *Oh, Jess.* He cupped her head in his hands. She was soaked with sweat, hair and clothes, through and through. He leaned over, kissed the tape covering her ear and spoke over the blaring alarm. "I'm so sorry. Don't cry. It's me. You're safe. Let's get this tape off your mouth, so you can breathe. Then we'll get your hands and feet. You ready?"

She nodded.

He worked at the wraps of gray duct tape. "Bubba, Cole, someone get an ambulance on the way? Get some water. Somewhere. Check around that old trailer for a working faucet. The house across the road."

"Bubba is on the phone right now." Cole put a hand on Wes's shoulder as he walked toward the front of the car. "I'll get the alarm and check for water."

Jess was in good shape, but the color of the car helped, white wasn't as hot in direct sunlight. A little longer or another day, one with the temperature in the 90s, he'd be putting her in a body bag.

Three layers of tape stuck to tape came off with little effort. The last wraps would have to wait, or hair and skin would come off with it. "Jess, I'm going to tear the tape just beside your mouth. Then we'll get some water in you. Can you turn your head? There you go. You ready?" He worked his fingers in next to her cheek, tore the tape and peeled it off her lips.

The alarm went silent.

She took two big breaths and coughed. "The water can wait until you get me out of here. That maniac said he'd be back to get me."

31

Wes squeezed Jess's hand one last time then closed the back door of the car. Cole sat behind the wheel. Bubba stood to Wes's right, staring off into the night above the levee. Wes elbowed him. "Hey, big man, you got Jess for me?"

Bubba nodded. "I got her. Already set up. After the doc sees her, she'll disappear into thin air. Here's your pistol. Still loaded. I didn't mess with it."

Wes took the weapon, dropped the clip for a quick look, then shoved it back home. The automatic held thirteen in the mag. He never carried it with a round under the firing pin. A baker's dozen would have to do. "I've been thinking."

"Again?" Bubba said followed by a short laugh.

Wes held the gun, testing the feel. Another day, he'd share the laugh with his friend. That was something Bubba used to tell him in Iraq when he voiced an idea. *You keep thinking, Wes. That's what you do best.* "I don't want Jess to just disappear. I want her dead until this is over. Make it public. Heat related dehydration, something, or nothing. Just get it in the papers. 'Woman found dead in the trunk of a car.' No explanation needed. There's a leak somewhere. I need to know she's safe. She needs to know too."

Bubba glanced at him then back over his shoulder at the car where Jess sat. "Agent Carr will have to call the papers, but I don't think that's a problem. He wants Meshach. If there's a leak and it's dripping from as high as you think, the coroner will need to be involved to keep the appearance of truth in the story. I believe the FBI has the means to make it happen."

"What are we forgetting? Did we stop the search for Jess?"

"We did. What else?"

Wes shook his head. "Standby the phone and be ready to come a runnin' if I call."

"You should let the Feds stake out this car. It's theirs now."

"Nope. He threatened my family. You heard what Jess said. My daughter, my grandson, my parents, you don't get to do that and walk away. I don't need a suit sitting in his car down the road. I do wish I had some night vision gear, though. One thing. You might ask Agent Carr if he'll meet me here at seven thirty in the morning. Just in case."

"Will do. You're nuts, you know?"

Wes let out a hard breath. "I know. Cole and Jess think so too."

"Just one more thing before I go. How'd you know Jess was in that car?"

"Look at the mud down the side. Red mud on white paint. Jess had the same color mud on her shoes this morning. She took a walk after we left your house and accidentally stepped into a hole at some roadwork, in the dark, not far from the hotel. I asked her about it just before she left for her run. Meshach must have driven through the same area. I just added two and two."

Bubba slapped him on the back and turned to get in the car. "You've still got it. Love you, bro. Stay low."

Wes slipped the pistol into its holster and walked toward the levee. The passenger door opened and closed behind him. The car pulled away. Tire noise faded over the next few seconds leaving the crickets and frogs free to sing without interruptions.

He couldn't see two feet in front of him. The porch light on the house across the highway gave off just enough light to deepen the shadows and make every step a new adventure. At the top, he squatted and sat on his heels, out of the skyline. Against the stars a man would be hard to distinguish, but not with a backdrop like ship lights or the communication tower's strobes flashing three miles distant.

Three sets of taillights were visible on the highway northward. One of them belonged to his rental headed for New Orleans and a hospital. That girl was hardheaded and insisted the ambulance be turned around in case someone who actually needed professional aid called for help. He loved it. Other than bruised fists, broken nails, sore fingertips from trying to gouge out Meshach's only eye, and a craving for water, she'd come through unscathed.

He touched his lips. Huh, like taking a nibble of a powdered sugar donut, she'd left a sticky remnant from the adhesive on the duct tape he'd removed from her lips. They would have to do that again. Soon. He tore his thoughts back to his task.

The old trailer house would be a logical place to hide and stakeout Meshach's car. After all, who would lie in the marsh with the bugs, mosquitoes, snakes, and who knew what else?

Wes would.

The man could arrive by automobile, but Wes suspected he was in the boat, either offshore or hidden out in the marsh somewhere. When Meshach beached the boat nearby, he wanted to be close enough to hear him breathe.

The GPS showed Meshach nothing he recognized. The track history on the Lowrance plainly displayed his last route so he knew the location of the fish camp, but how far was it from there to his car? Two miles? Maybe two and a half? Both of his navigation aids showed water close to the levee and the highway just beyond. The location would put him a little over three miles from the camp, a mile or less from the car, and for him, just a stroll away from ole blue eyes.

According to the sonar, six feet of water lay under the keel of the boat where he sat. Now, if that held true for the next half mile to the edge of the levee . . . Only one way to find out. He cranked up and engaged the outboard.

Ten minutes later, he nosed the boat into the bank and killed the engine. Using his handheld GPS display for light, he assessed his gear. He didn't need the cop's pistol and extra clips. Never go into a scrape with an unfamiliar weapon. Stay light. Then, he saw his ten-power, Leica rangefinder. That would be useful. He draped the lanyard around his neck and placed the monocular into his shirt pocket. A man with one eye didn't have need of binoculars.

After dragging the anchor up the levee twenty feet and shoving the flukes into the soft ground, he continued to the top and stopped, overlooking the highway. Cops travelled highways, but not the beaten path atop the levee where he stood. His car wasn't far, just around the long curve if the light in the distance belonged to the two-story house across from where he'd parked. He guessed roughly a mile, so no more than a twelve-minute walk. He set out at a quick pace.

The Altima came into view. He stopped a good five hundred yards out, took a knee, and scanned the area with the monocular — car, trailer, brick house across the high-way, then back to the car. No obvious tracks in the grass next to the Altima.

The car. The left passenger door window looked like a mirror, reflecting light from the bulb on the house across the highway, but not the driver's. He'd owned the car four days and had driven it twice. *Think. Was it tinted or not?* No, it didn't matter. Either the window was down, or the glass

was broken. If broken, why? Vandals?
Oh, my PI friend, you think I'm dumb.

Monday morning
One boisterous frog in particular spent the night a few feet from Wes. The thing sounded like it should walk upright and weigh sixty pounds. The Middle East had flies like Alaska had mosquitoes, but nothing compared to the mass of insects that had shown an interest in every inch of his exposed skin.

Bubba said he was nuts. Now, Wes wondered if he referred to going after Meshach alone or spending the night with the bugs.

The eastern horizon grew brighter by the second. Wispy haze drifted over the area. The humidity was thick enough to slice. Patches of green marsh grass and cane breaks were separated by water like a neighborhood by streets and cul-de-sacs. To his left, a dozen snowy egrets stood one-legged in a watery patch of grass. The levee rose to his right. He'd picked a good position on a dry strip jutting from the levee. Not bad for stumbling around in the dark.

A cockroach went about its business under the cover of darkness, like Meshach. He wasn't coming, not with a cloudless dawn in full glow.

Over the past hour, the traffic had increased. Turbocharged diesels whined and eighteen wheels pounded the pavement making it easy to distinguish semis from cars and pickups.

Wes rose and shook himself, brushing at his hair and clothes to rid both of crawly critters. A shower and a hearty breakfast would be the first order of business when he got back to wherever. Tony and Agent Collins had taken over Shanteel's place, uninvited, to dig into Meshach's computer, not to stay and use it for the night. Tony should be in a hotel, but where? Wes missed covering that tidbit of planning last night.

He turned on his cell phone and started for the highway two hundred yards distant. The waist-deep grass held heavy dew. His feet and pants were soaked in the first ten paces.

When the cell booted, he punched Tony's name. "Well?" was the first thing he heard.

"Nothing but bugs," Wes said. He topped the levee and paused. It really was a beautiful morning to look across the Mississippi River. The haze had settled into a thicker blanket, covering the waterway and making ships look like they floated on clouds.

"I'm at the Lighthouse Inn, several miles farther south, but I haven't slept. I've been waiting on you to call. Thank God, Jess is safe. You did good, Wes. Real good."

"Thanks, Tony. Did Cole or Bubba bring the car back to you last night?"

"I've got Cole's rental. You ready for me to come get you?"

"If you would, please. I'll be standing on the highway, I don't know, a couple of miles north of those fancy fish camps we were at yesterday. Meshach's white car is parked on the west side of the highway next to an old trailer house."

As he walked down the slope, he eyed the trailer. Someone had lived in it not long ago. The meter plugged into the box meant the electricity was still hooked up. As much mold grew on the sides and roof as the weeds in the yard.

"We found some interesting items on Meshach's computer. An auto-saved file, for one. He, someone, opened a new Word document and typed *Mars, Ursa, Nakika, Ace of Spades,* and a couple of others I can't remember, like doodling. He deleted the document, but the auto-save stored it. Anyway, they're platforms, rigs, production facilities, I don't know. Oil companies give their projects unique names. I don't know who owns the first three, but the last one belongs to Cole."

318

"He knows, of course."

"Everybody knows. He opened and accessed AIS too."

"What's that?"

"*Automatic Identification System:* it's a worldwide, integrated program used to track and identify any vessel enrolled and equipped. It's the same as a transponder in an airplane. Vessels can ID one another at sea, and the system can be accessed via the Internet and provides real-time information on a vessel's name, position or speed, any number of things. That's what Meshach did. I wouldn't be surprised to hear that a team of SEALs has been alerted and put on standby."

Cole had been right when he'd said Meshach's intentions could have national security implications. "Have you heard from Jess?" He walked a circle next to the trailer.

"She's OK. The doctor said she was good to go. She's at Bubba's place for now. Cole offered to fly her home, but she refused to leave. Can't imagine why." Tony's voice took on a conspiratorial tone.

Agent Carr arrived driving a small green Kia. He rolled down his window.

Wes walked in his direction. "All right, come on. I'll be waiting." He punched off and pocketed the phone.

"Good morning, Trent," Wes said.

"I don't see a scalp." He laced his hands over the steering wheel and leaned forward on his elbows. "Hop in. I'll give you a ride."

Wes took a knee at the window. "Thanks, but Tony's on the way. I have nothing to report, I'm afraid. A long night in the marsh."

"You did well recognizing the car. You saved that woman's life. A man who walks around with his eyes open, like you do, would fit into our program."

"I like my job. Besides, I have a degree in Marine Corps. I think your requirements are more stringent."

Trent nodded. "Your girl died. It was in the paper this morning. I've got an autopsy planned for this afternoon. With that said, we're trying to figure out a way to trap Lamech and Sullivan and get them into the open. You think of something, let me know. A question on that subject: would you be offended if I talked to Tony about employment?" The agent started his car. "If you have objections, of course, I won't mention it to him."

"Please talk to him. He's a consultant. I'll be jealous, though. A replacement will be hard to find."

"Thanks. Oh, we're going to haul Meshach's car off this morning. You might give a fingerprint sample today when you get a chance, so we can eliminate you."

Wes stood. "Right after breakfast."

Trent gave him a quick salute and drove off.

Wes moseyed back toward the trailer with thoughts of looking over the levee one last time before he left. Tony mentioned Jess had refused to leave. Good girl. He wished she would, but he was glad she hadn't. Now, he had to deal with *what-ifs,* if they didn't catch Meshach. How would he tell his daughter and son-in-law to be on the lookout for a one-eyed killer?

A metallic click jarred him. He'd been around guns all of his life. He knew the source. He prayed it wasn't the last thing he ever heard.

32

Meshach's knee pushed into the middle of Wes's back. The .45 pressing into the base of his skull hurt, but not as bad as his injured pride. One-upped by a psychopath. Again! Had Meshach been hiding in the trailer all along? Even last night when Wes had discovered the car and freed Jess?

Not a shot fired, either. Wes hadn't seen that outcome in all the scenarios his mind had produced.

Once they'd engaged, Wes lost track of time and events. Not a word spoken in anger, just a struggle as two men fought to stay alive. If that meant killing the other man, so be it. What felt like minutes might have lasted only a few seconds. Then his mind settled and he realized he had the advantage. He reached for Meshach's pistol lying in the grass. Another moment and two inches farther, and it would have been game over for the bad guy, but Meshach had pulled some kind of mixed-martial-arts move on him, reversed the hold, and grabbed the pistol.

Now, here he lay, the vanquished wallowing in *what-if*.

With his face pushed into the grass, Wes couldn't see. That didn't prevent him from hearing a slow-moving car along the highway. Had to be Tony looking for him. Wes prayed he'd stay put. God help them both if he decided to get out and wander around.

Just drive off.

The Corps taught recruits hand-to-hand techniques during boot camp, but like many physical abilities, if you didn't use it, you'd lose it. In Iraq, Wes had operated under one self-imposed rule: never let the enemy close enough to put a hand on you. He'd flunked this time.

Despite the obvious injury to Meshach's right hand, he'd used the fist like a battering ram. Wes took every opportunity to inflict pain and further damage to the bandaged area, but the man never acted like he felt a thing.

Stories of men doing superhuman feats, running on adrenalin — Sampson with God's power upon him — floated among troops in the Iraqi desert. As some war stories went, they grew with every telling.

Some he'd heard were true, some were not. Drugs could make a man crazy so that he would fight and kill with abandon, oblivious to wounds that would make a grizzly whimper. Meshach was methodical. No doubt evil, insane, but in control, and he had an uncanny ability to protect his eye. Wes had managed to break Meshach's sunglasses, but every other attempt he made to disable the man's vision Meshach thwarted.

The car stopped. A second later, another vehicle sped past, followed closely by a heavy truck with bad tread or a lopsided tire zinging every revolution. The sounds mixed into one and then faded.

Had a car door slammed? Tony? Did he get out of the car?

The pressure of the pistol eased and left the back of his head. Then it went off with a deafening explosion.

"Tony, run!" Wes screamed and tried to turn over, but Meshach had the advantage and hit him on the side of the face with the barrel of the gun.

Wes's world flipped out of control like it did the first time he jumped out of an airplane. Ground and sky inverted and spun. Two more rounds exploded from the .45 and rammed into the ground inches from his nose, jerking the sanity back into him just like the parachute did when it finally opened. What felt like a hot cigarette touched his right cheek as Meshach pressed the .45's muzzle against his skin. He shook his head and screamed and the pistol impacted the side of his head again.

"Keep it up," Meshach said and pushed himself away. "The fat guy in the hoodie took a round. You'll get one next. Come on, pops. Up. Walk."

Oh, Tony, Tony. Wes rolled to his right, onto his back. Meshach stood a couple of feet away, gun leveled at Wes's head. He knew he wouldn't survive lunging at the man.

Looking across the top of the barrel from the business end and into the lightless green eye of a murderer wasn't what Wes had envisioned. He did a quick sit-up with his knees pulled to his chest and stood without using his hands. He looked back over his shoulder for his techie but didn't see his body. The top of the levee spanned twenty yards, a long shot for a .45 automatic. Tony might be fine and just laying low, but Meshach seemed confident that his round hit home.

I'm going to kill you, Meshach. You shouldn't have left me alive. Whatever it takes, however long, I'll find a way.

"I love Louisiana. The sound of gunfire is as normal as the ding-dong-ding of church bells around here. Your cell phone, where is it?" Meshach had just shot a man, but he talked as calmly as if they were discussing what to have for lunch.

Wes felt his shirt pocket and inclined his head to indicate where they'd just come from, next to the trailer.

Meshach looked him up and down. "Show me. Turn your pants pockets out. Drop your wallet and back up."

Wes complied. His wallet landed in the grass next to his lip balm. He took three steps back.

Meshach bent at the knees. The pistol barrel never wavered. "Who was in the car? The guy you talked to?"

Wes couldn't think of any reasons to lie. "An FBI agent."

Meshach reacted with slight hesitation and a blank stare, but he didn't seem surprised. After pocketing Wes's wallet, he motioned with the gun which way he wanted Wes to go. "You're dumber than I thought if I have to tell you to move or I'll shoot ya."

Unless someone in the house across the highway witnessed the fight, saw his hurried ascent over the levee at the point of a gun, or saw Tony fall, pistol fire wouldn't even warrant a glance toward the report.

Wes didn't have to be told to stay away from the top of the levee. Deep weeds and grass made the walk a workout. A half-submerged refrigerator, the rotten hull of a wooden boat, sheets of corrugated aluminum from destroyed trailer houses, paper and plastic dotted the shoreline. All debris scattered by past hurricanes.

He didn't know a thing about Tony's parents or siblings. He had an older brother he'd mentioned in passing once, but where? *Lord, help me! What a mess!*

His left shoulder felt strange. He'd pulled something in the fight. Muscle shakes from fatigue quaked through his hands. Now that he had time to think about and assess the aches and pains, he was beat up and spent. He hadn't fought like that since high school, but then he hadn't tried to kill the kids he'd fought back then either. Looking back, he couldn't even remember why they'd fought.

The enemy had a face now. Short dark hair, a good start on a beard that hadn't been trimmed in several days, nose distinct but crooked from a poorly mended break. He looked like any man until the sunglasses had come off. A red spot replaced the left eye and the skin was drawn, like there wasn't enough to cover the hole where the eyeball had been, so the doctor had used a drawstring to pull it together. The wound didn't look like anything a plastic surgeon couldn't fix.

Wes realized Meshach relished the look. A reminder? Fuel to drive his hate?

They walked several minutes before the bay boat came into view, grounded against the levee. He'd yet to see a way out. A boat ride looked inevitable.

Meshach kept Wes alive. Why? Hostage? Save him for another fate? Wes wasn't going to complain about any options the man had in mind. He knew he'd barely slipped from the reaper's grasp. Time. He'd take all he could get.

Two kids trotted over the levee fifty yards ahead. Both boys were dressed in jeans, one in a red shirt hanging loose around his waist, the other, a pudgy kid in a white T-shirt a size too small. Their laughter stopped when they saw the boat. They pointed. The boy in the red shirt looked around and saw Wes and Meshach and nodded to his friend.

"I'll shoot both of them in the head." Meshach's tone remained flat, conversational.

Again, Wes didn't need to be told. Boys

first. As they approached, the kids glanced at each other. They looked fifteen, maybe sixteen, barely old enough to drive.

Meshach had already put Wes's pistol in the waistband behind his back. His pistol he'd stuffed in his belt, in front and handy.

Wes said, "Good morning, men," with as much sincerity as he could muster.

"Morning," the chubby kid said, almost a whisper.

"Isn't school in session?" Wes said.

"Yeah, but school stinks." The red-shirted kid flipped his hand and eyed the boat as he talked.

He'd called them men to bring them up to his level. The compliment went right over this kid's head. "I have news for you, boy. Dumb stinks too. You've got what, three more years of school and sixty years of living afterward, on average. That's a long time to be dumb. Go to school before you get in trouble."

He had their attention. They moved back the way they'd come, mumbling between themselves. Wes ignored them on purpose and picked up his pace. What they didn't know would hurt them.

"Real profound words for the boys there, pops. One of those kids will be a rocket scientist because of your advice."

A retort came to mind. He left it there.

Wes didn't have a gun to use against Meshach, but he possessed information. Throwing out a name, a place, an event in the man's life could buy seconds, minutes, maybe hours. But what should he reveal and how much?

When he reached the boat and looked back, the kids had left. He stopped. "What now, Elgin?"

Oh yeah. He'd hit a nerve. It wasn't much, a slight twitch in Meshach's neck muscles, but enough.

"You called her Jess on the phone a few minutes ago. Who you talking to? The fat boy I shot in the head? He was your computer guy, eh? Blue-eyes, Jess, she's one to pray. How about you? Do you believe in God?"

"Yes, I do, Mr. Fairchild? Do you?"

Meshach shrugged. "Of course. I make it a point to know my enemies."

33

Monday morning

Wes sat on a padded bench-seat in the front center of the boat facing backward. The prow held live-wells and numerous storage compartments, including the anchor's hold, all of them accessed by hideaway latches and watertight lids. The trolling motor was folded up, lying flat, and tied alongside the edge of the boat to his right.

Confidence and arrogance often had the same outward appearance, up to a point. Usually, the latter showed its ugly face when a man opened his mouth. At first glance, Meshach exuded confidence. The way he carried himself. The way he fought. No malice voiced, just matter of fact commands void of inflected tones or accents. He was as cold as an arctic winter.

Hard to believe he was only twenty-five. How had Elgin, the kid in the Cub Scout attire from the picture, become *Meshach* in such a short time? A close look at his dad would probably answer that question. If Meshach, at the age of twelve, killed his own father, then. . . . Wes didn't get that part. A boy's only escape from his dad was murder.

Was Meshach a product of his dad's environment? Was he any less at fault for his actions because of his childhood?

Meshach stood at the console. They faced each other. Wes tried not to stare, but that proved hard to do. The guy's eye watered continuously and he never blinked. How could he not blink? His injured hand shook every time he wiped around his eye. He steered with his left hand. The pistol lay in plain sight on the console. He didn't show discomfort, but the pain had to be excruciating. His skin had turned ashen. Infection?

Wes's hands were free, and he knew why. Meshach didn't trust himself to tie them.

When they departed the levee, Wes had to get on his knees before Meshach stepped into the boat. Then Wes retrieved and stowed the anchor. That task told him a lot. Knots tied at regular intervals along the length of the anchor rope and blue cloth wrapped around the anchor. He planned to use it for a grapple. From a boat? Now that Meshach had limited use of his right hand, he couldn't heave his makeshift apparatus.

Was that Wes's purpose? If Meshach couldn't throw the anchor with his injured hand, how could he climb the rope using the same hand?

The guy had lost his mind. Board a ship, underway, at sea. Then do what with it? The words Tony uttered went off like fireworks in his head. *Mars, Ursa, Nakika and Ace of Spades.* He was going to steer a vessel into an offshore facility. Meshach had accessed the Automatic Identification System looking for a weapon and a victim.

Sounded like a suicide mission, but the man didn't seem the type to give his life for a cause.

Did an environmentalist hire this nut job to cause a major oil spill in the Gulf of Mexico? Wes couldn't see it, but one more Macondo-type incident and Uncle Sam would shut down drilling offshore forever. The anti-drilling extremists would love that. Wes smelled someone really sinister, and he sat somewhere high atop a covert totem pole.

It was 8:20 AM and they were headed northwest on calm water. Meshach guided the boat down the center of the channels and wide around turns. They passed three boats, all of them traveling in the opposite direction. Wes averted his eyes. He wouldn't put others at risk to save his own bacon.

Meshach didn't act concerned or worried about much as they motored at a leisurely pace through cane breaks along the western side of the Mississippi River in broad daylight.

Wes prayed Tony had survived and alerted the cavalry.

He glanced left and right trying not to be too obvious about watching where they were going. A small manmade levee jutted into their path from the right. The builder may have had a purpose in mind, but Wes couldn't see it. Looked like Meshach couldn't see it either. If he stayed on course, he'd plant the bow of the boat right in the middle of it at thirty miles an hour. The sudden stop would be painful for them both.

Meshach wiped his eye and jerked the wheel left. The boat skidded by the outer reaches of the berm by mere feet. Wes prayed he didn't look so obvious in his surprise. He'd just seen a chink in the man's armor.

As quickly as he turned left, Meshach steered back right and cut the power. The boat dipped forward then settled. A camouflaged, three-sided boat garage without a roof lay just behind the small levee. It wasn't something Wes expected to find in the middle of the marsh. He'd seen one used on a television show about Louisiana duck hunting. The sides stood out of the water five feet. Camouflaged netting draped over a light PVC pipe frame flipped up and over the top of the boat, leaving a skylight to shoot from down the middle. A duck blind.

Meshach nodded at the structure. "Imagine that, Mr. Hansen. Right place, right time."

Every muscle in Wes's body tensed. Turn about and fair play aside, Meshach knew his name too. That gave more credibility to the threat he'd made against Wes's family.

Meshach turned the boat around and backed into the blind. He killed the motor. "Pops, pull the sides over the boat." He removed the key from the ignition, stuffed it into the left pocket of his pants, then picked up the pistol.

Wes did his bidding. Meshach kept his distance, moving from side to side and front to back as Wes worked the top over them. Pretty ingenious contraption — drive in, drive out, and never leave the boat. It even had a gate to cover the entrance. The thing would be worthless for hunting ducks without a couple of good Labradors to retrieve the fallen birds.

When Wes finished, Meshach gave a satisfied nod. "Looks like the posse will gallop on by this time." He motioned with the pistol again. "Back to your seat, pops."

Meshach made a point of using *pops*. Sometimes Wes felt old, like this morning when he'd fought for his life, but if Meshach thought the overuse grated on his nerves, he was wrong. Someday, in the not-too-distant future, he'd hear his grandson, Levi, use the title, and he'd think of this sorry excuse for a human being no longer.

A whisper of a breeze shook the camouflaged netting, like leaves of a tree playing with the shadows and sunlight on the ground below. Camouflaged though it was, viewed from the air the blind would present a blot on the natural scheme of things. An alert pilot would quickly see the difference.

Meshach sat on the outboard edge of the boat and wiped at his eye again. "You going to analyze me?"

"Nope." Wes gazed anywhere but at Meshach. The man acted cool on the outside, but what went on in the inside? Wes hoped the working jaw muscles showed inner frustrations. He'd be patient and wait to see what kind of questions he'd ask, if any.

A quick shadow passed across the boat as a pelican floated by. Wes gave thanks for the covering and shade. Baking in the direct sunlight, his thirst would be worse than it was at the moment. Looked like the bugs appreciated the shade as well.

Meshach unzipped his backpack and removed three pieces of his sunglasses. He held the broken frame together and tried to put the lens back in. Looked like a job for duct tape. Too bad. Must have used it all up. He dropped the glasses back in the pack and dug out Wes's pistol and a bottle of water. He put the pistol aside, held out the bottle, eyed the contents, then twisted off the top and took a long drink. He smacked his lips. "I filled this up at the trailer last night, right under your nose."

Wes would cede that point, but Elgin would never know. The man — no — the kid was a vengeful punk. The only difference between him and a five-year-old was one year, twenty times. Wes moved to the floor, sat, leaned back against the side of the boat and closed his eyes. He'd been up over twenty-four hours. He knew he could go fifty hours without sleep because he'd done it once in Iraq, but he was busy then, not sitting on his backside.

He had a long day in store, unless he managed to get himself shot before it was over. *Lord, my soul to keep . . . if it comes to that.*

34

Wes's mind snapped on like a light bulb at the flip of a switch. Humming? Meshach was humming? Wes didn't think the two were compatible: heartlessness and singing.

At least it wasn't *Taps.*

How long had he slept? It didn't matter.

This was one time in his adult life he wished he'd turned down a job. Then, maybe not. Sometimes the job found the man. This might be that time. If getting Meshach off the street was his calling, then so be it. He wished he felt more up to the task.

Could be his final calling. That would be disappointing. His daughter had decided to talk to him again, his grandson would be born soon, and he'd met Jess.

With the Good Lord's help, he'd get a chance to look back at the ordeal through a pair of 20/20 glasses. For now, he had trouble seeing a way forward.

He had to admit Meshach had one-upped him physically. To get out of this predicament alive, he'd have to outthink the man and catch him off his guard.

The breeze was barely noticeable and smelled musty. Meshach finished his tune. The silence was complete. He'd hoped to hear helicopters during the day, lots of them. The posse wouldn't gallop on by as Meshach had mentioned because they weren't coming. He was on his own.

He opened his eyes. The netting over the boat made the evening seem darker than it was. The sun was just below the horizon. Another time and another place and he might enjoy the sunset. He struggled to think if he'd ever had a worse day.

If Tony . . .

No! Tony was alive and intact until Wes heard the facts. Then he'd mourn or rejoice. For now, he'd remain optimistic and concentrate on saving his own hide. Tactical. Stay tactical.

He struggled to his feet and sat on the padded seat. He stretched. His neck hurt from sleeping with his head canted to one side. Something caught in his left shoulder again. Not a good sign.

Meshach sat at the boat's controls. He

glanced over the top of the GPS display mounted on the console and seemed to focus on Wes for an instant, then continued. The eye still watered. The "orb" Jess had called it. The term fit. Looked just like the business card. Meshach didn't blink. Weird. He seemed paler too.

The man was stoic.

Might as well get the ball rolling and see what it hits. "I had a good visit with Marlin Sands the other day. I saw Lane's mom. Even made a short excursion to the Valley of Fire State Park and looked around."

If Wes hit a nerve, it was numb.

He poked some more. "Monique wanted you to join her in D.C." Wes let his voice go up an octave. "Save the planet and the polar bears, that type of thing. Maybe you, Lamech and Sullivan could follow her on Chirp. Oh, wait. You already did."

Meshach looked up. "You don't know anything."

"I know you accessed AIS. Does Mars or Ace of Spades ring a bell? Why did you go after Bethany?"

Meshach acted deaf.

"She loves the dog, by the way."

Meshach took a deep breath. "You talk too much."

"Jess identified you. We found an old

340

picture of you and some other scouts at Lane's house. You only opened one lens cap on your binoculars. I see you prefer a monocular now. You were, what, twelve? That's about the time you took your last fieldtrip with your dad. Meshach, the man from fire."

Wes saw him grasp the .45. *Dear Lord.*

He didn't believe it. Meshach didn't even look up from what he was doing. Just pointed, pulled the trigger and set the gun down, like tapping the remote to change the channel from *Fox News* to *Duck Dynasty.* The bullet whizzed through the Plexiglas windscreen, passed inches from Wes's right ear and zinged off into the gathering dusk.

The report from the discharge had not cleared when Meshach spoke. "You remind me of my dad. He failed to take me seriously. I told him to leave me alone or I'd kill him. He didn't believe me. I told you that you talk too much. You do. Be quiet." Meshach started the engine. "Time to go. Open the gate, pops." He stood and grabbed the pistol again.

Wes turned mechanically, stepped onto the prow of the boat, and pushed the make-shift gate open. Meshach placed the pistol back on the console, engaged the outboard, and eased into the channel. He looked around as if undecided about a direction of travel, then pointed the boat southeast, back the way they'd come.

Wes sat, and the shakes hit him. The motor driving his heart and his nerves ran away with itself. He didn't see his life flash before his eyes, but he saw the muzzle blast from the pistol. Playing fifty questions with Meshach was the same as playing Russian roulette with a semiautomatic pistol — stupid.

The time had come.

The boat wallowed in the muddy water then slowly gathered speed. The outboard sounded like a vacuum cleaner with something stuck in the hose, then changed to a low, steady growl as the bow eased down and the boat planed out on the water's surface.

Wes looked forward and noticed something he'd missed. He'd even knelt on it to open the gate a minute ago. A loop of the anchor rope with one knot visible protruded from under the door to the hold. He turned back and glanced at Meshach standing erect at the controls, outlined against the southern edge of the waning sunset. The navigation equipment had his attention.

Wes didn't remember leaving the rope out, but there it was in plain sight.

The purpose he was supposed to serve in Meshach's scheme of things still eluded him. When Meshach pulled the trigger on the .45 a minute ago, he didn't know if the bullet would miss Wes or hit him in the head. Meshach didn't care anymore about shooting a man than he would when swatting a fly.

Meshach glanced up, eased the boat to the left, then leaned left to peer around the narrow windscreen. Wes heard a zip, a big bug, like a beetle. As a kid, he'd called them stinkbugs. Looked like it was doing 30 miles an hour and sounded like a dive-bomber. The thing hit Meshach right between the eyes. Sounded like a shot and set Wes in motion. He sprung for the rope and the anchor. He had two steps and a hard lunge to the left, off of the deck of the boat, to formulate his plan: *don't get tangled in the rope.*

As he cleared the hull, he dropped the anchor.

Hitting the water at forty miles an hour wasn't something a person would remember. Legs and arms and head yanked and twisted by their weight and the friction of the water pulled at his torso and limbs and brought his speeding body to a violent stop in mere feet. Wes gathered his wits in time to see the boat in a hard left turn, bow high, listed onto its side as the outboard forced the stern around. Meshach looked back his direction. Then, from out of the shallow water the rope sprang like a rubber band and stretched tight between the anchor and the bow. The boat changed direction like the end of bullwhip and left the water for air. Wes's last image of the wreck had Meshach upside-down in the air above the boat, arms and legs wide, headed for parts unknown.

Wes wormed his way through the water and mud into the tall grass. The motor sputtered and died. He ended up on the opposite side of the channel from Meshach. He didn't take a gander back and give the man a target to shoot at. Like Tony, until sight of his lifeless body proved otherwise, he'd consider Meshach alive and well — and armed.

Dry land and the highway lay a mile away, due north, and all of the distance consisted of either open water or grassy swamp. Nighttime settled in fast. Besides soaking wet, he'd soon be cold too. He tried to move his left arm and almost cried out at the searing pain in his shoulder.

Create distance and be quiet doing it.

Wes had no visions of being the disabled

and unarmed hero. Evade and escape. Live to fight another day. He crawled deeper into the swampy grass with the bugs and the crawly critters. After twelve hours with Meshach, he looked forward to their company.

35

Wes scurried through the ankle-deep water to the far side of the small island thick with reeds and cane, into the densest, tallest growth, and stretched out on his stomach. The direction he traveled took him toward the glow of lights along the levee and the highway, away from the last known location of his enemy. He'd put his back to another wide area of open water. If forced, he'd slither into the murky soup and disappear like he'd seen the gators do.

He strained to listen. What sounds were normal? Water lapped behind him. Frogs croaked, each one in its own cadence. So many crickets sang their grating screech sounded like one. Other moans and creaks penetrated the din from far and near. He couldn't determine their source.

Movement was easier to pick out than shapes, but he'd never seen a darker night. Again, he gave thanks for it. If Meshach had survived the carnage with his eye intact, the man wouldn't be able to see a thing.

An eerie quiet settled over the marsh as if the local population suddenly got a feel for an impending event or listened for the boogieman's approach as Wes did. It was a strange night in Louisiana when the bugs were silent.

A sky full of stars had faded to black along with the gray of dusk. *Clouds. Moving fast.* If he wasn't already wet, cold, and miserable enough, now the wind picked up. His hair, ears, and nose felt like icicles stuck to his head.

It was just as well that he'd lost his wristwatch. Negotiating the water and marsh to the levee was going to make one mile seem like fifty before the night was over. No use checking the time every five minutes and making two hours seem like ten. He prayed he could make it in two hours.

He put his mind back on the inky night around him. Grass and stalks of cane rustled and thrashed in the wind. Who was he fooling? He wouldn't hear a herd of buffalo coming now.

A deep rumble drew his focus offshore. Lightning flashed high above, giving depth to the darkness, followed by another ominous rumble and a clap of thunder. A tumultuous roar rolled down on him. The temperature dropped like he'd opened the refrigerator door and rain hit. The reeds and cane around him looked like they'd turned their backs to the wind and bowed into the shallow water. Big drops hurled to the ground by a driving gale pounded and beat him until he couldn't stand it any longer and had to push himself out of the marsh grass into the shelter of deep water. He pulled his shirt over his head. Submerged and out of the wind he felt like he'd slipped on a coat.

Men had died of hypothermia in warmer temperatures. The chills hadn't hit him yet, but he knew they were coming. He looked toward the levee. He preferred to do this in the daylight, but . . . Thank God he didn't have far to go. He struck out using a side-stroke, pulling with his right arm and scissor kicking. He pushed with his cupped left hand, working his arm at the elbow, careful not to move his shoulder.

How far? How long? Too far and too long. The wind, rain, and waves beat at him without rhythm so he didn't know when to breathe or hold his breath, and he couldn't see. He reached with his right hand for another stroke at the water, grasped a handful of mud and worked his way onto another island. He stood and slogged on. Meshach or no Meshach. He recalled an admonishment from Bubba from long ago. "You stop, you die. Get mad! Get mean! Survive!"

The wind drove him across another long section of marsh and back into the roiled water. He pushed thoughts of meeting an unfriendly critter out of his mind. Reptiles and rodents had more sense than to be out on a night like this.

He swam and swam. He must have entered the water in a curve, and he was swimming down the middle of a channel. He angled left and crawled out on his hands and knees onto steep, muddy ground. The levee!

He caught his breath and set out again. Scaling the thirty yards of mud to the top of the levee was like trying to climb a slide in his socked feet. His wet shirt and jeans stuck to him and hindered his movements. The jeans were stretched three inches longer than when he'd put them on and weighed him down with water and mud. The rain had let up, but the wind stole body heat. His feet grew in size and weight as mud stuck to his shoes, adding layer upon slick layer with every step.

He didn't hold much hope for what lay

ahead. He'd like to see the glow of light somewhere, the high beams of a car on the highway in the distance, something to give him direction and something to shoot for. He peered into the night from the top of the levee, overlooking the highway. The storm must have knocked out the power. An all-night convenience store shrouded in darkness lay just below. A Louisiana State Patrol car was parked at a pump.

He opened his mouth to scream for joy, but the wind snatched the breath away.

Wes approached the cruiser. The officer had his head down. Two men talked to the clerk at the counter inside the store. The officer glanced up, down, back up, then opened the car door and crawled out. The guy was all man and there was a lot of him. The black officer probably stood six-five and weighed two-sixty, if Wes had to guess.

He looked Wes up and down. "Wes Hansen?"

"That's me."

A big smile flashed white teeth. "I been praying you'd turn up."

"I hope you don't mind. I'm going to sit right here for a minute." Wes started to plop down on the concrete in front of the patrol car, and the officer moved to grab him and lighten his fall. The officer walked to his cruiser, leaned in, and retrieved his coat. He placed the black jacket over Wes's shoulders.

As soon as Wes felt the warmth, the shakes hit him.

"I'm Officer Lucas Jamison, Mr. Hansen. What can I do for you?" He knelt next to Wes and placed a big hand in the middle of his back. "Are you injured?"

Wes looked at the officer and then at the entrance into the store.

The two men inside opened the glass door and stepped out. The guy behind the counter stared through the window.

"Hot coffee would go a long way. Something to eat. I'm not wounded, but my left shoulder is a wreck. It's been a long day."

Lucas looked toward the two men and yelled, "Bring a cup of coffee, black. Something to eat, anything hot. A bottle of water too." He addressed Wes. "The power hasn't been out long, so hot shouldn't be a problem." He eyed Wes and canted his head. His big teeth flashed again. "Your shoulder isn't the only thing that's a wreck. You look like you tussled with a gator."

"I feel like the gator won. Can you do me a favor? My tech guy, Tony Moran, Meshach shot him, and . . . Can you call the FBI?

Ask for Agent Trent Carr."

Lucas nodded. "He's OK. He's fine, your guy. I worked the scene this morning, yesterday morning now. He's got a head wound. It's serious enough, but he's going to be fine. He's at West Jeff. The Lord looked after him."

Thank God! . . . yesterday? "What time is it?"

"Just after one."

The Lord was gracious. He'd lived to see another day after all.

One of the men from the store brought out a cup of coffee and two large pieces of sausage pizza. With help, Wes stood and walked around the officer's car to the back door. He sat in the back seat and sipped the coffee. Then he tasted the pizza. He couldn't remember tasting better pizza.

Lucas stepped to the front of the car and talked into his radio mic. He returned and squatted on his haunches beside the door. "Mr. Hansen, I'm taking you to West Jeff. Any objections?"

Wes fumbled with the shoulder strap and clicked the seatbelt. "Not a one. Could I borrow your cell phone?"

Officer Lucas pulled his phone out of his pocket and handed it to Wes. Then he pulled onto the highway and turned on the car's strobes.

Wes held up the cell phone. It was bigger than his iPhone. A Droid or some other brand he was unfamiliar with. He eyed the blank screen and realized it didn't matter whether he knew how to turn it on or not. His mind was just as blank. He couldn't remember Jess's phone number.

36

Tuesday morning

Wes opened his eyes and looked around the dark, windowless room. At least his eyelids didn't hurt. They were about the only two parts of his body to escape the abuse, and then just barely. His right cheek and that side of his head was black and swollen where Meshach had clubbed him with the pistol. He'd ignored the pain until he looked in the mirror. If he'd ever looked worse, he couldn't remember when.

He'd been in the hospital twice as a kid. Those memories smelled like disinfectant and alcohol and sounded like the control bridge in an episode of the old *Star Trek* series: *bleep-bleep, bleep-bleep, bleep-bleep.* Not much had changed.

He turned on the light, sat up on the edge of the bed and worked his limbs. All of them but the upper left arm and shoulder anyway. A dozen small wounds covered his forearms and hands. The latter were swollen and sore. Humans weren't meant to be wet for prolonged periods. Water weakened skin, making it easier to puncture and tear.

Agent Carr stepped into the open doorway. He smiled. "Good to see you, Wes. Can I come in?"

"Good morning, Trent." Wes waved him in. They shook hands.

Trent brushed back the bottom of his lightweight, tan jacket at his waist and pulled his khaki pants up his wiry, hipless frame. "Did you get some rest?"

"I got to sleep about three or so. After the doc poked me all over, and I'd had a hot shower."

Trent checked his watch. "It's seven twenty. That's not much sleep. How are you feeling?"

"Like one of Saddam's SCUDs hit me. I hurt in places I forgot I had."

Trent pointed at one of two small, padded, blue armchairs at the foot of the bed. "Mind if I sit down?"

Wes shook his head. "Of course not."

An orderly walked in carrying a brown plastic tray holding a large covered plate, a small bowl full of fruit, and small plastic containers of milk and apple juice.

"Thanks," Wes said.

The guy left the tray on the rolling bedside table and took his leave.

Trent removed his trademark pad and pencil from his shirt pocket. "Talk to me."

Where to start? Facts? He had few, but he could make some educated assumptions. "Meshach planned to hijack a large vessel, tanker, freighter. I don't think it mattered which, and use it as a weapon to hit an offshore oil facility. The anchor rope on the boat had knots tied in it at useful intervals and blue cloth was wrapped at strategic points to silence the anchor. A makeshift grapple, if you will. His target might have meant more to him than his weapon of choice because of his obsession with Cole, but who knows. If you'll remember the file Tony and your agent found on his computer, he had many options in mind."

Wes took a deep breath. "I think you can close one missing person, slash murder case, and one first degree murder. Meshach didn't come out and say it, but he killed his dad. His only admission to anything I asked came when he compared me to his father. He threatened his dad if he didn't leave him alone. His dad should have listened. He told me I talked too much and implied I didn't take him seriously, like his dad. Looking at that situation from the outside, ten, twelve years ago, you might have let Meshach walk and called it self-defense."

Trent scribbled on the pad for another moment and looked up. "The murder?"

"Yeah. Lane Woodard, last week, here in New Orleans. He and Meshach went to school together. They had a chance meeting that got Lane killed. Dig around and I'll bet you'll find confirmation."

"I remember Lane's name from your notes. His mother got us Meshach's real name from the picture. I'll need to call her."

Wes didn't tell Liz he'd get her son's killer. He didn't have anything to apologize for, but he felt obligated to her. Maybe because he'd met her, witnessed, and empathized with her grief. "If you don't mind, I'd like to talk to her first. Jess and I will fly to Vegas tomorrow and sit down with her."

Trent eyed him a long second and nodded. "Meshach's character?"

"None. His feelings are cold, numb, and hard as a brick. What drives him? Again, who knows? Ideology, money, revenge, or just because he likes what he does. It's anyone's guess."

Wes picked out a grape from the bowl, then put it back. "Did you find his boat?"

Trent nodded. "We did, early this morning, right where you told Officer Jamison it

357

would be. I'm afraid we didn't find our man, though. I've got a team headed out there to drag the area for his body. I'll let you know what we find, if anything."

Wes knew it. There was always a glitch. No body, dead or alive, no closure.

Trent looked up from his pad and blinked. "How did you get away?"

"God sent a stinkbug to help me."

Trent's head canted to one side. His nose crinkled, hinting at a subconscious thought about sniffing at a bug. "What?"

"We left our little hideout and cruised down the middle of the channel. I can only guess at our speed, but we clipped along at a good pace. I noticed a small loop of the anchor rope sticking out from under the hatch where the anchor was stored. I was mulling that over when I looked at Meshach. He leaned to look around the windscreen, and a big bug hit him in the forehead. I grabbed the rope and dove off the boat with the anchor. The rest is a blur. The anchor must have buried up in the mud and when the rope pulled tight, the boat flipped. The last time I saw Meshach he was airborne and at the mercy of speed and gravity."

"What made you think of something like that?"

Wes had been wondering that very thing.

"I didn't think. It just happened."

Trent wrote on his pad again.

Wes doubted the scribbling referenced the lack of forethought as to why Wes did what he did.

"What else? Did he mention Lamech or Sullivan?"

"No, but I threw their names at him. He never blinked. Speaking of, he doesn't blink . . . ever. Tears run from his eye like a leaky faucet. He wears the dark glasses for a reason. He has to. And he's wounded. His right hand was wrapped in a bloody cloth. I'd say he's right handed too. He was awkward using his left."

After a moment, the agent shook his head and said, "He's crazy if he thought he could pull off something like hijacking a ship alone."

Wes knew that was where he'd made his biggest mistake in evaluating Meshach. "Be careful. You and I think people like Meshach are crazy. He is not. He's insane, possessed, or both. If you don't find his body, assume he's planning his next whatever. Don't confuse him with crazy. He's calculating and void of emotion. Another thought. He was armed with a 1911 frame .45. A fancy piece, like a Kimber maybe, with rose-colored wooden grips, and he's got my Springfield

.45. We know he took the cop's service piece, though I never saw it. How is that guy, by the way?"

"He succumbed to his wounds yesterday afternoon." Trent flipped his pad closed and stood. "I wonder why he kept you alive."

"The one time I tried to draw him out and get him to talk, I nearly got perforated in the forehead. He picked up the pistol, pointed it my direction and pulled the trigger. Like wiping his nose with the back of his hand. He didn't care if I lived or died, so who knows. I didn't complain."

"I'll bet not. Wes, go home. We've got this from here. You've done good work and deserve a rest. Do me one favor, though. The next time you're down this way on business, call me so I can put on extra agents." He smiled again. "You've got my thanks and my number. Call me if you think of anything else."

They shook hands again and Wes said, "No, actually, I don't have your number. I don't even have clothes." Wes pulled at the backless gown he wore. "I think I know where my cell phone is, but Meshach has my wallet. My travel bag and computer case are in my rental car and Cole or Bubba has it."

"I'll call Bubba for you. Tony has my info.

He's, well, he's . . ."

"He's what?"

"You'll see. It's crazy, plum crazy. Go see him. He's in room 117." Trent waved and walked out.

Wes didn't let the suspense build very long before he chose the only option available and peeked under the stainless lid covering his breakfast: a broccoli and cheese omelet. It went down well, even without his usual dose of salt and pepper the hospital dietary staff conveniently failed to provide, probably by design. The bowl of fruit and the drinks proved to be apt additions.

As he finished and pushed away the tray, Cole knocked. "Hey, are you up for some company?"

"Come in here. You brought my suitcase. Did Trent call you?"

"No. I thought you'd need it."

"We must have *ESPN* then. I'm threadbare. Actually, I'm worse. I'm bare. Set that up here for me."

Cole placed the bag on the foot of the bed. "That's good humor — *ESPN*." He had on the same Wranglers, cowboy boots, and camo cap but had changed to a white, vented, Columbia fishing shirt.

Wes unzipped the travel bag, removed a

change of clothes and his shaving kit, then eased off the bed. "If you'll excuse me a minute, I'm going to get out of this airy garment and brush the fuzz off my teeth. Then, I want to go see Tony."

Cole held out his hand.

Wes stopped and grabbed it. They shook.

Cole's eyes held Wes's a long moment. He said, "You went above and beyond."

"I didn't plan it that way, Cole. It just happened."

"Your kind never plans it, but when you're forced into a tough situation, you don't shy from the task either. Go on. Get dressed. Jessica and Bubba are on their way too."

Wes eased into the bathroom and changed. He wished he had an extra pair of shoes. His were soaked. He put them on anyway and stepped out.

Cole scanned him from head to toe. "You look rough, my friend. Are you OK?"

Wes tossed the gown on the bed. "I did something to my left shoulder. They want me to have an MRI today, but I'm going to wait until I get home. After that, I'm well. How about you? Business as usual? How's your daughter?"

"Bethany is fine. Thanks for asking. Business is not as usual. That Meshach character pointed to some deficiencies, industry wide.

Operating overseas, history prepares us for such efforts from the more radical types, but here at home, we don't have a history yet. We have work to do." He glanced at his watch. "I have to leave soon for a meeting with the Bureau of Ocean Energy Management. I have something for you before we go see Tony too." He removed an envelope from his back pocket and handed it to Wes. "You didn't send me a bill, and I don't want one. Don't try to give the check back either. Cash it. You'll find an offer of employment in there as well. Take your time. Recuperate and think on it."

Wes slid the envelope into the pocket of his shirt. "Thanks, Cole. I'll consider your offer."

What kind of position could an ex-Marine turned PI fill in Cole's organization? The answer could wait until he looked at Cole's proposal, and he wouldn't do that until he was alone.

A nurse walked in carrying an iPad. She looked at the empty bed, at Cole and Wes, the vacant bathroom, then back at the bed. Her eyes narrowed. "Where's my patient?"

"You're looking at him," Wes said.

She blinked then pointed at the empty space between the white sheets. "Are you kidding me? Get back in bed. You can't leave until the doctor releases you."

"Ma'am, I'm going down the hall to room 117 to see my friend. I'll be back." He edged toward the door. "Promise."

Cole led the way.

37

The door stood open. Wes knocked and eased into Tony's room. "Anyone home?"

Tony gingerly glanced up from his plate and what looked to be common fare for patients this morning: an omelet. He smiled. "Hey, Wes, Cole." He held up his fork in salute. He had on a gray hoodie fitted with a zipper. No wonder about the hoodie because his head looked like a mummy with unfinished wrappings.

A sharp pang of guilt twisted Wes's stomach. "Man, Tony, how are you?"

"Twenty-two stitches and a headache."

The bathroom door opened and FBI Special Agent Stacy Collins stepped out. Wes almost didn't recognize her. He had to think about the name of the pants — capris — in red, a yellow blouse, flip-flops, and a beautiful head of golden hair that hung to the middle of her back. The look and the attire didn't fit his idea of an agent's dress code, but maybe for a techie.

"Good morning, Wes." She glanced at Cole. "I don't think we've met. I'm Stacy."

Cole nodded. "Cole Blackwell. My pleasure. Tony, I hate to barge in on your meal, but I wanted to shake your hand. I promise I won't shake hard." He reached across the bed and they clasped hands for a brief moment. "Good job. Great to see you're still with the breathing. I have to excuse myself. Business calls. Stacy, again, my pleasure. Wes, I'll be waiting for your call." He nodded again and stepped out.

Stacy walked around Wes and stood next to Tony.

Wes scanned the room for Tony's ever-present computer but didn't see it. "Sorry, I guess I should have asked. Did we interrupt official business, Stacy?"

She sat on the edge of the bed and took Tony's hand. "Oh, no. I'm off." She smiled.

Tony grinned so big it must have pulled at the stitches because his face quickly morphed into a grimace. Wes hoped his expression didn't show his shock. No wonder Trent had said Wes would have to see it for himself. Crazy.

Must have been love at first byte. He had to control the urge to laugh. He'd tell Tony that one later.

Good for them.

For now. "Tony, I don't know how to apologize."

"Then don't. You didn't shoot me. That nut did. Tell me you got him."

"I wish I could. They haven't found his body, if there's one to find. We had a little boating accident, but I didn't wait around to check for survivors. Tell me about your head."

"The round grazed the right side, just above my ear, and laid open the skin, like a scalpel passed through. I never saw the guy. Just a buzz, like a big bumblebee zipped by, and I was down. I heard you scream my name . . . and the gunshots afterward. I thought he killed you. I was a bit more cautious sticking my head up the second time. I saw you two walking along the edge of the levee in the distance." He took a deep breath. "Then I realized I was bleeding to death and tied my hoodie around my head. I tried to drive myself to the hospital. Big dumb. I barely remember calling 9-1-1. Cole's rental car is a mess. It's still parked along the highway."

Stacy raised her hand then let it fall back onto her lap. "I'm going to take care of that this morning."

The rapid *squeak, squeak, squeak* of

rubber-soled shoes on the tile floor outside the room fit someone on a mission. The squeak stopped and Jess peeked around the doorjamb. "Ah!" She glanced back down the hall. "Bubba, he's in here."

Jess walked up to Wes and stood shoulder to shoulder with him, her hands by her side. Her smile was beautiful. Her blouse matched her blue eyes. She gave Tony and Stacy a quick wave. "Good morning, everybody." After a second, she glanced up at Wes and held up her fist for him to bump with his. He did. Her eyes sparkled then seemed to dim. She reached up and caressed his bruised cheek.

Bubba lumbered in dressed in a blue suit, white shirt, and a yellow and red tie. "Good gracious, what a sight," he said. "You need to borrow some of the gauze wrapped around Tony's head and cover that beat-up face. How are you?" Bubba squeezed and yanked on his right hand so hard Wes felt it in his left shoulder. "You scared us. Welcome back."

"Thanks, Bubba. I'm glad you're not wearing that fancy get up to a funeral."

Bubba hesitated and his voice lost its energy. "Me too, bro. Me too."

Wes had tried to make light of the events,

but the attempt only served to dampen the mood.

None of it made sense. Tony had been shot in the head, shoulder surgery looked like a strong possibility for Wes, and everyone in the room was happy. All things being relative, everyone knew the outcome could have been much worse.

Bubba's cell rang. "Excuse me a minute," he said and stepped into the hall.

Jess put her left elbow against Wes's ribs then bumped her left fist with the palm of her right hand. She had just elbowed him without actually elbowing him. His comment about Bubba wearing his suit to Wes's funeral hit her harder than he had thought. He smiled at her.

"That was not funny," she whispered.

"I know. Sorry."

Bubba stepped back into the room. "Tony, turn on the television. You yahoos made the news."

Tony reached for the controls. "What channel?"

"Try the local, *Fox 8.*"

Wes, Jess, and Bubba moved around to the head of the bed. Tony scrolled through the channels. The television flashed to a live shot from a helicopter as the camera zoomed in on a capsized boat floating on muddy water. The white hull and the out-board's lower-end and prop were exposed to the morning sun. Two small craft floated nearby. An inset picture of Wes in desert camouflage holding his M4 occupied the upper right corner of the screen.

He looked like a kid back then. He had been a kid.

The scene took Wes back to the previous night. Viewed on television, the tall green grass, tan switch cane, and water looked less menacing. He scanned the north side of the island for where he'd crawled out of the dense growth into the water. There was no telling how much he'd accidentally ingested during his swim. It hadn't tasted as muddy as it looked now.

Despite the beating the storm delivered, the marsh appeared to be untouched.

His peripheral vision suddenly came to life again with the pair of bluebonnet eyes locked on him. Wes knew why the camera captured Lane Woodard smiling, standing next to the black-haired beauty with her eyes locked on him. Pride and hope for a future with the woman he loved.

Wes had a few things he wanted to say to Jess.

A lady's voice broke in and the picture changed to a typical news broadcast desk and a serious looking, dark-haired lady holding up a piece of paper to read. "Sorry. We're having audio difficulties. We'll go to our D.C. affiliate, *Fox 5*. On the ground is our own Anne Greenway. Anne, are you there?"

"Great, we missed it," Tony said.

"Maybe not," Stacy responded and patted his leg.

The screen changed again to what looked like a cool morning in Washington. The reporter turned her head away and let the wind blow the blond strands of hair out of her face then looked into the camera. "I am here Courtney. We're waiting for a statement from the Secretary of Homeland Security, J.S. Berger."

"Anne, give us a feel for what authorities believe this alleged terrorist had planned."

Everyone in the hospital room exchanged glances.

"Well, they have the scoop, and they're running with it," Tony said.

"Yeah," Bubba said. "More like a scoop of manure. The guy is already a terrorist."

The camera panned to the front of a business. It looked like the secretary and his wife leaving a downtown restaurant. The redhead had her arm in the crook of his elbow. Public figures were never safe from the press.

"Well . . ." The reporter glanced at the door. "One moment, Courtney." She approached him on the sidewalk, holding out the mic. "Mr. Berger, a second of your time. Please!"

The camera zoomed in on the swarthy figure in a black trench coat, loosely belted at the waist. He took the woman's hand from his elbow, held up one finger, mouthed "one minute" and faced the camera. He blinked and took a deep breath.

She jerked the mic back to her lips. "Mr. Berger, what can you tell us about events unfolding in Louisiana this morning? Has your department been in touch with Mr. Hansen in New Orleans? Our sources tell us he's being treated for injuries. Has Elgin Fairchild, the man who called himself Meshach, been captured? What's being done to secure our oil supply? There's speculation the price of a barrel of oil could jump five dollars today. Any comments?" She held out the mic again.

"Anne, this is still a developing situation. The FBI and Coast Guard are on the scene. I'd be remiss in commenting until all the facts have been gathered and assessed."

The mic returned. "Again, has DHS or another agency spoken to Wes Hansen about further threats? Our sources tell *Fox 5* that this terrorist planned to ram a drilling platform that would have resulted in a spill to make the BP incident look mild in comparison." She poked the mic back in his face.

"Again, I will not comment on these islands or platforms or rigs or whether they were part of the suspect's plans. My source puts Mr. Hansen in the Venice area, so as soon as he's available, the proper authorities will follow up with pertinent questions." He nodded at the reporter and held up his hand. "I'm sorry, but . . . ."

The television went mute. Tony tossed the remote onto his lap. "Did you guys hear what I did?"

"Yes," Jess nodded. "He said island. Who calls them that? That's like the president calling the Navy guy a corpse-man instead of a corpsman."

Wes walked to the foot of the bed and turned to face the group.

Bubba glanced at Tony, Jess, then at Wes. "Bro, what did I just miss?"

"Bubba, first, one of Lamech's posts read *your isle of choice.* Second, and I don't think anyone else caught this, the reporter said I was in New Orleans being treated for injuries. Here I stand. Berger said I was still in Venice, according to his source. My cell phone is still in Venice. I lost it yesterday morning when Meshach and I went at it. It's laying in the grass next to that brown trailer house."

No one in the room was privy to the conversation Wes had with Cole from Las Vegas. Cole mentioned that he and the secretary went to school together. Looked like Cole was the one who needed to set up a long-time friend.

Wes would have to see what the initial *S* in the secretary's name stood for too.

Stacy hopped up from the bed and grabbed her purse. "If you'll excuse me, I have to call Trent." She stepped into the hall.

Bubba held out his hands, palms up. "Is the guy that dumb? He's not that dumb. Come on. The Secretary of the DHS is not involved with Meshach. He is, isn't he? I need to go look in the mirror and slap myself."

Jess stepped up beside Wes.

Bubba headed for the door. "Bro, shake my hand. Are you going to stop by before you leave? I'll understand if you don't, but Rae will be mad if you take this beauty here and run back to Colorado without saying good-bye." He took Jess's hand and kissed her on the forehead.

Wes glanced at Jess and raised an eyebrow. She raised one in return and put the ball back into his court. "We'll have to talk about it," he said, "but I don't see why not."

They shook hands again. "Love you both. I have to go put these duds to good use." Bubba took his leave.

Stacy stood against the far wall in the hallway talking on her phone. She shook her head when she saw Wes looking at her.

Tony pushed up in the bed and motioned toward a pair of wooden clothes lockers in the corner of the room. "Jess, would you mind getting my computers out for me? There are two of them in the case in the left closet. Let's look into this Berger guy and see if we can find Lamech's identity through him. He'd make the Hansen team three, bad guys zero."

"Sorry, Tony, I'd love to boot-up with you, but I don't work for Wes anymore."

Tony's brows furrowed. "You don't?"

"Wes fired me three days ago."

Tony's eyes darted to Wes then back to Jess. His voice went up two octaves. "Why?"

Wes slipped his right arm around Jess's waist and turned her to him. "So I can do this." She tilted her head up. He put his lips on hers and held them for a long moment.

Not hungry, but a final guilt-cleansing soft-ness he never thought he'd experience again. He let her lower lip go and whispered, "I'm glad you washed the sticky from the duct tape off your lips."

She bit his lower lip, held it between her teeth, and whispered back like a ventrilo-quist, talking around his lip, "I'm never let-ting go."

"Of my lip?"

"Or you."

Meshach eyed the Snowy Egret standing stiff-legged in the marsh grass six feet away. The bird stared at the ground, its head cocked to one side. It had moved once in the past three hours to gobble up a big black grasshopper that made the mistake of land-ing within reach of the bird's sharp beak.

If the egret was unaware of Meshach's presence, the Feds in the helicopter flying an ever-changing grid pattern over the top of him wouldn't see him either. They'd ar-rived at first light. That meant Wes had survived. Disappointing, but then, maybe not. Half submerged in water and covered in thick mud, he could lie unseen for hours. He had already. Too easy.

Earlier in the morning a second chopper had hovered high above the capsized boat.

No doubt some fair-haired news reporter getting her fifteen minutes of fame bumping her gums about the who and why of it all. The authorities knew his identity now.

Whatever.

Local Mounties in a bay boat traversed the area around the wreckage. One man stood on the bow and one stood aft probing the muddy water with grapples for a body they'd never find. He had to give it to them. They were persistent.

The first grays of dusk finally covered the eastern skyline. Just a little longer and he'd slip into the marsh and disappear. The first order of business: a shower and change of clothes. Then, he'd secure transportation north to Denver and pay Wes's daughter a visit. Have a chat. Yep, talk about her dad, Meshach's oldest, dearest friend.

The helo flitted off into the sunset. The boat's engine spooled up and roared away. Someone had pulled the plug on the search. Perfect. He would swim to shore before nighttime settled in. The egret took flight as he pushed into deeper water. Meshach found an easy rhythm and set out. Ten minutes later, his feet found bottom. He stood, waded ashore, and plodded up the slope through the deep weeds and brush.

Heavy trucks and passenger vehicles

pounded the highway, traveling in both directions. Bumming a ride should be a snap.

Then he heard them erupt and knew he was in trouble. His mom had warned him. *Next time, Honey, you might not survive.* He'd stepped on them, somehow, somewhere. One, two, three stings on his neck and face. Then a hornet hit his lower lip and he slapped at it and the floodgate opened. They swarmed his face and upper body. He spun and ran for the safety of the water, but . . . like . . . the ground jumped up and slammed him in the face. Numb, he rolled onto his back. Darkness gathered, but this was different. Final. Eternal.

ABOUT THE AUTHOR

David Arp spent the last 35 years working drilling rigs from the US to the Middle East to the vast oceans offshore. His love of reading fostered a passion for writing. He lives in Colorado with his wife, Karen.